Bones Were Free

Thérèse St. Clare

This is a work of fiction. All names, characters, places, and incidents are either the product of the author's imagination or are used fictitiously. Any resemblance to actual persons, living or dead, businesses, companies, organizations, events, or locales is entirely coincidental.

Library of Congress Registration Number: TXu 1-880-306

ISBN-13: 978-0615904016 (Amazon.com)

ISBN-10: 0615904017

This book is dedicated to my beloved daughters, K.T. and K.C.

Without your editorial and publication design services, it would not have been possible.

Thank you for your encouragement, support, and patience....

Chapter One

"Wrong, wrong, wrong! That's all wrong, girl friend!"

As Bernadette Julien assessed her image in the mirror, she didn't need Valerie, the friend who had taught her to be fashion savvy, next to her right then to know the outfit was definitely not flattering. The mirror in her bedroom wasn't full length but the way it was positioned on the wall provided a view of the outfit to her knees. Bernadette turned one way and then another to see her image at different angles and every angle came back with Valerie's voice clearly yelling at her, "Wrong, wrong, wrong! That's all wrong, girl friend!"

Bernadette was what the fashion advertisers discretely referred to as full-figured. Alone in her bedroom, Bernadette was more honest, more critical of herself. Even though it wasn't the most flattering uniform, she knew it wasn't just the outfit making her look ridiculous. She was downright fat! The outfit just didn't make any effort to help her attempts at hiding the fact. Based on her last annual check-up, even if she lost eighty pounds, Bernadette knew she would still be on the high side of any doctor's weight chart for her height. Dragging this outfit out the top of the closet and donning it once again confirmed the verdict her doctor repeated this year just as he had for the past ten years. She was overweight.

The cotton candy pink and white seersucker waitress outfit sported a white mock apron with ruffles that were positioned in all the wrong places for her full figure. When her mother's older brother, her Uncle Aaron, got her a job at his buddy Joe's place the summer she graduated from high school, she had been happy to wear the outfit and earn the money she needed to pay for her books and to cover her miscellaneous college fees. Now, over ten years later and accustomed to wearing only fashions that complemented her figure, Bernadette was sickened by the thought of going into public wearing the waitress' uniform. Looking at the pink and white cloth stretching across her midriff, she remembered an incident from her childhood, the incident that had first caused her to be self-conscious about her weight and to start hating the color pink.

Bernadette's mother loved pastels on children, especially pink for little girls. From the time Bernadette was born, it seemed she was always clothed in pink which earned her the nickname Pinky among her closest relatives. For her sixteenth birthday, her parents had given her a pink jean set and it had immediately become her favorite outfit. When the extended family was invited to the Labor Day barbecue her parents always gave, Bernadette wore the pink jeans and matching jacket confident she looked her best. At one point, everyone had gathered in the den to watch a family movie. After seeing the film, the adults retired to the outside patio to play cards and the children were left to entertain themselves in the den. Soon Bernadette and the older children were at a folding table focused on putting together a jigsaw puzzle. The younger children were on the floor on the opposite end of the den playing pick-up sticks. Bernadette hadn't paid careful attention to what the younger children were doing but got suspicious when she heard her little sister, Cecelia, start to whisper. She didn't know what they were up to until Cecelia tapped Bernadette on the shoulder.

When Bernadette turned in her chair, the younger cousins were gathered around her in a semicircle with Cecilia at the center. As soon as she turned, Cecelia had a pick-up stick in each hand and was waving them rhythmically in the air leading the group in a song, a parody she had made up from one of the songs that had been sung in the film. Bernadette was smiling at her little sister's creativity until she heard the words, "Pinky is shaped like a round chimney!"

Cecelia and the gang she had gathered kept repeating the sentence like a chant. Then Cecelia's hands fell to cross against her stomach and she began laughing hysterically. Everyone in the den joined in. Bernadette wanted to die of embarrassment.   Not only did Bernadette stop wearing pink, though it broke her mother's heart, but she tried to lose weight for the first time. Trying to lose weight in a Creole household was as challenging as an adult traveling from New York City to Los Angeles on a tricycle.

When she entered the kitchen the next morning to take her place at the breakfast table she stated emphatically, "Mama, I only want one hard-boiled egg and a slice of plain toast for breakfast."

Her mother turned upset and questioned, "Bernadette! Honey, are you sick?"

"No, I'm starting a diet today. I just want to lose weight."

Hearing that, her mother was satisfied that her eldest daughter was in good health and turned her attention back to preparing breakfast for the family. As she placed the filled plates on the table, Bernadette looked down and saw her mother had completely ignored her request. Bernadette's plate was piled with two fried sunny-side-up eggs, cheese grits, two buttermilk biscuits slathered with butter and filled with her grandmother's homemade fig jam, and six slices of crispy fried bacon.

"Mama, I can't eat all of this! I said I want to lose weight and this is more calories than I need for the entire day!" She pushed the plate away from her in disgust.

Her mother pushed the plate back in front of her.

"Bernadette, honey, I'll never forget what happened when I went to the grocery by myself for the first time. I was six years old and I remember that day just like it was yesterday. Money was tight, but my Mama always found a way to fill our bellies. She told me to go to the grocery and ask the meat man for some soup bones. What I didn't understand is why she didn't give me any money! Well, I figured she just didn't have any to give me right then and that didn't matter anyway. You see, back then people tried to help each other. You could run a tab at the grocery and just pay them whenever you got the money. They didn't even charge you any interest. People were just nice like that... Well, I went in that grocery thinking I'd have to tell the cashier to put the soup bones on my Mama's tab. But, when the meat man gave me the package, he had written on it 'no charge.' That's right! That package of soup bones wrapped in freezer paper had 'no charge' scribbled on it with that big, black marker he used to quote the price. I didn't have to pay a dime!

When I got home I asked my Mama why it was no charge, and she explained it's because you have to pay for meat but bones were free! She told me to remember that when I went to school. If anyone teased me about being fat to tell them you have to pay for meat but bones are free.... You remember that too, Bernadette. Bones were free back then. No one wanted to be skinny! Nowadays, they even make you pay for the soup bones but meat is still higher. Yes, ma'am, meat costs a lot more than bones! Remember that, Bernadette! Now, honey, eat your breakfast before you get weak. I want to see that plate clean. Like the nuns used to tell me when I was in school, 'People in China are starving.' So, you don't ever want to waste what's put in front of you."

Bernadette's face was glum, and she was about to push the plate away once again and refuse to eat it when her father gave her a stern look.

"That's right, Bernadette. When I was growing up, men didn't want no skinny woman." He purposely used the double negative to emphasize his point. "No indeed! Now, you eat that good breakfast your Mama made for you right now and get all that stupid dieting nonsense out of your head.... Baby girl, you're fine just the way you are."

Glancing across the table at her sister, Cecelia had a smug smile on her face, and Bernadette knew she was laughing at her again. When Cecelia stuck her chin out towards her indicating she had won another skirmish between the two sisters, Bernadette wanted to reach across the table and slap the satisfied expression off her face. Those images of Cecelia first taunting her in front of the relatives and then gloating over Bernadette losing her food battle with their parents replayed in her mind as well as other things Cecelia had done over the years.

She began wondering why she was standing in front of this mirror upset about wearing this awful outfit and why did she ever agree to work the spoiled brat's shift? What compounded the hurt she was feeling was her physical features compared to Cecelia's. Bernadette had inherited the larger build and looks of the women from her father's side of the family while Cecelia had the more petite build and delicate features of their mother's. "Call it sibling rivalry, call it jealousy, call it whatever you want as long as you truthfully called it for what it was," Bernadette thought. Cecelia didn't deserve the sacrifice she had agreed to make.

Disgusted, Bernadette was about to slip out the outfit and tell Cecelia she had changed her mind and was not going to work the breakfast shift for her at Joe's when the reason she had agreed to do so in the first place swung her door open and came bouncing into her bedroom.

"Aunt Ber'dette, Aunt Ber'dette," her two year old niece Miki was calling. "Maw-Maw says come eat!"

As the toddler ran towards her, Bernadette stooped to capture her in her arms. Lifting her and planting a kiss on the soft, chubby cheek, she responded, "Ok, Miki. You go tell Maw-Maw I'll be right there."

After hugging her tightly and planting butterfly kisses in the crook of her neck causing the toddler to squeal, Bernadette stooped again placing Miki back on the floor and watched as the chubby little figure with bouncing dark curls scampered from her bedroom to deliver the message.

Since Miki came along, everyone now called Bernadette's mother Maw-Maw, a Creole nickname for grandmother. Bernadette loved her niece and wanted to ensure Miki had everything she needed. When Cecelia got pregnant, she had been expelled from the private Catholic high school. She was scheduled to take her GED tests that morning. If she passed, she would be able to start college the following fall. Neither of them wanted to leave Joe shorthanded on one of his busiest restaurant days. He had been too kind to both of them through the years. Looking back in the mirror for the last time, Bernadette knew this wasn't about Cecelia. It was for Miki's future and wearing this hideous outfit was worth the sacrifice for her precious niece. She tried to keep that thought as she drove to Joe's that morning in her pink and white uniform. It was time for the round chimney to report to work.

Chapter Two

Clark Laurent woke that morning the same way he did every morning – sunlight streaming through the bare windows in his bedroom and the aroma of his favorite French roasted coffee perking. Coffee perking always helped his day start right. He had grown up in New Orleans East but his grandmother, who lived in one of the older sections of New Orleans called Gentilly, would pick him up every day from his elementary school. He would stay at his grandmother's until his mother got off from work. Rather than taking the interstate home, his mother preferred to drive down Gentilly Boulevard until it turned into Chef Menteur Highway. He often heard her say, "After a hectic, stressful day at work, I don't want to deal with those fools speeding like they're crazy on the interstate and cutting in front of me." She wanted a relaxing drive instead. Her favorite part of the trip had become Clark's as well. When they crossed the Danzinger Bridge, they could smell coffee roasting from the plant located on the Industrial Canal and bread baking from the factory on Downman Road. Clark couldn't think of more pleasant scents to wake to except one, the scent left on his pillow cases and sheets after a woman had shared his bed.

The problem is he always woke up alone. He was careful not to spend an entire night with anyone he dated. It didn't matter if they had sex at their place or in his condo. At some point during the night, he would either leave their pad and return home or wake his partner and have a pre-paid cab waiting to take them home from his condo. In his mind spending the entire night in someone's arms represented the start of a permanent commitment, one he wouldn't make until he knew he had found the right person. Lately, he regretted that the space next to him in the bed was empty when he woke. He was at a stage in his life that he was ready for more.

He thought about the previous evening. He and Patricia had been seeing each other for over ten months now. He turned onto his left side and imagined her sleeping soundly beside him. Somehow the image only gave him a sense of sexual satisfaction. He couldn't put his finger on it, but something didn't quite click though she seemed to be a nice person. She had mentioned the lease on her apartment was expiring and began hinting in little ways for a long term commitment. Each time she started a conversation in that regard, a warning bell went off in his head, and he hesitated to take that next step. He knew in that moment he would eventually break off this relationship as well.

Tossing off the covers, the cool air from the air conditioning vent rushed across his nude body causing him to shiver. It was rare for him to feel a chill. The times it did were always an omen of something about to change in his life. Clark shrugged the notion aside attributing it to his newfound knowledge that Patricia wasn't the right one either. After all, it was a Saturday. He wasn't even going into the office. He probably just had the temperature set lower than normal. Pulling on a pair of sweat pants, he climbed the stairway to his kitchen and poured a cup of the strong brewed coffee, added cream, and stirred in a teaspoon of sugar.

His condo was in a complex in the old warehouse district where renovations of abandoned buildings into luxury condos and apartments were making some very sharp entrepreneurs billionaires based on the price he had paid for his two bedroom unit. He particularly loved the entertainment area. When you first climbed the stairs, you entered a large living area with a wall of French doors that led to a lanai. The view of the Mississippi River at night was enchanting. Even stepping out onto the lanai in the morning light was invigorating. He enjoyed the many images that were so familiar, so much a part of his native city: the distant whir of vehicles speeding across the river bridge, the sounds of tug boats blowing their warning horns to ensure a safe passage as they pushed barges on the river, doors slamming on delivery trucks bringing fresh baked pastries to local coffee shops for the early morning breakfast crowds and crispy po-boy breads with soft centers to neighborhood restaurants to prepare for the lunch demands.

He stood by the railing sipping the coffee and watching cars speed across the Crescent City Connection, the official name of the Mississippi River's bridge. He pictured Patricia by his side, his arm circling her waist taking in the scene together. No matter how hard he tried, he couldn't visualize her truly loving the moment or putting on sweats to join him for his morning run on the levee. He didn't imagine any of the women he had dated fitting into that scene. Wearing designer sweat suits at a gym and walking on treadmills in an air conditioned environment would be more of an expectation of their status than to exercise outdoors. Of course having a massage, a fresh fruit plate, and a bottled sparkling water with a hint of fruit essence would complete their perceived workout. None of them would have been willing to work up a real sweat with him. Disgusted, he downed the last of the hot liquid and went back to his bedroom to dress. He wasn't up to the morning run alone and needed to meet the gang at Joe's for their monthly breakfast. No time for fantasy right now.

Stepping out of the elevator, Clark stopped by the security desk and slipped Adrian, the night shift guard, a bill. It was comforting to know he could just slip a robe on, kiss his date at the elevator, and Adrian would take things from there. Adrian knew Clark's routine well. As he monitored the security cameras, he would ring for the cab as soon as he saw Clark's entrance door open. The ladies always assumed Clark had gone through special planning just for them. Thinking that Clark had called for the security guard to greet them to ensure their safety and had arranged to have a car waiting, made the ladies feel like princesses. Adrian always walked them to the cab, opened the door for them, tipped his hat politely wishing them a good night and saying it was such a pleasure to see them again before closing the door and signaling for the driver to move out by a slight tap on the rear panel. None of them guessed this was a scene that had played out the same way on so many occasions that it was well orchestrated at this stage.

No words needed to be spoken between Clark and Adrian. Anyone watching the exchange would think the two men were just doing a handshake instead of slipping a bill from one's palm to the others. The bill was Clark's way of saying thank you for being discrete. The tip of his hat was Adrian's way of acknowledging he appreciated the extra cash.

Clark stepped through the leaded glass entrance doors from the main lobby and took a moment to once again observe the morning bustle of a city that always had something on the move. Turning to his right, he walked half a block to the secured parking lot, punched in the gate code, and walked a short distance to retrieve his car from his reserved spot. That was the only drawback to the condo. He had wanted the parking to be adjacent to the building and covered so you didn't have to brave the elements. Other than that, everything else met the specifications he had given to the realtor. What had sold him was the view. He definitely would exchange the minor inconvenience for that image. Turning the key in his Corvette, he shifted into drive but had to wait for the iron security gate to swing back before pulling into the street and heading towards the New Orleans neighborhood called Mid City.

Chapter Three

Arriving at Joe's restaurant, Clark grew frustrated about the only thing he didn't like about Joe's, the parking lot. It was rare to find an empty spot, and he hated parking his car on the street. This morning played out the same way again. He drove into the parking lot and curved through towards the back exit but not a vacant spot was left. The closest empty parking spot he found was two blocks away. He didn't mind the exercise; he just hated not being able to keep an eye on his car. Joe's restaurant was famous in the Afro-American community. Even tourist had heard by word of mouth that it was one of the eating places you should not miss if you visit New Orleans. What bothered Clark was the neighborhood had changed since Joe first opened his doors. Clark was always careful not to leave anything of value within sight, but in this area, the target was the car itself.

By the time he entered Joe's, his mood was not his best. First, the realization this morning that Patricia was just another passing fancy, then having to sit with his car out of easy sight.

Bernadette had just recorded the tab in the register and counted out change for Lisa. She was bent over with her head under the counter to stash excess bills in a safe Joe had installed when she heard the bell jingle indicating a customer was entering the restaurant. From under the counter, she was surprised that Lisa greeted the customer with an animated lilt in her voice which was atypical of her usual manner.

"Hi, Clark! The guys have been waiting for you! Having your usual today?"

"Thanks, Lisa, but no! I think it's time for a change. May I see a menu?"

"Sure. Right this way."

Hearing a voice reminiscent of Luther Vandross, her favorite male artist, Bernadette knocked her head against the post supporting the countertop in her rush to catch a glimpse of the customer. He and Lisa were turning down the far aisle with booths along the windows by the time she was able to spot them. If Valerie had worked that shift, she would have slammed her hip against Bernadette's and said, "Damn! That man is FINE!"

Having died unmarried at only 54, there were always rumors that Luther Vandross was gay. Eyeing this guy taking a seat next to two gentlemen that had arrived a few minutes earlier, Bernadette knew there was nothing gay about him. As he raised the coffee cup Lisa had set in front of him to his mouth, her eyes were drawn to perfectly formed lips under a trim moustache. The way his shoulders filled the black slim fit polo shirt he wore and his biceps stretched the cuff of the sleeve showed he worked out regularly, obviously not from need but a commitment to fitness.

The bell rang again and Bernadette turned to see an attractive, slim lady in an expensive business suit standing inside the door waiting for someone to approach and seat her. Obviously not a regular customer, Bernadette smiled and greeted the patron, "You may sit anywhere you like."

"Thank you," she smiled back but something in the expression told Bernadette the smile she returned was forced. She glanced about the restaurant and her eyes fell on the guy Lisa had called Clark. After staring at him, she strutted to the only empty table left in that aisle, her hips swaying and her six inch heels clicking on the tiled floor. She slowed her pace as she passed Clark's booth. The man seated next to Clark didn't miss her as she passed, but Clark seemed oblivious to her arrival.

As Allison walked up to present another tab to Bernadette, Bernadette focused back on the business of running the restaurant for Joe.

Chapter Four

To say Clark was distracted and not in tune to his friend's conversation was an understatement.

"Hey, man! What's wrong with you this morning?" Willy spoke impatiently as he jabbed Clark's right side so hard with his left elbow, Clark winced.

"After that, I can tell you what's wrong. I have a set of bruised ribs," Clark responded looking at him annoyed.

Sitting across from the two of them, Michael got a good laugh watching the antics of his two friends. It was reminiscent of their college years.

Willy continued, "Man, you didn't even smile at that fox that just passed. She was trying hard to catch your eye and you didn't give her the time of day! What's wrong with you this morning? Man, if she had given me the look she gave you, I would leave you two in this booth, and I'd be sitting at that table for two with her. You sick or something?"

Willy tried to discretely glance backwards and check the lady out again. The look she gave him made it obvious his attention was not the one she was seeking. She pointedly turned her gaze to the back of Clark's head before looking down to study the menu again. Without looking first, Willy grabbed Clark's arm causing the coffee cup he was lifting to his mouth to tip and splash, most of it falling onto the napkin in his lap.

"Damn, Willy, what the hell? One more time and, man, you're on my list! What's your problem this time?"

Clark was irritated as he dabbed at the wet spots on his shirt and tossed the soiled white napkin on the table. He motioned for Michael to pass him the clean one from the empty spot. Glancing at Willy, he gave him a stare indicating that better be the last time he touched him today!

"Man, you need to check her out! I wish she was looking that way at me."

Clark looked at Michael with an expression that, after four years of college together, said everything without the need for words, "Is it worth my while to turn around or has Willy not had some in so long, anything works for him?"

Understanding the signal, Michael spoke for the first time on the subject, "She is hot! I wouldn't mind tapping her myself but I can tell she doesn't want me either… Every time I glance that way, her eyes are like darts!"

"See, man! See! I told you!" Willy chatted with such animation Clark knew nothing was going to calm down the excitement he had over this woman. He wanted to change his seat and join Michael in the opposite side of the booth but the move would be a signal to the lady that he was interested and was positioning himself to sustain eye contact. Reluctantly, he shifted in the booth so he could easily glance over his left side.

Her expression and coy smile definitely signaled her interest. The way she eyed him back then reached over to remove her brief case from the chair opposite hers and place it on the floor before taking her fork to pick a berry from the fresh fruit plate she had ordered was the signal to please come over and interrupt her. Clark noted her suit, shoes, hairstyle, brief case, and cell phone sitting in easy access on the table. He surmised correctly she was a pharmaceutical representative in town for a few days and had appointments that morning with doctors at the medical complex nearby. He turned back as their waitress approached and placed his order. Michael placed his as well. It was Clark's turn to get back at Willy. He took his right elbow and knocked it hard into Willy's left side to get his attention.

Willy turned from staring backwards at the lady and responded, "What?"

"Close your mouth until your food comes. You're holding up progress, man. Give Lisa your order!"

Michael laughed at the comment and Willy looked at Lisa apologetically before ordering his usual. Once the waitress walked away, the conversation continued between Willy and Clark with Michael watching his two friends entertain him, occasionally laughing at their exchange.

"So, what you think?"

"Think about what?"

"Think about what? Man, you mean to tell me you're not going over there? You crazy? Don't you see the looks she's giving you? I know you could probably have her TONIGHT if you wanted to. You are actually sitting there telling me you're passing that up? Man, you need to make a doctor's appointment if you're passing on that... Something is seriously wrong with you!"

"You know one night stands were never my style! You also know I'm dating Patricia right now and, even if I wasn't, I'm just tired of it!"

"Tired of what? You're burnt out already at your age? Are you saying you need some of those pills they advertise on television?"

Michael had to comment on that one, "Willy, you're asking for it now! I wouldn't go there."

"We're friends. If he's having problems or caught some disease, he can confide in us. I'd understand. That's the only reason I can think of he'd pass up on that."

Willy glanced back one more time and saw the lady gathering her things. He leaned over and whispered into Clark's ear, "Hey man, she picked up her stuff and she's about to pass our booth!"

Purposely glancing down at Clark to give him one final chance, she angrily picked up her pace and walked over to the register when he didn't return her gaze. Clark watched the exchange with the lady he assumed was the cashier though it appeared she was running the restaurant that day instead of Joe, the owner. The patron was taking out on the cashier the fact that she felt rejected by Clark. Clark could tell by the exchange nothing she apparently had for breakfast pleased her. The lady in charge remained calm and professional lending her undivided attention and nodding at appropriate times to indicate she was listening. When the patron pulled out her credit card, the cashier indicated with a wave of her hand there would be no charge. She scribbled something on the bill then stuck it into the collections bin. The patron chattered on a minute or two more and the cashier indicated again with a wave of her hand that it was no charge. When the patron couldn't get the cashier riled, she stuck the credit card back into her wallet, tossed the wallet into her purse, and gave Clark a scowling final glance before stomping out the restaurant.

"See what you did, man?" Willy spoke contritely but loudly into Clark's ear.

About to lose his last shred of patience, Clark spoke first to Michael, "Remind me never to sit next to him again"

Turning his attention to Willy, their faces were almost touching as Clark responded angrily, "Did what?"

"Man, you upset her!"

"Upset her how, Willy? Unlike you, I'm a little more selective. Just because it's free doesn't mean you bring it home! You need to hang a sign on your door. I can see your slogan, 'Got a stray pussy, drop it here.'"

Michael laughed before adding, "Whoa! He got you there, Willy. We all know you don't pass up anything! You're the poster child for venereal diseases."

Willy answered indignantly, "Man, that's wrong! You both just wrong.... Hey, remember that song Glenn's mother used to be singing when we went over to his house about love making the world a better place. All I'm trying to do is to make the world a better place by comforting those in need."

Clark looked at his friend and shook his head. Willy was mixing pop music with a bible phrase. He chose his words carefully before replying, "You keep spreading your love, but for me, that's not my scene. I'm tired of taking a woman to dinner and all she orders is a salad and then picks at it all evening. I'm fed up with the trophy wife images. I'm sitting in a restaurant wanting to order an appetizer, steak, baked potato, and maybe dessert too and she's sitting across from me wanting a salad. Right then, I know she's just going to pick at that salad all night. I'm fed up with that type of date. I want someone that's going to chow down with me. I want to take out a woman I know is enjoying herself! Like this one you're calling a fox? Look at our plates – omelets, bacon, and sides of pancakes. What did she do back there? She picked at a saucer of fresh fruit slices, barely touched a slice of plain toast and nonfat yogurt, and then complains to the cashier about her food. How can you mess that up? It doesn't even have to be cooked. I don't need that in my life, and I'm fed up with it!"

Michael could empathize. He was beginning to feel the same way. It seems they were meeting too many women that were artificial. He longed for the real thing too.

Willy was still being Willy. He motioned to Michael and started laughing, "Check out the chick at the register. Mike, Clark should take her out. I bet she would order more than a side salad."

Turning to face Clark, he continued, "What about her, Clark? You want to date the ham hock?" Willy was bursting with laughter by the time he finished his sentence.

Michael turned to his left and paid attention to who was at the register for the first time. He couldn't help but agree with Willy, "She didn't get that weight ordering salads." Michael started laughing too.

Both continued laughing heartily and giving each other a high five.

Clark couldn't believe the two clowns sitting with him. While Michael was always amused by Willy's behavior, most of the time he aggravated Clark and today even more so. His father had drilled into him that a man should be a woman's champion and guardian and here Willy was poking fun at a woman he didn't even know just because of her size. He was working on Clark's last nerve and Clark was fed up with him. Turning to face Willy, he hissed, "She's the same size as your Mama!"

"Man, don't you talk about my Mama!" Willy's facial expression became serious for the first time that morning.

"I'm not TALKING ABOUT your mother, William! I'm making an observation...." Clark used the name Willy's mother always called him as emphasis. "The point I'm trying to make is you love your mother. Your mother is the same size as that cashier. Why are you ready to ask me to step outside over your mother but you're sitting here making fun of a lady that's the same size? If you love your mother, why would you not date someone like her? I saw your parents' wedding picture. Your mother was as skinny as Glenn's wife before she had four children.

"Man, like I said. Don't you talk about my Mama!" Willy turned away slightly but kept checking out Bernadette. It appeared he was contemplating what Clark had said.

Michael jumped in to try to ease the tension that was quickly building addressing his remarks to Willy. "He has a point, man! Think about Glenn's mother too. We all would beat the crap out of anyone that made an ugly comment about Mrs. Eleanor, and Mrs. Eleanor is larger than your mother and that cashier."

Mentioning Glenn upset Clark even more, "Think about Glenn now. Remember when we drove down to Houston that weekend for the Saints game? He looks miserable and it's all because he married the same kind of woman that just walked out of here! Like I said, man, that's not for me!"

Chapter Five

Clark hated he had made that comment about Glenn and wished he could have taken the words back as soon as they were spoken. The four of them had met at college. They were the only black males that year that had registered for engineering majors at the traditionally white university. They formed a quick bond and supported each other, studying together and using their joint knowledge to ensure each passed every class. Of the four, Glenn was the only one that accepted a job out of town after graduation. With a degree in chemical engineering, one of the major oil companies quickly grabbed him up and he moved up the corporate ladder faster than he ever imagined as part of their corporate diversity initiatives.

Of the three, Glenn was Clark's confidant, the one he could truly open up with and share his dreams. The feeling was mutual. It was the visit to Houston and staying at Glenn's place that triggered Clark to start reassessing his own life and what he really wanted.

During their college years, Glenn had tried repeatedly to date a girl named Gwendolyn. They had swung by the traditional black university one weekend and Glenn had met Gwen at a party the Alpha Kappa Alpha's had given for their pledges. Fair skinned with blondish hair and light green eyes, Gwen was considered a high yellow in the Creole culture and wouldn't give poor Glenn with his medium brown skin tone the time of day. When the word spread that a major oil company had recruited Glenn and made a salary offer higher than any Afro-American had previously received, Gwen was suddenly all over him. Within six months of graduation, Clark found himself serving as the best man at Glenn's wedding. Within two years, they had a daughter. Glenn took one look at Angelique and was stuck for life. Anything Gwendolyn demanded, he gave in. All she had to do was threaten him with divorce and not being able to see Angelique and whatever she desired was hers.

When they first arrived in Houston, the three admired everything Glenn had achieved. He had a beautiful home – six bedrooms most with private baths and three luxury cars in the garage. There was the S.U.V. equipped with all the latest features including a built-in child seat. Glenn and his wife each had the car of their dreams for the times they went out alone. However, Clark could tell the man was not comfortable in his own home. The house was a showcase, just like his trophy wife. It was not a home. Angelique was confined to a children's den on the second floor. No dolls would be caught lying on the sofa in the formal living room in this house. No bikes or roller skates would ever be left behind in the driveway. You won't find water toys hanging on the backyard fence to dry. No pictures drawn by their daughter were stuck on the refrigerator with magnets, and Clark knew they never would be unless in a custom frame and matching the decor. There was not a speck of dust to be found anywhere. Everything was picture perfect, like the window of a fine furniture store. Even the inside of the refrigerator didn't say home. No leftovers in plastic tubs or expired jars of condiments you never seemed to be able to finish. Clark wondered when and what they ate.

Gwen had gone out to tea with her club while the guys were at the football game. Post the game, they were hanging out in Glenn's den drinking beers and talking over old times before the trio drove back to New Orleans. The minute Glenn heard Gwen's car coming up the drive, he literally jumped into action. He had been holding Angelique on his lap letting her munch on animal crackers. He quickly passed her to Clark, got on his knees and scooped up any crumbs that had fallen on the carpet. He placed napkins under each can of beer and warned Willy to take his feet off the coffee table. He gathered all excess trash items, ran to the kitchen, and dumped all tell tale remnants in the garbage can. By the time Gwen made her entrance, the scene was picture perfect, picture perfect in Gwen's eyes. Clark could tell Glenn was on edge waiting for her to find the one thing he may have missed. Nothing to be left behind though Glenn paid for a maid service to come in twice a week and paid extra for the morning after service if they gave a party or had guests at the house.

Maybe Clark was more sensitive of the comment he had made because of the conversation he had with Glenn the night they arrived. After everyone else had settled in, Glenn and Clark had hung out in the den. Glenn had shared everything that was going on in his life – marriage, family, and career. He wanted more kids. In fact, when he agreed on the house plan Gwen had chosen, he thought they would have four kids and he didn't have any objection to each having their own bedroom. Despite using the most expensive skin creams available, Gwen had a stretch mark that hadn't faded from Angelique and was adamant she would not risk any additional blemishes to her figure. She told Glenn it was too hard now finding the right bikini to hide the awful scar when they attended pool parties and barbecues during the summer. Obviously he was heartbroken at the thought his house would never be filled with the patter of little feet. It was also frustrating he had paid for and had to keep up the ongoing expenses of heating and cooling a house with a square footage far beyond their needs.

The main struggle he was facing was his family. He had been offered another promotion but would have to move to Europe for a three years tour. His father had recently been diagnosed with cancer so he wanted to stay close to home where he could see him often and support the family through this medical battle. Because of the money, Gwen was pressuring him to take the job. She was also the envy of the wives in the club she had joined. There was no way she was going to let him pass up the chance for her to live in Paris and visit Europe during his stint. She had already hired a French language tutor for Angelique and instead of the toddler being able to watch cartoons on Saturday morning, she was forced to listen to tapes and work with her personal coach. Clark could tell he did not want to relocate at this time but by the end of their visit, Clark knew Glenn was going to sign the papers to authorize the start of his relocation process.

The way Clark was viewing Glenn's life he had married a trophy wife and became a prisoner in his own castle. Glenn was successful in his profession but not happy except for his one little shining star, Angelique. What was most frustrating is that Clark had no advice to give his friend. All he could think of to tell him was, "Divorce the bitch!" Seeing how he adored Angelique, Clark knew it would make Glenn's life even more miserable. Gwen would use the child against him every chance she could. Driving back from Houston, all Clark could think of is that he would not let the same thing happen to him. When he looked at the lady that gave the cashier a hard time, all he could see was an image of Gwendolyn. No way would he fall into that trap.

Chapter Six

All three of them had obviously been reminiscing about that weekend in Houston and each had their own thoughts and memories about Glenn's situation. Michael was the first to speak.

"Clark, do you know if he left for Europe yet?"

"He should be leaving in about two weeks. I talked with him the other night. They have the house leased furnished as is and were packing some personal items for storage. They'll be staying in a corporate apartment while in Europe unless he chooses to get his own housing."

Willy spoke then, "With that wife of his, she probably won't be satisfied unless she gets to do her own thing.... I really miss Glenn."

The trio fell into a spell of silence once again. This time Willy broke the silence.

"Remember when we were in college and we would all go over to Glenn's house when it was time to study for exams? Mrs. Eleanor would bake a batch of walnut, chocolate chip, oatmeal cookies. As soon as we hit the house, that smell would be filling the air. Man, didn't her kitchen smell good? She wouldn't do like Gwen did when we first arrived. Remember she put three cookies each on a china saucer so delicate, I was afraid to pick it up when she brought them to us. It was those little tea cookies too, not those jumbo ones like Mrs. Eleanor use to bake. You could tell Gwen just picked them up at some fancy, overpriced bakery. Mrs. Eleanor would have flour in her hair and a smudge of dough on her cheek. You knew she made her own cookies. Then she would put a whole tray in front of us and say, 'Help yourself, boys!'"

Michael had to share his memory. "The best time, to me, was when we pulled the all-nighter for the senior exam. We had eaten the entire double batch of walnut, chocolate chip, oatmeal cookies she had made, and we had completely wiped out every drop of milk in their refrigerator. It must have been two in the morning, and all of us were having problems staying awake. I think Willy dropping his textbook on the floor caused her to come and check on us. She came in, took one look, and took the tray back to the kitchen. It seems in no time at all, she had whipped up a batch of tea cakes and two big pitchers of lemonade. Just the scent of them baking in the oven got us going again and it was enough sugar between the cookies and the lemonade that none of us needed any sleep. I did better on that test than any other I took that semester."

Michael laughed at the memory.

Willy added, "My grandmother used to make us tea cakes and lemonade before she passed. Mrs. Eleanor's tasted just like my grandmother's."

After another short silence, Clark finally spoke. "That's what I'm talking about! I want to find a woman that knows the difference between a house and a home. I want my kids to know what it's like to smell real cookies baking in the oven, and I don't mean buying one of those ready-made rolls out the refrigerator case at the grocery. You know the ones I'm talking about? They advertise them on television all the time. All you have to do is peel off the wrapper, slice them up, put them on a cookie sheet, and stick them in the oven. I guess the house smells good, but it's not the same.… They're not like Mrs. Eleanor's."

Willy broke the silence this time. "You know. I've been thinking. Glenn is all the way in Houston, and now he's going to Europe for three years. Man, what kind of friends are we? I need to go over and check on Mrs. Eleanor from time to time. That's the least I can do for my friend. You know. Go check on his mother and make sure she's doing okay and not needing anything."

Clark looked at Willy like he was a space monster. "Man, you are so full of bullshit I can't believe it!"

"What? What?" Willy looked from Clark to Michael and back again trying to understand.

Clark continued. "Just like your love is going to better the world and you have to comfort those in need, right? You are going over there for one reason and one reason only. You want to start bringing up all those memories in hopes Mrs. Eleanor is going to bake you some cookies. You ain't doing a damn thing for Glenn. It's all about you, Willy! If you go over there and try to get that lady to bake you cookies with all she's doing to take care of her husband, I'm going to call Glenn even if he's in Europe and tell him what you're doing. Man, I don't know why I stay friends with you!"

"Come on, Clark! You wouldn't do that! Huh, Michael? Clark wouldn't do that to me?"

Willy looked really scared that Clark was going to tell on him. Michael was trying to hide his amusement that a batch of cookies could turn a grown man into a jelly doughnut but wasn't doing a good job at it. Clark glanced at him shaking his head in disbelief that Willy grew that concerned.

Disappointed he might not get a batch of homemade cookies, Willy started sulking, "Damn, those cookies were good! Glenn should take some of his money and set up his Mom in her own business."

Silence fell again.

Lisa walked up at that point and asked if they wanted anything more. All three shook their heads indicating they had their fill. After leaving the bill on the table and walking away, Willy jabbed Clark again. Michael burst out laughing when Clark slammed both of his hands on the tabletop before getting out of the booth motioning to Michael to move over and taking a seat next to him.

"Hey, what's wrong, man? Why you changed seats?"

Clark just stared at him a second before turning to Michael, "He just doesn't get it, does he? Does he ever get it?"

"What? Get what? Are you complaining about me jabbing you again? Man, I had a good point!"

"Like what?"

"You two think the ham hock knows how to bake cookies?"

All three of them turned to look at Bernadette. With the mock white apron on the front of her uniform, they each could visualize Bernadette in the kitchen just like Mrs. Eleanor. Their looks turned to one of longing as their senses recalled the scent of milk chocolate chips melting in the oven and walnuts roasting. It was heavenly taking that first bite of a warm, crisp cookie followed with a gulp of cold milk.

Clark spoke first, "You know.... If you ignore the uniform and don't focus on her weight, she's really an attractive lady."

Willy started acting up again, "Man, I think you passed up the fox because you want to go out with the ham hock."

Michael started laughing.

"What if I do? Why is that so amusing?" Clark challenged, the lectures from his father motivating him to be the lady's champion.

Michael had to speak this time, "Come on, Clark. You're not serious. I'd bet money on it."

Willy was quick to chime in, "Me too."

Clark rarely acted impulsively but something was triggering his protective instincts where this lady was concerned.

"How much are you willing to cough up? It would have to cover her costs and mine. Are you ready to put your money where your mouth is? If not, I don't want to hear another criticism of that lady."

Michael looked at Clark a little confused studying his friend's face. Something else was going on here but he couldn't put his finger on it? Having known Clark for so long, one thing he was sure of is that Clark probably couldn't put a finger on it at this stage either. Still not thinking he was serious but his gut feeling was to egg Clark on and let this play out, Michael stepped up to the challenge.

"I'll put up a C-note." He studied Clark's reaction as he said it. Seeing how serious he was, Michael knew it was time for the teasing to stop. He wished he could make Willy understand that but the guys knew Willy well.

"C-note for what?" Willy questioned not following the exchange that just occurred between Clark and Michael and glancing between the two of them hoping for some direction.

"When I take a woman out, I don't bring her to cheap places. Unless each of you coughs up at least a hundred, I can't ask the lady to go out with me."

It's a good thing Clark had changed his seat. No way even his ribs could have taken the jabs from Willy at that.

Willy finally understood, "Clark, are you saying you will go out with the ham hock if each of us puts up a hundred dollars?"

"That's exactly what I'm saying and if you call the lady a ham hock one more time, it'll cost you two hundred," Clark stated to Willy in no uncertain terms.

Michael glanced at Clark again. He was positive now something more was happening here.

Willy couldn't pass up this challenge. He pulled out his wallet, sorted through the business cards as well as the money he had and finally dropped five twenty dollar bills on the table.

Michael looked between his two friends for a minute before following suit and dropping two fifties on top of Willy's before setting the ground rules. "You have to take her out within two weeks and I expect a photo of the two of you together at the restaurant as proof! It better not be an edited version either."

"No problem!" Clark picked up the stack of bills and stuffed them into his own billfold before turning to look at the cashier. Now was the biggest challenge. Could he convince her to go out with him?

Chapter Seven

As soon as Clark rose from the table, Bernadette knew something was amiss. When she first started working at Joe's, Joe took her under his wing and trained her himself. On her first day, she did nothing but follow him around learning the restaurant business. At one point, he brought her to the cashier's station. From that vantage point, you could see everything going on in the restaurant. Joe challenged her to look around the restaurant and tell him what she saw. Having graduated valedictorian from her high school, Bernadette wasn't accustomed to feeling stupid but she definitely felt stupid at that point. She felt like she was trying to solve one of those children picture puzzles, the kind where you find the hidden objects. Because she was still looking at things from a patron's viewpoint, she had no clue what Joe expected her to say. Joe let her case the joint for a few minutes before he started her first lesson.

Calling her by the nickname he had given her the first time they met Joe explained, "Peaches, ya're not here for the salary I'm paying ya'! Ya're here for the tips. A good waitress can make a killing on tips. There's a lot of well off people that come in here and they can give ya' some really nice tips! A good waitress can also make or break a business. She leaves just as big an impression on a patron as the food. So, ya' got to learn to read your customers."

Joe framed his hands together like an artist judging a scene in preparation for putting his brush to the canvas before continuing. He started pointing things out to her.

"See the man in the suit in the far corner. He keeps checking his watch. That means he can't be late for something important but he was hungry and needed a quick bite. To get a good tip, he doesn't want to have to look for ya' to get what he needs or his check. Keep everything flowing to him fast and offer him a cup of coffee 'to go.' He probably will need it.... See that couple in the booth. Ya' can tell by the way the lady smiles coyly every so often, closes her eyes, and sometimes even blushes that they are on a date so they want to be left alone. Don't go up and interrupt their conversation. Wait until it looks like they ran out of things to say, then ya' be right there to fill the gap so things don't get awkward with nothing but silence between them. If it gets too quiet and they don't have anything more to talk about, they start thinking that maybe they're not right for each other and they associate that memory with coming here. If the memory is bad, they will hesitate to come back. Then you may have lost a good customer.... See the four guys laughing and talking at the window table. They're watching the women passing on the street, talking about them, and sharing stories about women they went out with. Smile when ya' wait on their table. They won't mess with ya' because they know I don't allow that in here but they want to flirt with ya' a little, Peaches, so smile at them real pretty.... See the man by himself in the suit sipping his coffee slowly and reading his paper. He's in no hurry so don't try to rush him. When he looks up to find you, that's his signal he's ready for something else but get there fast. He has a routine and he likes to keep to it.... And always wear your school I.D. Lots of folks may give ya' a little extra knowing ya' working ya' way through college."

Bernadette was shocked at how differently she could see the pulse of the restaurant with the little knowledge Joe shared. The lessons continued, and eventually she became so good at handling things, Joe would leave her in charge for him on occasion. Because of these lessons, she had been monitoring the exchanges between the three guys in the booth. She could tell their conversation had been all about women and relationships. What she couldn't figure out despite having over four years of experience and tutoring under Joe is how she connected to their discussions. It had perked her interest so she had watched them even closer.

Bernadette hadn't missed a single glance or stare that had come her way. She got a little unnerved when all three of them were staring at her at the same time at one point. She had watched interestingly the exchange between the irate lady in the business suit and the gentleman named Clark now walking towards her. From the corner of her eye, she knew he had observed everything that transpired between them when the lady checked out. She wondered what relationship, if any, may have existed between the two of them and if he was not satisfied with the way she had handled things. Had the woman sent him a text message? Was he coming over to complain too? She had given the patron her entire meal for free. What more could they possibly want? Well, now she felt confident she was about to find out everything. As the gentleman came closer, she started getting butterflies in her stomach, which was odd. With her experience, she had learned how to handle any customer situation that came up. She shouldn't be nervous at all, but for some reason she couldn't fathom, she was.

"Excuse me, Miss." Clark didn't recognize his own voice. Why was it quivering? He sounded like a Catholic grammar school student about to ask a girl to dance with him for the first time. Acknowledging that feeling caused Clark to feel off his game. He was accustomed to women approaching him so why was he so nervous approaching this cashier?

"Yes, sir. How may I serve you today?" Bernadette was shocked that her voice came across as calm and professional as she faced him despite the turmoil in her stomach. After hearing how strong she sounded, her confidence level was restored until the gentlemen uttered the next sentence.

"I was wondering if you were free next Friday night. If you are, would you grant me the pleasure of your company for dinner?"

Bernadette could feel the blood draining from her face. She thought she was going to faint. That is the last thing she expected the gentleman to say. Glancing at his comrades in the booth, she realized they were watching her reaction and everything the gentleman was doing. She knew exactly what was going on. She had experienced that before and it made her transition from being nervous to being angry. She thought she had been in a real relationship and she had been working hard at it. Then she found out it was only the same inconsiderate, juvenile-acting, stupid guy stuff that she knew was playing out right in front of her eyes, the same kind of foolishness that ended with her quitting the first job she had right out of college.

Chapter Eight

Bernadette had majored in computer science with an emphasis on Information Technology (IT). Not wanting to disappoint her parents, she had gone to work for the son of one of her parents' closest friends instead of accepting a position at a major corporation in their IT department. After several years in corporate America, the guy had secured a minority small business loan and risked starting his own firm. His main clients were other small businesses that needed custom built computers and software programs based on their specific needs. After going to a few kick-off meetings with the owner, she had fallen in love with her job and was glad she did accommodate her parents' request and had joined his team.

Bernadette enjoyed the independence and opportunity for creativity she had instead of being in a rigid, dictated environment. She would go back to work and develop the coding based on what was needed whether printing their payroll checks based on spreadsheets, sending out bills, or creating mailing lists in a database for promotional material. She loved being able to do her own thing and the look of satisfaction from the customer when she delivered the final product. It also gave her an opportunity to learn marketing skills, an area she had not studied in college. Based on word of mouth, the client base of the small firm grew and the owner was able to give her progressive pay increases until her salary matched the initial offers she had been received from larger companies. It was still not the financial position Bernadette wanted to be in so she could get her own apartment and purchase a new car, but she was saving towards those goals.

After the initial meeting with the client, Bernadette was also required to work up a specification list based on the amount of data that needed to be processed and the level of literacy the client had. If during the interview session she sensed the client enjoyed typing commands, she would not build in as much mechanization into the software programs. If she had to point out the power button to the client and explain the log-in process, she built a lot of function keys into her software so they could just press a button and everything would magically happen. She never envisioned the interpersonal skills she had learned as a waitress was a transferrable skill based on her college curriculum. She had even called Joe and thanked him for the lessons he had shared. The skills she had learned about reading people and their positive and negative reactions along with her ability to modify her approach served her well in her new career.

Part of her job involved getting the hardware built once the customer's software specifications were determined. The owner had hired two guys that actually ordered the parts needed before building the client's computer from scratch. The firm was still very small. In fact, other than the owner, Bernadette, the two hardware geeks, and a secretary, there were no other full time employees. An accountant was paid on an hourly basis to keep up with the book keeping requirements for the firm and a local copying firm consulted with the owner to print any specific items on an as needed basis.

Bernadette was working late one night, and the only other person in their tiny leased space was Gregory, one of the hardware geeks. He knocked on Bernadette's door but didn't wait for a response before barging in.

"Hey, babe, how are you doing tonight?

Greg didn't even talk to her unless they were discussing customer specs. In fact, he typically came across as outright rude. Bernadette didn't know how to react to the greeting and didn't have any time to waste thinking about it. Her initial thought was Greg must be drunk the way he was looking at her. She knew Greg and Kevin, the other hardware guru, often went to Happy Hours after work and was wondering if he had come back to the office to wrap up some things after partying.

"I'm fine, Greg. I just have an awful lot of coding to finish to get these specs to you guys on Monday so we can meet the deadline I promised the customer, so if you don't mind, please excuse me. I need to wrap this up."

Bernadette didn't want to come across as rude but needed to be firm. They had never had any casual conversation before and this was not the time to start.

"I know you have a minute for me!"

Greg walked over to her desk and sat on the edge. Bernadette could do nothing but look at him and deal with what he wanted so she could get rid of him as quickly as possible.

"Ok, Greg, but only one minute!" She clicked "File, Save" to ensure she didn't lose the coding she had just completed and turned to give him her undivided attention.

"I was thinking that maybe you and I could go out sometimes."

Greg had reached over and was moving his index finger slowly up and down Bernadette's forearm. Bernadette didn't have to think about it anymore. She knew without any doubt that Greg must have been drunk and he was making her very uncomfortable, especially since only the two of them were in the office suite that night. She knocked his hand off her arm and stood up to make more of a point.

"I don't think that would be a good idea, Greg. I don't believe people who work together should be in a relationship! So, if you would please excuse me...."

Bernadette walked over to her office door and opened it indicating clearly it was time for him to leave. She didn't know if she really believed what she had said or not but had heard it on a soap opera one time and it sounded like an appropriate response based on the situation. She had come to the conclusion in later reflection that her response was sophisticated and mature, especially for someone who had never been in a situation like that before.

Greg did get off the edge of her desk but leaned close to her as he walked out. He was so close, their lips almost touched as he whispered, "Think about it." He winked before walking out the door.

Bernadette quickly switched the knob to the locked position. Sitting back at her computer, it took her several minutes to compose herself. She couldn't regain her focus until she heard Greg's car pulling out the parking lot. She wondered if she should report it to the owner. What if a similar situation would come up with a client? If she did report it, would he have second thoughts about her ability to meet and deal with clients? Bernadette shrugged the incident off to Greg being drunk and went back to work. Nothing serious had happened so she never mentioned the incident.

After that fateful Friday night, Greg began initiating more casual conversations with Bernadette. For Valentine's Day he brought both her and the secretary flowers. The secretary had an arrangement of pink carnations. Bernadette was given a dozen American Beauty roses. Greg continued trying to get her to go out with him and approached her every time they were alone. Bernadette finally gave in.

For their first date, Greg suggested they go to a Happy Hour. Since Bernadette had never been to one, she went along with the suggestion to satisfy her own curiosity. Though Greg encouraged her to take advantage of the 'two for one' specials, Bernadette had never drunk in public without being with her parents. Knowing she had to drive home, she settled for a virgin pina colada. The free appetizers were great, but other than the food, she never felt comfortable the entire evening. It seemed there was little she could offer up for conversation that Greg would follow and that was a skill she had learned well dealing with customers at Joe's. After sitting and trying to make small talk for over an hour, Bernadette made an excuse about needing to get home by a certain time, thanked Greg for a wonderful time, and headed out.

That night in bed she thought about the evening. Bernadette had gone on her first real date. She had been out with guys before, who were basically the sons of her parents' friends escorting her to events like her high school proms. It wasn't real dates. Somehow, she didn't think this is how it should feel. She was tempted to call Valerie and bounce everything off her friend but didn't know if she had enough to share yet. The other thing that bothered her is the fact that she hadn't mentioned

Greg to her parents. This is the first time she was hiding something from them, another sign that something wasn't quite right about this first date.

The next time they went out, Greg asked Bernadette to decide where they should go. There was a movie she had been dying to see and suggested that. At the concession counter, Bernadette wanted to order the jumbo popcorn with the free refills but hesitated. To her surprise, Greg turned to her and asked if she mind buying that size and share. Maybe they had some things in common after all. Bernadette became so engrossed in the movie that she didn't pay attention to the fact Greg ate very little of the first bag and none of the refill he got during intermission.

The third and fourth dates were Happy Hours on a Friday evening after work at different venues, but it proved just as awkward between them as the first date. Their fifth date was complements of the owner of their firm. There was an exhibition at NOMA, the New Orleans Museum of Art. To get a free advertisement in the program, he had purchased tickets for all his employees. Bernadette met Greg at the museum one Saturday afternoon. It seemed Greg wanted to speed through the exhibit at a faster pace than Bernadette thought made sense, especially when they arrived and she saw the price the owner had paid for their admissions. To be able to report back on their experience to the owner, Bernadette wanted to peruse every plaque, sit through the mini film presentations throughout the exhibit, experience the hands on activity, and attend the special lecture at the end of the self-guided tour. Greg seemed agitated she wanted the full experience. When she got in the line for the lecture, he made some excuse about having another appointment, excused himself, and said he'd see her at the office on Monday.

That night in bed, Bernadette wondered why Greg never asked for her home phone number. Thinking about the times they went to Happy Hour and her failed attempts at keeping a conversation with him going, she shrugged it off. What would they discuss if he did call?

The next time Greg asked Bernadette out, he suggested the buffet at one of the casinos on the west bank. Since their office was located close to the Mississippi River Bridge, Greg suggested they ride over together and he drop Bernadette back at the office after to get her car. It didn't make sense for her to waste her gas. The drive over was made in almost total silence. Bernadette kept trying to bring up topics she thought would interest Greg but received very trite responses. At the buffet, Bernadette had gone back through the line for a third time when it dawned on her Greg had stopped eating and was just sitting there watching her totally bored. Catching his expression as she bit into a fried chicken leg, she decided it was best to skip dessert. When they got back to the parking lot by work, it was already dark. Greg didn't pull into his assigned, reserved spot but into the spot where the lights illuminating the parking lot were the brightest. He sat silently for what seemed longer than normal, then suddenly turned towards Bernadette and kissed her lightly on the lips. He didn't touch her or look at her after but sat silently once again staring out the window on the driver's side. Bernadette didn't know how to respond. The kiss wasn't what she expected. It felt more like something a sister and brother would exchange. The only difference is that it was on her lips instead of her cheek. She felt disappointed. She thought her first real kiss would generate more feelings within her.

With Greg not speaking and just staring out the window, Bernadette glanced over trying to ascertain what she should do next. She thought his expression spoke volumes and it clearly indicated he was sorry for what he had done. It was the same expression she'd seen on patrons at Joe's restaurant who had ordered the wrong dish. She didn't want to get out the car saying nothing so she whispered good night softly before opening the door and stepping out the car. Greg didn't even wait to ensure she had got into her own vehicle safely. As soon as she cleared his car, he backed out the parking spot and sped away.

The following Monday Greg was acting like his old self again. He completely ignored Bernadette unless they had to attend a meeting. His behavior wasn't really that unusual since he never came on to her if others were around.

On Thursday of that week, Bernadette had to leave work early to escort her mother to a doctor's appointment. She had driven only two blocks when she remembered she had left her cellular phone on the corner of her desk. She had plenty of time to drive back to the office. When she entered the building, she could hear Greg and Kevin arguing. She wasn't the type to ease drop but something told her to position herself so that she could hear the conversation. Greg was the one that sounded upset.

"The bet was all my expenses would be paid. I'd also get twenty dollars and a five dollar bonus if I kissed her! Look at the camera I sat up. See that! I even kissed the fat cow! You owe me, man. Pay up!"

"How many dates you went on? You had to go out six times. These receipts only have dates for five times."

"That's because one of the dates was using those dumb, free museum tickets! You should pay me a bonus for that. I spent hours walking through that museum with her. She had to read everything. You'd think she was going to be tested on the material or something. You're getting off cheap. For dinner, I took her to a buffet. Can you imagine what your payout would have been if the fat cow ordered a la carte?"

"Alright! Here's your money. You won fair and square. I never thought when I made the dare you'd go through with it. I believe you now. You would do anything for money!"

Bernadette stepped from behind the cabinet where she had positioned herself and purposely clicked her heels hard on the linoleum floor as she walked to her office so the two geeks would hear her. Greg came running into her office behind her.

"Bernadette, what did you hear? Whatever you heard, I can explain. "

Bernadette grabbed her cellular phone, pushed past him, and walked toward the parking lot. Greg was running behind her pleading for her to talk with him. She acted as if he wasn't there. Both Greg and Kevin knew the owner was almost like family to her. She never responded or looked at him. She thought she'd let them sweat it out wondering if she would report them.

When she went to work on Friday, Bernadette kept the door to her office locked. She ignored Greg's knocking and any phone calls from his extension. She purposely left work on time so she and the secretary would walk out together without Greg approaching her and starting a personal conversation. Over the weekend, she thought about the situation and decided to resign. She couldn't continue working with people that juvenile. The summer intern she had mentored was about to graduate and could step in to replace her with minimal training. That would be the easiest thing for everyone. When she sat down with the owner to turn in her resignation, she could see through the one window of his office that Greg was in the hall outside pacing up and down. When she came out the meeting, she saw he had gone back to his own office but looked up at her with a worried expression as she past his door. Bernadette knew that was the last time he and Kevin would play a prank like that anymore.

Chapter Nine

Bernadette tried to remain calm as she fought to think of the right words to tell Clark to take a flying leap. When she thought she had formulated the perfect sentences, she looked up to focus her anger on him but something drew her eyes to the portrait of Joe on the wall behind Clark. One of the short order cooks he helped through college had graduated in art and painted the oil of Joe as a tribute in appreciation for all Joe had done to support him finishing school. It seemed the eyes in the portrait locked with hers letting her hear Joe's voice.

"A good waitress can also make or break a business. She leaves just as big an impression on a patron as the food…. They associate that memory with coming here. If the memory is bad, they hesitate to come back. "

Bernadette had already processed the credit card transaction for the three guys. The order was one of the highest bills she had rung up that day, and they had left Lisa a fifty percent tip. Think, Bernadette, you're only here for one morning. Why let the stupid actions of these men you have never seen before and will never see again matter? Why let their juvenile behavior cause a day that had started out bad to get even worse? Why make Joe lose good customers and the waitresses lose good tippers just because you're riled up? Cool down and think of how you can salvage this.

Looking into the man's eyes, Bernadette recognized something different than she had seen in Greg's. Clark was just as ill at ease as she was over the situation. She needed to do something to lessen the tension building between them. Maybe being forthright was the best road to take. Having glanced towards the booth the three men had occupied, she softened her expression. Michael had twisted back into a semi-normal position while Willy nearly hung over the low wall between theirs and the next booth. Bernadette sighed and nodded in their direction.

"It seems your friends have a strong interest in whether or not I say yes?" She winked at Clark and gave him her most practiced waitress smile, the one Joe had taught her to use to get the big tips.

Clark grinned with embarrassment and dropped his head down a little to his chest. Bernadette looked at Joe's picture once again and knew she could actually salvage this. She had been taught by one the best. Most restaurants fail within the first few years, and Joe had been in business over forty years now after surviving some hard times and tough competition. She coaxed herself on, "You know the game they're playing, and you know the rules so you already have the upper hand in this." She couldn't wait to tell Valerie about this one the next time they had lunch together when Valerie asked her what was new.

"Hey, buddy. Why don't you tell me what the bet is and maybe we can figure out together how you can go back to the booth and save face with your friends and I don't get embarrassed either in the process? What do you say?"

Clark couldn't believe how astute this lady was. He bit the left side of his lower lip and his eyes shifted to the left as he tried to think of a comeback. Damn, he felt like Willy and he never thought he'd go that low in life. It was hard for him to face the lady when she had called his poker hand so his only option was to lay his cards on the table.

"Miss, first of all, I'm begging you to please accept my apology because you're right…. I am asking you out because of a stupid bet! For reasons I'd rather not go into, the bet is whether or not I had the balls to be bold enough to come over here and ask you to go on a date with me. At the loss of those two characters who have given me the worst case of indigestion this morning than I have suffered my entire life, I now have two hundred dollars in my pocket. It's ours to spend if you're willing to suffer my presence and go out with me just one time…. I'm a man who loves to eat and I'm looking for a woman that will match my appetite. There's a new restaurant on Magazine Street called Blaine's. I've been dying to go there…." He emphasized again as if spending time with a man as gorgeous as what stood before her was going to be a big sacrifice on her part, "If you can put up with my presence for just ONE evening and, if you like fancy places… and I hear this is now one of New Orleans' best, what do you say the two of us go out and have a free meal on those two jokers waiting impatiently to hear if I pulled this off?"

Clark presented his case as if he was at a high school debate competition before waiting for the rebuttal. Bernadette could tell by his eyes and body language that he had spoken truthfully and had an earnest appeal.

"Looking for a woman that can match your appetite? Hmmmmm!" She couldn't let that comment get by so she had to make him suffer a bit more. "That sounds like the bet has something to do with you taking me out because I'm FAT? Am I right?"

Clark had to grin. He closed his eyes and his left hand massaged his forehead. "Damn," he thought to himself. He had never met a lady like this before and somehow he knew that he never would again.

Seeing his embarrassment, Bernadette didn't force him to come up with another reply. Bernadette could tell he wasn't a bad guy, just a guy that got stuck in a stupid situation with no way to save face and get himself out of it.

She had heard of Blaine's and had been dying to go there herself. She had been intrigued by the feature story she had read in the newspaper on the owner who was also the head chef. Apparently the guy was a retired police officer who always worked the night shift. He had never adjusted to sleeping in the daytime and ended up spending his entire mornings watching cooking shows and competitions. His only background in gourmet food preparation was the television series and what he had been taught about Creole cooking by his mother. Yet, every food critic had said his food rivaled those of chefs trained at the best culinary art schools in the country. She had looked up the menu on the internet and, when she saw the prices, she decided going there would have to wait until she was celebrating a special occasion. The price range was definitely not in the same league as Joe's place.

Two hundred dollars! Remembering the menu, she thought about what two hundred dollars could buy. That would definitely cover everything she wanted to try plus this guy's meal as well. It should even cover a couple of glasses of wine each as well as the tip. What the heck? Even if the total went over, she didn't doubt the man standing by the register would have any problems paying the difference based on how he was dressed and the tip he and his friends had doled out. She wondered what Valerie would do in this situation. She felt Valerie would say to go for it but should she? She thought about the menu again and how much she wanted to try this place out and here she was given the chance to go for free. Glancing at Joe's picture, she could sense his approval too.

"Ok, buddy, you have a deal." As she extended her right hand to shake his, she said, "By the way, my name is Bernadette."

Seeing his sigh of relief as he stopped rubbing his forehead, looked up once again, and took her hand gratefully using a strong grip, she knew she had done the right thing. She didn't have to look at Joe's picture again to know he was smiling.

"Bernadette, it will be my pleasure.... Thank you! My name is Clark Laurent."

"Glad to meet you, Clark Laurent," Bernadette replied with a genuine smile as she realized she actually was.

"Would seven next Friday work for you?"

"Make it seven thirty, and I'll meet you there," Bernadette replied.

Clark pulled out his blackberry and made notes on his calendar. Looking up, he asked, "Shouldn't we swap cells just in case something comes up and one of us has to cancel?"

Bernadette gave him her number. She pulled her cell phone out of her apron pocket and typed Clark's number in as well. However, she was thinking all the time during the exchange that in case something comes up really meant in case I chicken out and I don't want to go through with the bet."

Clark let out an audible sigh of relief and flashed Bernadette such a genuine smile that she felt she was going to look forward to this date.

"Until Friday?" His facial expression was far more relaxed.

Bernadette glanced at Joe's picture once again. The vibes seem to say, "Peaches, give him your most flirtatious smile."

She did and replied, "Until Friday…. So, what are you going to tell your two friends when you get back to the booth?"

Clark glanced over his shoulder and saw Willy staring with his mouth wide open in anticipation. Turning back to Bernadette, he bit the left side of his lower lip, his eyes shifted slightly to the left before an idea came to him, and he poised a question.

"Bernadette, have you ever made walnut, chocolate chip, oatmeal cookies from scratch? From scratch, I mean measure the flour, sugar, crack the eggs and such?"

Bernadette was a little taken aback. That was the second time this man had caught her off guard. What a strange question to ask? She glanced at Willy again, and her gut feeling was cookies had something to do with this bet.

"I know what from scratch means!" She replied pretending to be a little insulted that she wouldn't. "I do make truly homemade oatmeal cookies! My cookies aren't just baked at home," she wiggled the index and middle fingers of each hand in the air to demonstrate quotation marks, "from a mix or out one of those tubes. My Dad loves them and oatmeal is great for reducing his cholesterol so I make them fairly often. I use a recipe my grandmother handed down to me so they taste just like the ones he remembers eating as a child…. I do add either walnuts or pecans to the recipe. Most of the time, I use walnuts because it's the healthier of the two nuts but my Dad loves pecans and, on occasion, I use both…. I never made them with chocolate chips but I don't think it would hurt to throw a few into the dough."

Based on Clark's reaction, she thought she had just handed the man a winning lottery ticket.

With the sexiest smile he had shown that morning and in that Luther Vandross' tone of voice, he advised, "When I get back to the booth, I'm going to tell them we have a dinner date set for Friday night and that you make the best walnut, chocolate chip, oatmeal cookies in the world! Thank you, my lady!"

With that odd statement, Clark kissed the back of her hand before releasing it and turning to return to his booth. Something about the way he said, "My lady," gave Bernadette a sense of pride, like she had just met a knight in shining armor. She didn't feel at all the way she had felt that awful weekend when she had learned of the cruel joke Greg and Kevin had played on her.

She watched the interactions when Clark sat down. Lisa walked over immediately and poured hot coffee to top off his cup. The guy who had been hanging over the low wall to the aggravation of the patrons in the adjoining booth started chattering like a chipmunk occasionally slapping Clark's upper arm. Clark sat slowly sipping the coffee and seemingly ignoring the guy's questions. He let the guy chatter on and on until Clark could tell his impatience to know what had happened was about to result in an embarrassing outburst. Downing the last drop, he finally stood, picked his keys up off the table, and locked eyes with the guy who had moved to the edge of the seat when Clark stood. Bernadette could tell Clark did not utter more than two sentences before turning away from his two friends and walking toward the restaurant's rear exit. The guy who had been hanging over the wall stared at the other gentleman across from him in the booth and said loud enough for the whole restaurant to hear, "I knew she can bake cookies!"

It gave Bernadette a sense of pleasure and confidence she had made the right decision. It appears this Clark was a man of his word.

Chapter Ten

By Friday morning Clark would describe himself as energized. He woke before the percolator had filled the apartment with the aroma of coffee brewing. Donning his favorite sweat suit, he had gone for a quick run on the levee before returning to his condo to shower for work. When he reached the lobby of his complex, he didn't hesitate to call out greetings of "Good Morning" to those he passed. Adrian studied him warily. The behavior was atypical. Clark was always polite, but he seemed happy! Adrian checked his log to make sure he hadn't forgotten events of the night before. The log confirmed what he remembered. Though Clark appeared to be riding high, he saw no indication in his log he had called any cabs. Even when he had, his spirits were usually not that high the next morning. He watched Clark as he continued across the lobby and through the leaded glass doors. Maybe he won a lottery, Adrian thought before once again focusing on closing out his paperwork from the night shift.

Bernadette's work day was a typical Friday fire drill. The marketing department was dropping change requests from customers at a faster pace than usual. It was a good thing the Information Technology section where she worked was fully staffed that day. Bernadette knew the pace would slow after lunch when they all started leaving early to kick off their weekend plans. That made Fridays even more hectic because you often had to clarify with them the customer's intent before they disappeared and left her stuck with ambiguous orders. She was just beginning to wind down for the day when her cellular phone began vibrating.

"What now?" Bernadette thought. She prayed it was not another last minute fire drill that would cause her to have to work late that night. She was tired and just wanted to go home. Picking up the cell angrily, she punched in her security code and saw a meeting reminder pop up. What meeting could she possibly have that was not on her work calendar? She always reviewed her agenda the night before to ensure she would be prepared for the next work day, and it was extremely rare for any meetings to be scheduled late on a Friday afternoon. The reminder only showed, "Blaine's – 7:30 p.m."

"Damn!" Bernadette uttered aloud.

"You okay, Bernie?" Her co-worker Faye poked her head out of her cubicle to check on her. She had never heard Bernadette use a four letter word in the years they had worked together even though what she heard was mild by today's standards.

"I forgot I have a date tonight!"

"A date?" That was two shocks in a row. Faye had never heard Bernadette ever mention going out with a guy. The only plans she ever discussed surrounded family events and her niece Miki whose pictures covered every spare spot in Bernadette's cubicle. At that, Faye had to stand up and walk around to fill the only means of exit out of the cubicle. She had to learn more.

Glancing up, Bernadette was sorry she hadn't taken a second to think before blurting out the words.

"Nothing serious! I worked one of my old jobs last Saturday for my sister and ended up with a dinner invitation. That's all!"

Faye was not about to let the conversation end that easily. For the first time since she's known her, she could sense that Bernadette was nervous. Even when she had made a presentation to their Chief Executive Officer (CEO), Bernadette was calm and delivered the presentation professionally as if it was part of her daily routine. Faye could never have remained that calm in front of the CEO. She had been biting her nails watching Bernadette's delivery. There had to be something more to this.

"A dinner invitation? So, why the 'damn'? Sounds like a fun evening for a change."

Bernadette fidgeted with items on her desk avoiding looking at Faye. After she moved her tape dispenser to a third location and still seemed not pleased with the arrangement, Faye took the lead.

"Someone you don't know?"

Bernadette was embarrassed to admit she had accepted an invitation from a complete stranger so kept her head down and moved the tape dispenser to a fourth equally unsuitable location.

"I don't know him well," she responded her voice cracking.

"Wondering what to talk about?" Faye prompted realizing this was very likely Bernadette's first real date. "Just use your old waitress' charms. Think of the guy as your customer and you'll do fine!"

"Customer interactions at the restaurant were pretty short though and here meal conversations always surround the business. What do I say to fill what could be over an hour?" Bernadette again blurted out her concerns before she thought about the comment she had just shared. She didn't want to appear vulnerable to Faye. She was the team leader in her IT section. Would she appear incompetent or weak to someone she had to lead?

Faye pulled up a chair so her comments were to a friend instead of providing feedback to a coworker. Faye talked about some of her first dates and before long, she had Bernadette laughing at the ones that definitely had not gone well. After listening to Faye's experiences, Bernadette felt less apprehensive about meeting Clark. She also reminded herself this was only a one-time event so it wasn't a big deal. Glancing at her watch, she made a quick call to let her mother know she wouldn't be home for dinner before heading to the restaurant.

The energized, elated feeling Clark felt all day was slowly being replaced by a feeling he couldn't identify. Anyone observing would comment Clark was getting nervous. Though they were supposed to meet at 7:30, Clark arrived at the restaurant by 7:00 and took a stool at the bar.

"Another bourbon?" The bartender kept the bottle at a slight tilt waiting for Clark to confirm.

"Yes, thanks," Clark replied downing the remainder of his first drink before the bartender refilled his glass.

Clark had checked in at the hostess stand specifying he wanted a secluded booth, not one of the open tables, before taking a spot where he could watch Bernadette's approach. When he spotted her, he wasn't sure at first if it was the same lady. The navy blue jacket dress she wore was extremely flattering. The jacket had side front panels with spaghetti striping that created a slimming effect. The collar and sleeves sported a white stripe which made a striking color contrast. The heels were practical shoes you would wear in an office environment. The look was more appropriate for a board room meeting. This was not an outfit he expected a waitress to have in her closet. He pictured what she would have in her wardrobe for church on Sundays or other outings would be a bit fancier. Grabbing his drink, he called to the waiter to add the two to his tab before meeting Bernadette at the hostess stand.

"Hi!" Bernadette forced a smile eyeing his drink and wondering if his nerves were as much on edge as hers.

The hostess grabbed two menus and requested they follow her. Bernadette fought the urge to jump when she felt Clark's hand lightly touch the small of her back as they followed the waitress to a booth at the far corner of the establishment. She started to request a location that would feel a little less intimate but was unsure how to word the request with Clark standing so close to her. She took her seat quickly and immediately opened the menu and began studying it.

"Care for a drink?" Clark broke the silence as he took the seat opposite her in the booth.

"Just a glass of red wine would be fine," Bernadette replied trying to calm her voice.

"Merlot?" Clark questioned wanting to confirm her preference.

"With a twist of lime. Thank you."

Clark placed Bernadette's drink order when the waitress approached and requested they have a few more minutes to study the menu.

Bernadette couldn't help but comment on the selection of appetizers.

"The crab cakes with the remoulade sauce sound great."

"I was looking at those too but can't decide between the crab cakes and the mini fried crawfish pies."

"I was also thinking about the crawfish pies." Bernadette responded but was shying away from ordering the pies because you had to eat those with your hands. Even though this wasn't an official date, she still didn't want to do anything to embarrass herself. But surely Clark would use his hands too. Crawfish pies were made like fruit turnovers which didn't lend well to a fork and knife scenario. Not in her family anyway.....

They glanced up and eyed each other at the same time.

Bernadette started to laugh and spoke first, "We could order both and share. Didn't you say you wanted a woman that would match your appetite?"

"Sounds good to me," Clark laughed back. "I don't want to return even one penny to those two jokers."

Bernadette's words had set the stage for the entire evening. From then on, the ice was broken, and the mood was like two old friends reuniting after not seeing each other for years. They ordered the specialty bread as well - a warm, crusty French bread coated with roasted garlic and served with an herbed olive oil for dipping.

All guests were treated to the chef's choice salad – baby spinach leaves tossed with fresh Ponchatoula strawberries, toasted almond slivers, finely chopped red onion, and a raspberry vinaigrette dressing.

Bernadette ordered the calf liver in an orange sauce served with a side of roasted corn grits cooked in heavy whipping cream. She told Clark her mother cooked liver smothered the usual Creole style so was curious to have this version of the dish. Clark agreed that the liver, being a signature dish, was one they had to try and ordered the breaded veal with oyster stuffing, another dish they both had selected. As everything was served, they requested extra plates to make it easier to split the dishes. They were even in tune over the desserts, splitting pecan pie topped with cinnamon ice cream and bread pudding with a rum sauce and whipped cream.

Over dinner, the conversation first turned to cooking. They compared their favorite family recipes with the descriptions Chef Blaine had on the menu. At different times throughout the evening, Chef Blaine appeared checking that the patrons were pleased and granting an opportunity for the three of them to pose for the coveted photo Michael and Willy needed.

Conversation turned to other aspects of family life. Bernadette shared stories of summer vacations on her grandfather's farm in Opelousas, Louisiana. Clark told her he had a cousin and family living in Ville Platte, a short drive north of Opelousas and he had attended family reunion picnics there. When Bernadette mentioned swatting mosquitoes at the drive-in, favorite movies became the topic.

By the time the waitress asked if they wanted the check, they both hesitated.

"How about a night cap?" Clark offered.

Seeing the line of folks waiting for tables, Bernadette's waitress training kicked in.

"We're keeping the chef from pulling in more business," she nodded at those impatiently eyeing their booth and hoping they would hurry and leave.

Clark glanced towards the bar area which was also full. Reluctantly, he pulled out his credit card and handed it to the waitress.

"I had a wonderful evening, my lady." His eyes showed he meant every word he said.

"I did too," Bernadette replied not even trying to hide the obvious pleasant surprise the evening had become from sounding in her voice.

They were sitting quietly smiling at each other when the waitress brought the receipt for Clark to sign.

As they walked together to the front door of the restaurant, Clark's hand on the small of her back seemed natural to Bernadette this time. Once outside, Clark broke the silence.

"Where did you park?"

"Not far. I'll be fine." Bernadette quickly responded. She would feel awkward having him walk her to her car. After all, this wasn't a real date. It seemed better to part outside the restaurant.

"We should do this again sometime," Clark stated surprised that he meant every word.

"You'll have to trick your friends into making another bet," Bernadette joked about the offer before continuing, "Thanks for dinner. I hope you have a wonderful weekend."

Not sure what else to do or say, she turned and started walking towards her car. Clark called out wishing her the same and watched until she closed the door of her vehicle and the parking brakes lit before he turned and walked in the opposite direction towards his Corvette.

As Clark walked across the lobby floor alone that night, Adrian was disappointed. Not having to order a cab meant he wouldn't get a wad of bills the next morning slipped in his hand. Eyeing Clark, he was confused for the second time that day. He thought he would detect disappointment in Clark's face as well but his steps were light and he seemed content. Adrian pondered Clark's behavior for a moment before focusing back on monitoring the security screens.

As Bernadette pulled up the covers in her bed that night, she thought about the evening. She looked at Clark's number in her cellular phone and debated whether to hit the delete button or to save it in her contact list. She couldn't recall having such a nice time in years, but she also had to remember this was just a bet. Remembering the incident with Greg and Kevin, she punched the delete key before rolling onto her side and falling into a deep sleep.

Chapter Eleven

Clark stirred Saturday morning when the phone rang. It didn't take much for him to fall back to sleep the first time. By the time the caller had tried to reach him the third time, he gave up, got out of bed, and answered.

"Hey, man! Why aren't you here?"

Hearing Willy's voice on the line, Clark glanced at the clock and saw it was at least twenty minutes past their scheduled meeting time at Joe's.

"I'm walking out the door now," he lied. Hanging up the receiver, he quickly dressed and headed to Joe's. Driving over, he wasn't thinking about the bet at all but only on whether Bernadette was scheduled to work that morning. He was looking forward to seeing her again.

When he arrived, he was disappointed to see Joe at the register. Taking a seat next to Michael, Clark glanced at the staff door whenever it swung open, hoping Bernadette would be the next waitress to appear.

"So, how was it?" Willy was the first to pop the question to Clark.

"We had dinner," Clark stated trying to sound nonchalant as he disgustedly tossed the receipt on the table for Willy and Michael to review. He hated to be reminded of the fact the wonderful evening he had experienced was tied to a juvenile bet. Pulling out his cell, he showed the picture he and Bernadette had taken with Chef Blaine first to Michael then to Willy.

"You looked like you were enjoying yourself!" Willy seemed astounded.

"I did. Bernadette is a nice lady. The food was great. We had pleasant conversation. It was a nice, quiet, laid back evening."

Michael could sense something more after studying the photo and watching the exchange between Clark and Willy but made no comments. Instead he quickly turned the conversation to their typical topics to distract Willy. That didn't take much and the morning slipped into the usual banter among the three friends.

Miki jumped onto the bed waking Bernadette.

"Aunt Ber'dette! Maw-Maw made French toast for breakfast and sausage. She has the little round ones I like to eat with my fingers. Wake up, Aunt Ber'dette. Come eat!"

"Stop jumping up and down on the bed, Miki. You might fall off. Tell Maw-Maw I'll be there soon."

As she watched Miki scurry from her bedroom, Bernadette thought about last Saturday when she was at Joe's. She wondered if Clark and his friends were there and discussing the evening they had shared. Thoughts of Greg and Kevin came to her, and she began imagining them making fun of the time she and Clark had spent together. She had truly enjoyed herself and didn't want those past images of her and Greg to spoil the memory of the evening she had with Clark. At that moment, Miki bounced back into the room.

"Maw-Maw says your French toast is getting cold!"

"Tell her I'm coming right now." Thank goodness she had Miki to distract her.

As Clark walked past his secretary Monday afternoon, she shoved five notes from Patricia into his hand.

"Please call her as soon as you can. The lady seems worried."

Sitting at his desk, Clark eyed the notes. He hadn't thought about Patricia at all. Typically, he would call her by Thursday morning and make some plan to see her over the weekend. He had looked forward to the dinner with Bernadette so much and had such a nice evening that making other plans had totally slipped his mind. His company was already in strategy alignment sessions for the next year. Between the presentations he had to prepare and make, work had occupied him. He eyed the notes sorting them over and over. Picking up the phone, he dialed her work number unsure of what he planned to say.

"Clark? I was so worried when I didn't hear from you. Are you okay?"

"Sure…. I'm fine."

The line went silent for a minute. When Clark didn't offer anything more, Patricia continued, "Well, I need to get back to work, and I know you're busy too. You probably had to work this past weekend?"

He did, but he also felt guilty that he had made time for the dinner with Bernadette. Another awkward pause, and Patricia broke the silence again when Clark neither confirmed nor denied he had spent the weekend working.

"So, I'll see you next weekend?" Another awkward pause followed.

"Sure…." Clark answered trying to sound enthusiastic about the future date.

"Okay, then…. Call me by Thursday!"

As Patricia hung up, Clark's mind wandered to Bernadette. He wondered what she was doing right then.

Monday morning at Bernadette's office started differently. Faye was waiting at Bernadette's desk, eyeing her approach over a cup of steaming coffee.

"You look like you survived. Can we go to lunch, and you share all the details?"

Bernadette couldn't help but grin at the look on Faye's face.

"We can go to lunch, but no juicy details to share. It was a very pleasant evening. The guy is a great conversationalist. The food was outstanding. I had a good time."

Bernadette pulled out her cellular phone and scrolled through all the pictures of Miki before finding the one with her, Clark, and Chef Blaine.

"Damn!" It was Faye's turn to react strongly. "Tell me you're seeing this man again."

"Nope! It was a one-time invitation for dinner. His number is already deleted."

"What a waste." Faye turned and walked to her cubicle shaking her head. Bernadette knew Faye would not get much work done that morning.

Looking at the photo in her cellular, Bernadette started to press delete on that as well but didn't. He is gorgeous she thought.

"Thanks for the memory," she whispered before closing the screen and focusing on the change requests pouring into her inbox.

As Clark walked past the secretary Friday afternoon, she shoved three notes into his hand though he was carrying a mound of binders. I know you're just getting out of the budget meeting, but this lady has called three times. She said you promised to call her no later than yesterday morning, and she hasn't heard from you. Clark looked apologetically at the secretary and promised he would call her right away. In his office, he tried to think of what he would say to Patricia. Before he could dial the number, his phone rang. When he picked up the receiver, Patricia was on the line, and her impatience was quite obvious.

"You promised to call by Thursday so why didn't you?"

Her tone was different from her usual shy, sweet, accommodating style. In fact, listening to her voice reminded him of Glenn's wife, Gwendolyn.

The red flag was rising, but knowing he was the one at fault, Clark felt he should tread softly but also affirm exactly where their relationship stood. They weren't married. They weren't even engaged. In fact, they had held no conversation whatever about any type of commitment, but her voice sounded accusing as if Clark had to account for all his actions to her.

"If I recall, Patricia, I didn't make that promise.... YOU requested I call by Thursday."

As soon as Clark said the words, he wished he could have taken them back. He had planned to take a softer approach but was so perturbed by her attitude he had emphasized the words "I' and "you."

"Damn, Clark!" He chided himself silently trying to think of how he could recover the moment. Before he spoke, Patricia clearly indicated her outrage.

"Maybe you need a little time alone to think about what I mean to you!"

Patricia was the one now emphasizing the word you. Clark started to reply he had already started down that path two weeks ago but caught his tongue in time. He began comparing the wonderful evening he had spent with Bernadette with the times he and Patricia were together. All he could remember from their outings together was the sex afterwards and even that memory wasn't the best out of the ones from his past. Trying to recall a more positive aspect to their relationship, the silence between them went longer than it should have. Tired of waiting for Clark to state he did not need time to reconsider their relationship, Patricia sought to save face.

"Clark, I don't think things have been working out as well as I hoped. It's been nice but it's time for me to move on." She waited impatiently to hear his reaction to her threat.

Clark found himself thinking, "No loss on my part," but responded instead, "You are a wonderful person, Patricia.... I wish you the best."

As his ear drum almost shattered from the sound of the receiver slamming down, Clark recalled the evening he had spent with Bernadette again. When she bit into her crawfish pie, the crust broke and sauce spilled down her chin. He chuckled at the memory. Patricia would have been embarrassed to the point they probably would have had to leave the restaurant. Bernadette was the complete opposite wiping it from her chin and licking her finger commenting the sauce was so good she hated wasting even a drop. Opening his desk drawer, he spotted two tickets his boss had given him to a riverfront festival that weekend. He had forgotten all about them knowing it was something Patricia would never agree to do. He wondered if Bernadette was free. There was only one way to find out.

Faye heard Bernadette's cellular phone ringing. Seeing Bernadette on the far end of the office talking to the Director of Finance, she ran over to Bernadette's cubicle and answered on her behalf.

"Hello."

"Bernadette? This is Clark." The voice sounded different, but Clark first attributed it to the transmission.

"No, this isn't Bernadette. It's her friend Faye."

"May I speak with her please?"

"She's in a meeting right now. May I take a message?"

"Ask her to please call me. I'm wondering if she's free and would like to attend the food festival being held on the riverfront this weekend."

"She'd love to! She was just telling me she had no plans for the weekend and was hoping for something to do. Give me the details, and I'll pencil them in on her calendar."

Clark hesitated but since he wasn't giving out any personal information, he provided Faye with the details and requested she have Bernadette call him back to confirm.

"No problem…. I'll have her call you right away!"

"What are you doing on my cell?" Bernadette walked up right when Faye was flipping the phone closed.

"Is his name Clark?" Faye asked excitedly.

Bernadette motioned for her to sit down and to quiet down before the entire office heard.

"The guy I went to dinner with was named Clark. Why? And why were you on my phone?"

"He called. He wants you to go to that food festival with him on the riverfront. I wrote down all the details on your calendar. I told him you were just telling me that you didn't have anything to do so would love to. He still wants you to call him back though. I guess to work out the details."

"How do you know I don't have any plans?"

"Because you never have adult plans. All you talk about is the baby and doing things with her. Don't you think it's time to do something for yourself?"

Bernadette wanted to strangle Faye. They had always got along well but she never thought of her as a friend because they didn't hang out together outside of work. In that moment, she realized Faye was not just a coworker and that she was also right. She wasn't sure how she felt about the invitation and was curious if it was tied to the initial bet. But, based on what Faye told Clark, it would be impossible not to accept without causing him insult. Concerned others may have heard her conversation with Faye, Bernadette waited until most of her coworkers had left for the evening before returning Clark's call.

"Clark, this is Bernadette. You called earlier?"

"Yes, my lady. Thank you for returning my call."

Bernadette blushed hearing the words my lady. Something about the way Clark said it made her feel special.

"I'm glad that person Faye gave you my message. Is she a close friend of yours? She said you were in a meeting. I never pictured Joe calling meetings at the restaurant, but I guess you have to conduct strategy sessions no matter what business you're in."

"Oh, my God," Bernadette thought, "Clark thinks I actually work at Joe's." For some reason, she didn't choose to correct him at that point.

"Are you free for the food festival?"

"I've seen it advertised on television. I've never gone before and it looks like fun. I'd love to go. Suppose I meet you at noon tomorrow at the Poydras St. entrance to Spanish Plaza?"

"That time and location should work out fine. I'll see you then."

As they hung up, both Bernadette and Clark were smiling and so was Faye whose ear had been on the edge of the cubicle listening the entire time.

Chapter Twelve

The weather Saturday morning was perfect for a festival. Sunny with just enough cloud coverage not to let the humidity New Orleans was noted for become too unbearable. When Bernadette arrived at Spanish Plaza, Clark was waiting for her at the main entrance just as they had planned. He waved as soon as he spotted her.

Since he had jogged over from his condo, he was wearing tennis, a pair of jogging pants, and a short-sleeved T-shirt. Bernadette couldn't help but admire the muscles in his upper arms bulging out the sleeves.

"Is this another bet?" she questioned as she walked over to him. She had to get her mind off his physique.

"Yes. It's a bet I'm making right now with you."

"And that is?"

"I bet you never had alligator sausage."

"In fact I haven't."

"Then that's the first booth we're going to. I haven't had it myself. "

Clark handed Bernadette a brochure indicating where the various booths and kiosks were located so they could plan their next stop. Walking side by side, they headed towards the open park along the Mississippi River levee.

The sound of the bells ringing at St. Louis Cathedral signaling vigil mass would be starting shortly was the first indication to both Bernadette and Clark of the time.

"I didn't realize it was that late," Bernadette checked her watch to confirm the time.

"It's not late. The festival doesn't close down for another two hours, and then there's a jazz concert in Jackson Square." Clark looked concerned she appeared to be considering calling it a day.

Bernadette was having a great time and had never attended a concert in an open park. Just when she was making up her mind about whether she would stay, a voice screamed out.

"Girlfriend, you still wearing pink?"

She knew that voice anywhere.

Turning towards the sound, she greeted Valerie, "It's only a trim! Even you think that's okay, Miss Fashion Model!"

Bernadette and Valerie hugged before Valerie stepped back and eyed Clark from head to toe.

"Now, who is this hunk of man by your side? You've been holding out on me? Has it been that long since we talked?"

"Valerie, this is Clark Laurent. Clark, Valerie and I have been friends since college."

Bernadette didn't try to explain who Clark was because she could tell Valerie had already made up her own mind about them and, once Valerie determined something, nothing would sway her in that regard. Clark and Valerie shook hands while Valerie was still unashamedly indicating her admiration. Since Valerie appeared to be alone, Clark did the only gentlemanly thing that was appropriate.

"Valerie, Bernadette and I are about to go over and grab seats for the jazz concert. Would you like to join us?"

"I'D LOVE TO," Valerie emphasized each word assessing Clark's physique one more time, "but I have some friends from out of town waiting in line at the beignet shop so I need to go…. You two enjoy yourselves and, Bernadette, you call me, girl!"

Valerie pointed her index finger at Bernadette as she spoke the last sentence indicating they definitely needed to catch up. As she walked away, she did glance back a couple of times checking out the couple.

Sitting on the steps behind the fountain across the street from Jackson square, Clark posed the question while they were waiting for the concert to begin.

"So, you and Valerie met for the first time attending college?"

"Yes, but it's a miracle we became friends based on what she did."

Clark glanced at the makeshift stage with electrical lines still being pulled into place, "Looks like we have the time. Care to share the story?"

Bernadette exhaled and smiled as relayed what had happened between them to Clark.

"It was my first semester, but based on my class schedule, I could go to Joe's, help out with the breakfast crowd, get home to change clothes, and still get to school on time. I got to work and found out one of the ladies had called out ill. The place was packed that day and Joe was shorthanded. I offered to work later than usual so I didn't have time to go home and change."

She tilted her head towards Clark and added before continuing, "Trust me. After this happened, I kept a set of clothes in the trunk of my car so I'd always be prepared if it happened again."

Though he didn't comment, Clark thought, "Spare set of clothes in the car? Not a bad idea."

"Being the first day of school, I was a little self-conscious about having to show up in my pink waitress uniform, but I didn't have a choice. It wasn't long before I was so engrossed in my schedule that I forgot I was wearing the uniform. When I got to my last class for the day, I spotted someone I figured was the instructor coming down the hall so instead of taking time to walk to the back door of the class, I entered the front. That meant I had to strut across the front of the class to the only empty seat left which happened to be right across from Valerie."

Clark smiled and turned his full attention to Bernadette knowing the best part of the story was about to be told.

"As I sat down, she started talking in way too loud a voice. I know everyone in the classroom could hear her. At first I didn't know what was going on because she started out with, 'Wrong, wrong, wrong! That's all wrong! Girl, when you walked in the room, I had to stop and think. I must have gone to a party last night. I was trying to remember how much I had to drink. Even though I'm from Mississippi, I know about those New Orleans' drinks and I have had my share. But I'm checking my calendar, and I didn't party last night. So this is so confusing…. I didn't have anything to drink and here I am still seeing a pink elephant! How am I seeing a pink elephant and I'm not hung over? That dress is wrong, wrong, wrong. That's all wrong. I thought rural Mississippi was bad, but girl, where are you from? You look like you stepped off the set of one of those country television shows. You just don't have the big wig to go with it.' I was so embarrassed! Everyone in the class started laughing, and they didn't stop until the instructor walked in. The class finally settled down, but I was at the point I was fighting to keep from bursting into tears."

Clark's face changed to a puzzling expression, "The first time you meet, she calls you a pink elephant in front of your peers, and you pick this girl to become your friend?"

"She became my best friend!"

"Your BEST friend?" Clark thought about the support system he had in college and wondered what institution Bernadette had attended and the toxic environment that existed on her campus that, despite Valerie's actions, she was still her top choice.

Knowing what he must have been thinking, Bernadette hastened to tell more, "It's what she did after that changed everything between us."

"I'm Catholic so excuse the expression but, right now, I'm nominating you for sainthood. You bring a whole new level to the forgiveness theory and turn the other cheek."

"I'm Catholic too but it wasn't enough to get me a crown in heaven yet!"

The two of them laughed together before Bernadette continued, "When the instructor started his introduction, she reached across the aisle and put her hand on top of mine.... I started to slap her hand away but the gentle way she squeezed mine made me turn and look at her instead. She held my gaze and her eyes got moist as she whispered, 'I'm sorry, girlfriend. I acted like a real ass. Forgive me?' Though her language was appalling, I could tell she truly meant every word. After class, we hung out together in the hall for a while and just talked. Valerie kept apologizing and I can't repeat the words she spoke to anyone who had been in the class and made a passing comment. My torturer became my ally especially once I told her why I was dressed that way. After that day, we were inseparable. I used to hang out in Valerie's dorm room sometimes to complete assignments. We studied for tests and exams together. I was best at mathematics and sciences while Valerie leaned towards English and the arts. We complemented each other well. I spent many nights on campus with her instead of driving home."

"The two that were with me at Joe's that morning. We had the same relationship in college. We didn't start out calling each other names though."

They laughed together again.

"So, how many hours do you have left before you get your degree?"

"I earned my degree years ago," Bernadette cocked her head at him and smiled.

"If you don't mind me asking, why are you working at Joe's if you attended college?"

"I'm not. I did work at Joe's to earn extra cash while in college, but I'm not there anymore. I just happened to fill in for someone that morning as a favor so he wouldn't be shorthanded."

"Fate," Clark whispered softly though still unaware of how strong that would come into play.

They began talking about their careers. Bernadette was fascinated about the various aspects of engineering. Clark had discussed engineering as an applied science and pointed out various applications to her within their view. Bernadette discussed aspects of her IT world and Clark related items she mentioned to his current project. They were so engrossed discussing the software impact on engineering, the band starting up startled them. Laughing at how work had consumed their off day, they turned their attention to the entertainment. Fireworks lighting the sky above the river signaled the end of that day's festivities. As they walked along the river's levee back to Poydras Street where Bernadette had parked her car, they passed the theaters at One Canal Place, a shopping and office complex at the foot of Canal St. where it meets the Mighty Mississippi.

"I've been dying to see that movie," Bernadette pointed to the billboard on the outer wall.

"I like foreign films if they don't have subtitles. If I wanted to read, I'd stay home with a novel. "

Bernadette hadn't thought about subtitles that way before but Clark made a good point. Subtitles frustrated her as well. It seemed no matter where she sat, someone's head blocked the one word she needed to read at a critical point in the film. Bernadette walked closer to the poster and read the fine print.

"This one is in English."

"Would you care to go Wednesday after work? They have a 7:30 showing." Clark offered after checking the listings.

"Wednesday would be great."

"It's a bet then."

"And the bet is this time?" Bernadette tilted her head waiting for how he would tie that theme to a movie.

"I bet you can't go to a movie without ordering hot buttered popcorn."

"You win that one," Bernadette smiled.

"It's a date then because I can't either."

They shook hands on it.

Wednesday night, Bernadette and Clark met at the theater about 7:00 pm. Bernadette walked up to the counter to purchase the tickets, but Clark quickly placed his hand over hers.

"You paid everything at the food festival. It's my turn." Bernadette offered.

"Sorry. I can't go out with a lady and let her pay." Clark gave Bernadette a look indicating that was totally unthinkable and a point not to be argued.

"But, I'm not your girlfriend," Bernadette argued despite the scowl on Clark's face.

"You're a friend and you're a girl so that makes you a girl-friend." Clark laughed at his own logic.

Laughing herself, Bernadette decided not to argue the point.

The smell of fresh popcorn bursting from the pan turned their attention to the concession stand. When Clark was about to place an order for two mediums, Bernadette pointed out if they shared the large that they'd get free refills. Clark had no problem with that logic, and he juggled the drinks while Bernadette handled the popcorn and napkins.

After the movie, Clark asked if she wanted to walk down to the beignet shop for coffee. Sitting along the river, they discussed the film and others they had seen in the past. Their interest had been peaked by the preview of another foreign film starting Friday. Walking back to the complex, Clark suggested they catch dinner and a movie that Saturday night. Bernadette readily agreed.

So began a friendship that filled a gap for companionship in both of their lives….

When Clark walked across the lobby that Saturday night alone again, Adrian started to call out to him. This was the third week he was not accompanied by a lady friend. Something had definitely changed but prying into the personal lives of the residents, even though he felt close to Clark, was not appropriate. He turned back to his duties regretfully knowing he was about to miss another big tip.

Chapter Thirteen

Bernadette and Clark were attending a reveillon dinner. Traditionally, a reveillon was the meal following midnight mass on Christmas Eve that broke the fast Catholics were required to perform in order to receive communion. Today, it represents a special menu local restaurants offer during the holiday season that consists of five courses and includes wines to accompany each.

"Clark, no!" Bernadette was adamant placing her hand on top of the bill. "We've been hanging out together for months and you never let me pay for anything. I'm paying tonight. Let me do it as a Christmas present to you. Please...."

"Well, if you want to do something for me, there's a favor I need but was afraid to ask you."

"What is it?"

Clark moved her hand aside gently.

"Because it's the holidays, I feel obligated to invite my boss and his wife over for dinner. Do you mind helping me plan it?"

"A dinner party? I'd love to! You're not thinking of catering it, are you? Just tell me what time it needs to be ready. I'll cook everything and deliver it in time for you to warm it up."

Clark seemed a little uncomfortable with Bernadette's suggestion.

"Clark, what's wrong?" Bernadette could tell her response was not what he had in mind.

"I was thinking that.... Maybe you could help me cook it at my place?" Clark kept his face down taking a longer time than usual to calculate the tip, sign the receipt, place his credit card on the tray, and set the tray in easy reach of the waitress.

Bernadette was glad he was not looking at her at the moment. All the time they had spent together was always in public. She had never brought him home to meet her parents since they weren't actually dating. He had never invited her to his place. They were friends so she couldn't understand why she felt uncomfortable. She could sense Clark was uncomfortable too, but what was the big deal about going to his place? Friends should be comfortable in any environment.

"No problem," Bernadette finally answered in a shaky voice and avoided his glaze as well.

"Would next Saturday be ok?"

"Sure…. We need to plan a menu…. Do you have a full set of pots and pans or do I need to bring anything over?"

"I should have everything you need there. The kitchen is fully equipped. Can you come over about 10:00 that morning? We can finalize the menu, go shopping, and then start cooking? Think that will allow adequate time for dinner to be complete by 6:00 p.m.? Assuming when they arrive, we'll have cocktails first…. We probably won't actually sit down to eat immediately so we would have a buffer."

"That should be fine."

Clark scribbled his home address on the back of one of his business cards and handed it to Bernadette.

"I can draw you a map if you're not familiar with that area of the city."

"No, you don't need to…. I should be able to find it with no problem."

"There are several visitors' parking spots so you shouldn't have any problem parking at that time of morning. At night, it becomes an issue, but once you arrive, we can take my car."

"Sounds good."

The entire conversation was held with no eye contact and both wondering why they seemed to be feeling uncomfortable with the idea.

Saturday morning, Bernadette easily found the building where Clark lived. As he mentioned, five of the reserved visitor spots were still available. She felt self-conscious as she walked into the elegant lobby. Stopping by the security desk, she identified herself as Clark's guest. After scanning a pre-printed list, the guard indicated which elevator Bernadette needed to use and advised he had programmed the elevator to stop on Clark's floor. As Bernadette entered the elevator, she noticed there were no buttons she could press to select a floor, only an LED panel indicating which floors it was passing. When the elevator stopped indicating the fifth floor, Bernadette cautiously stepped through the doors.

"Good morning!"

Clark was waiting for her in the hallway.

"Good morning to you! Did the guard warn you I was on the way?"

With a grin, Clark replied, "It's part of the building's security system. I'm right down the hall this way."

As they were walking towards the apartment located at the corner of the floor, Bernadette had to pop her other question.

"Did you engineer that high tech elevator?"

"No, that's not my line of work," Clark spoke over his shoulder as he punched a code into the panel next to his door. Bernadette heard a click which allowed Clark to turn the handle. He stepped aside so she could precede him.

Once inside, all Bernadette saw was a long hall with a stairway rising on the left side.

"Let me give you the grand tour."

Bernadette followed Clark as he moved down the hallway. Monochrome was the only way she could describe the first floor, but it all seemed to say Clark to her. He must have hired a decorator because everything she saw looked like it could be pictured in a magazine. All the walls on the first floor were painted a deep tan. The first door on the right was a guest bedroom. The comforter was gorgeous. The material was a rich jacquard and silk dyed in shades of brown, beige, and cream with gold thread accents. Bernadette wanted to pass her hand over the satiny top but resisted. The next door on the right housed a full bath but not the way Bernadette typically thought of a bathroom. The tub, walk-in shower, and toilet were inside but what was odd is that the sink was located in an alcove to the left of the doorway outside. As they continued down the hall, they arrived at a short stairway.

"That's the master suite," Clark stated and turned back to lead her to the upstairs wing of the condo. He seemed embarrassed for Bernadette to see where he slept. She realized the room held memories he probably would never share with her, but you can't see memories, and she really wanted to check it out.

 Bernadette took a longer peek inside before turning to follow him back towards the front entrance door. For some reason, she was disappointed she didn't get to see more of his bedroom. What commanded her attention were the windows. She saw his bedroom windows went from the ceiling to about waist high but were completely bare – no window treatment at all.

"They must be coated with something," she thought. Otherwise, people could see everything going on in your bedroom. That should be no concern of hers, but she felt bothered by the thought nonetheless.

Following Clark back to the entrance door, they climbed the stairway, now on their right, to the main floor above. At the top of the stair, Bernadette caught her breath. Hearing her, Clark led her to the lanai.

"That's the same way I felt when I first saw this view."

"Clark, I could sit out here forever."

"Then, let's plan the menu here. I have coffee brewing. Care for a cup?"

"Sure."

Bernadette followed him back into an area that was ideal for entertaining. A sofa and two overstuffed arm chairs faced the French doors that led to the lanai. Beyond the sofa was a dining area. As they walked through the dining area, the kitchen was on the right and a powder room was on the left. After pouring two steaming cups of café au lait, they went back to the lanai. While enjoying the view, they planned the evening meal based on what Clark knew of his boss' taste having observed him at business events.

Bernadette suggested a crab and corn bisque for starters. Clark commented he loved that type of soup but hated the mix of textures – the kernels against the creamy soup always seemed at odds. When Bernadette advised her mother had taught her to make it with creamed corn instead of the whole kernels, Clark quickly agreed. They planned for the soup to be followed by a spinach salad with honey roasted pecans, golden raisins, red onions, and bleu cheese dressing. The entrée would be baked catfish with a shrimp and crawfish sauce. Wild rice and green beans sautéed in olive oil and garlic with toasted sliced almonds would be the sides. They went back and forth on the desserts. Bernadette wanted to do a bread pudding with a whiskey sauce. Clark wanted a carrot cake. Somehow they ended up with walnut fudge brownies a la mode. Completing the grocery list, Bernadette dropped the pencil on the side table and leaned back enjoying the view one more time.

"How can you stand to go to work in the morning? I don't think I could ever leave this place."

"The motivation is continuing to pay for the note on it so I don't have to leave it permanently," Clark chuckled.

"Good point," Bernadette replied before finishing her last sip of coffee.

"Ready to make groceries?"

Bernadette laughed at an expression that was purely used by natives to New Orleans. In New Orleans, you never shopped for groceries, you made the groceries.

Picking up their coffee cups, she left from the lanai and went into the kitchen rinsing them in the sink and placing them on the top shelf of the dishwasher.

"That's different," Clark thought to himself. The women he usually brought over never lifted a finger. They always expected him to wait on them. Grabbing his car keys off the counter, he led the way back to the entrance door.

When they arrived at the parking lot and Clark pulled the cover off his Corvette, Bernadette would have whistled if she had ever mastered that skill as a child. She hadn't even touched one let alone been a passenger. Clark walked to the passenger side, opened the door for her, and didn't close it until she was completely settled in with the seat belt buckled. As he pulled through the drive gate, Bernadette wouldn't have been surprised if Clark had mashed the accelerator to the floor but he was a cautious driver. No stunts or racing on his part. With his engineering background, she could tell he just enjoyed driving a well-made machine.

With the friendship they had developed these past four months, anyone watching them shopping through the grocery together would have mistaken them for a married couple. They selected the freshest looking green beans together and squeezed Vidalia onions to ensure no soft spots. They argued over whether the amount of pink in the flesh of the catfish filets indicated which was the freshest. Bernadette had to pull the heavy whipping cream carton Clark had tossed into the basket back out to check the date before selecting another one from the back of the refrigerated case. Finally, they had everything they needed and headed to the checkout.

Back at the condo, Clark showed Bernadette where everything was stored in the kitchen. As he began saving the refrigerated items, she grabbed the chopping board and pulled out a knife. Taking the bag of onions, she began to peel the first one.

After closing the refrigerator door, Clark called out with panic in his voice, "NO!"

Bernadette was startled thinking she had selected a knife he didn't want her to use. He gently took the onion from her hands and chided, "That's my job. Ever since I was old enough to use a knife, my sisters put me in charge of the onions. They couldn't stand the scent on their hands. They tried rubbing their hands with lemon juice. They tried that old Penny Prudence tip too, the one where you first wet your hands, pour salt on them, rub it around, then rinse. They claimed they could still smell the onions so the onions, the garlic, and peeling the shrimp are my job. That's not for ladies."

Bernadette smiled at the fact he was not going to park on the sofa and take a nap but truly intended for them to cook the dinner together. They quickly split up the responsibilities and went to work. Before long, the aromas of stock boiling for the soup, seasonings sautéing for the shrimp and crawfish sauce, and chocolate baking in the oven filled the air.

When the soup was done, they each tasted it and both frowned.

Bernadette spoke first, "It needs a little something more." Conscious of her weight, she didn't want to suggest adding more butter. "Maybe a pinch of thyme? And another dash of cayenne pepper?"

Clark took a second taste before facing her and saying, "We can, but I think we need to throw in another stick of butter."

Bernadette started laughing, "That's the Creole way, isn't it? If it doesn't taste right, add butter. If it still doesn't taste right, add more butter. Third time, try a pinch of sugar.""

"Sounds like my aunt's house," Clark laughed with her. "My Dad was watching her prepare the macaroni and cheese she brings to my grandmother's for Thanksgiving and he told me, 'It's only once a year so he didn't think anyone would get a heart attack that day.'"

"I've been trying to get my mother to change the way she cooks for years, but when I get home, it's always the same Creole dishes I grew up on."

"You stay with your parents?"

"Yes…. After college, I started saving to get my own place. By the time I could afford it, circumstances had changed at home… and I was needed there… so I stayed…."

Clark started to comment that he admired her for doing so, but Bernadette had turned pensive and something told him not to pry but to leave her alone with her thoughts. He didn't want to overstep the boundary of the friendship they were developing. Whatever it was, she needed to tell him in her own time. She finally broke the silence.

"One night, we were all looking at television, and the commercial had this beautiful bowl of steamed broccoli. I told my Mom I would love to have some for dinner. When I got home from work the next night, she was so proud she had made broccoli for me, but it didn't look anything like the ad. She told me, 'Bernadette, when I went to the grocery, I asked the vegetable man about this broccoli you saw on television. He told me how his wife fixes it at home…. This healthy eating sure is costly. I had to buy another pound of butter and two bags of cheese.'"

Clark started laughing, "So no steamed broccoli…. And, to top it off, she fixed cheese with broccoli instead of broccoli with cheese?"

"You got it!"

"That's exactly how my aunt fixes hers…. I splurge when I eat out, but I do try cooking healthy when I throw something together at home."

"One thing I make for them that they like is my oven roasted rosemary potatoes. They prefer those over my Mom's creamed potatoes now. I have one success story."

"That sounds good!" Feeling there was more behind the story Bernadette had just shared, Clark paused a moment before he continued. He hesitated to raise the idea remembering how uncomfortable they both seemed when he first suggested Bernadette come over…. Finally, he just blurted it out, "Do you like grilled salmon?"

"I love salmon."

"I make a mean grilled teriyaki salmon…. Why don't we eat in one night? You do the roasted potatoes, I'll grill the salmon, and we'll try real steamed broccoli."

Bernadette laughed. "That sounds like a winner. I'm in."

Clark relaxed hearing the honest enthusiasm in her voice at his suggestion. Of all the activities they had done, this day turned out to be the best time the two of them had together. Both had been raised in families that loved to cook and each had stories to tell on the subject. It also seemed they talked nonstop on a variety of subjects as they walked through the steps of meal preparation working side by side, laughing if they occasionally bumped each other in their haste. By 6:00 that afternoon, all was well under control.

"Time for me to head out," Bernadette stated as she pulled the apron off, folded it, and placed it on one corner of the kitchen counter.

"Head out?" Clark questioned obviously confused as he was setting silverware on the placemats on the dining table.

"I need to get out the way before your guests arrive." Bernadette stated adamantly. Knowing his boss was bringing his wife, Bernadette was sure Clark had invited a woman to join him to complete the foursome. She didn't know what type of woman he would date and, for some reason, couldn't bear the thought of finding out. She wanted to make her exit in time not to meet her.

"I apologize if I didn't make it clear about this evening, but after helping prepare all of this, I fully expected you would join us for dinner…. I need someone to keep the conversation on track. If you're not here, the boss and I will start talking business, and his wife will be bored to tears. That would not make for a memorable evening for her, and I'm sure he'll be told about it."

Bernadette glanced at the dining room table and saw Clark had set the table for only four people. She saw him looking pleadingly at her to stay. When the intercom announced the arrival of Clark's boss, he glanced at Bernadette again.

"I sure would like to get their feedback, especially on the extra butter." She winked and gave Clark the winning waitress' smile she had learned at Joe's.

Releasing an audible sigh of relief, Clark bounded down the stairs to greet his guests.

When Clark came back to the main floor and introduced Robert and Angela, Bernadette's apprehension melted quickly. She expected an elderly, white haired couple and was concerned she would not be able to converse on subjects of interest to either of them. Instead the couple was middle-aged. She and the wife were immediately at ease and even hugged when Clark made the introductions. Clark poured cocktails for all of them before they sat down for the first course. With Clark's looks and position, Bernadette knew he could easily nab any woman he wanted and always pictured a slim, tall, model at his side. Neither Clark's boss nor his wife showed any indication of surprise when Clark introduced full-figured Bernadette.

Clark knew the dinner was a hit when Bernadette offered to serve seconds and both readily agreed. By the end of the meal, Bernadette was promising to E-mail the recipes. The two couples retired to the lanai for a night cap. Leaning against the railing enjoying the sight of a paddle wheeler slowly floating down river, Clark felt content for the first time in his life with Bernadette at his side. The scents of a home-cooked dinner wafted onto the lanai. He was surrounded by a boss he also counted as a friend, mentor, and confidant and a woman that shared his interests. He admired the way Bernadette had played hostess. She was adept at keeping an interesting conversation flowing. He could tell his boss was obviously impressed. The evening had gone surprisingly well. Life was good!

Chapter Fourteen

Over the holidays, Bernadette and Clark did not see each other on any regular basis. Between work demands, family events, and personal invitations they each had to honor, time flew by. It was the middle of January before they fell once again into their old routine.

At dinner one night, Bernadette could tell something was bothering Clark.

"Having issues at work?"

"No," he answered absent mindedly.

"Having issues with me?"

"No! Definitely not." Clark perked up at the comment and began studying Bernadette trying to tell where the idea originated.

"Something isn't right. You look like someone ran over your dog. And, since I've been in your apartment, I know you don't have one."

Getting the laugh out of him she needed, Clark opened up.

"My sister got engaged for Christmas. I should say *officially* because she got her ring. They had met with the priest over a year ago and have been going through all the requirements so it's not unexpected her wedding is next month."

"So, you don't like the guy?"

"I told her, with her spoiled ways, that's probably the best she can do!"

Both Bernadette and Clark laughed at that.

"I have to take full blame. The guy she's marrying is named Cedric. He was my best friend in grammar school. I convinced him to do me the favor of taking her to her high school prom. I picked him because he's a geek. I knew he was someone I could trust. I didn't expect them to actually like each other and to start dating afterwards. I guess I can't complain about him since I was the one that introduced them."

"So, what's the issue?"

Clark started fidgeting. After announcing her plans, his sister had caught Clark alone, looked in his face and ordered, "Don't you dare bring one of those stuck-up bitches along like you usually hang out with. I don't want any airs at my wedding. I want to have fun!"

"I need an escort." He took a deep breath and shifted his eyes so he wouldn't see the rejection he expected before continuing. "Would you mind going with me? I'm going to be the best man…. I don't have a list of all my duties yet, but I'd appreciate your help getting through that day."

Bernadette hesitated at first. Then she remembered the dinner party with his boss over the holidays and how well it had gone. That helped her feel more confident about meeting Clark's family and being able to help out that day as well.

"Get me the date and the dress code and I'll check if I'm free."

Clark perked up again. Looking at Bernadette, he advised, "I'll have my sister put you on the invitation list. It's in Lacombe. You may need to drive over that morning by yourself. My sister wants a country style wedding. Since I need to help with the cooking, I'll probably drive over Friday night. I offered to help pay for a caterer and a hall; but she wants it at our aunt's house, and my parents agreed."

"Lacombe?" Bernadette knew the general location of the town on the North Shore of Lake Pontchartrain but had never visited the area.

"It's not that far. I'll make sure you have easy directions to the church, and I'll do all the driving once you meet me there."

"Lacombe? Isn't that like an hour's drive from here?"

"Probably…. Changing your mind?"

Clark looked so pitiful, Bernadette couldn't deny his request. Seems that was happening more and more often lately.

"No, I'll still go." Seeing his smile made her feel she had made the right decision. That smile could get him anything he wanted, she thought. Thank, God, she was fat and they were only friends. Else, she'd probably be knocked-up just like Cecelia had been and what a disappointment that would be to her parents.

Knowing he could count on Bernadette to get him through another trial, Clark was his old self again.

Somehow, hearing her being added to the formal invitation list made Bernadette grow apprehensive.

The week before the wedding, Bernadette and Clark were having dinner at Blaine's.

"What time are we meeting next Thursday night? Are you going to park at the condo since it makes sense for us to ride over together?"

The blank, cold stare Bernadette gave him prompted Clark to continue in a cautious tone of voice, "Did I forget to mention you're expected at the rehearsal dinner?"

Bernadette almost choked on the food she was about to swallow.

"YES! I think you did." Going to a wedding was one thing, but the rehearsal dinner was more intimate. Only the closest of friends and family were usually invited.

"You're invited," Clark responded nonchalantly and speared a shrimp hung on the cocktail glass.

"Clark!" Bernadette was becoming impatient.

Clueless, he looked up and questioned, "You had plans?"

"No. I don't have plans but I've never met your family. Are you sure they're expecting me? Shouldn't that night be for just the wedding party?"

"My family never does anything in a small way. It will be a lot more than just the wedding party at the church and at my aunt's house afterwards. Relatives are already arriving from out of town. Besides, it'll be good for you to meet all my sisters beforehand."

"All your sisters? How many do you have?"

"Six."

"Six? Any brothers?"

"No, I was the only boy."

Bernadette couldn't imagine growing up with six siblings in the same house. Cecelia was enough to make her wish she was an only child.

"Six sisters?"

"Don't start laughing when you hear their names."

Bernadette was curious. The look she gave Clark told him he had to tell her more.

"Both of my parents' names start with Cs and they named all of us with Cs as well."

"I like that idea," Bernadette answered intrigued and trying to think of eight other names that the family may have used as Clark continued.

"My mother used to embroider. The letter 'C' was one of the prettiest in her eyes. My parents are Calvin and Camille and my sisters, in order of their birth, are Colleen, Constance, Corinne, Catherine, Candace, and Cher. Cher, the spoiled baby, is the one getting married. It means beloved one but I think the devil played a part."

"So where do you fall in the line?"

"At the point my father and, especially my mother, had given up on having a boy."

Both Bernadette and Clark laughed at that.

"I am number six. The first six of us were each born two years apart. I think my parents intended to be done after they finally had a boy because I was five when Cher was born. We all spoiled her rotten so this wedding is going to be a circus."

"I have only one sister and no brothers. Her name starts with a 'C' too. It's Cecelia. My father is Bernard; but since he was named after his father, everyone just calls him Junior. I'm not sure some people even know his real name…. My mother's name is Audra."

"Bernard…. Bernadette? Were you named after your father?"

"Yes. My Mother got the idea after seeing a movie about the saint."

"So, you and your sister were close in age…"

"No, we're nine years apart. I don't think my parents thought they were going to be blessed with any more kids so she's spoiled rotten too. I can relate to your situation."

As she spoke the words, Bernadette recalled the cruel comment she had overheard about her mother. Since it had been so long between the two of them, the family had given up and thought her mother couldn't have any more children. One Christmas they spent with her Dad's family, she had overheard her paternal grandmother telling her aunt that she thought it was because her mother was so obese that the layers of fat were blocking the sperm from finding the egg. The two had burst into laughter, but Bernadette didn't find the comment at all amusing. Her aunt had responded, "Junior loves his little, fat wife," and they laughed again.

Clark detected a change in Bernadette's mood but attributing it to sibling rivalry he lifted his wine glass in a toast, "To spoiled rotten baby sisters. May we continue to survive despite their impact on our lives."

Thinking about how having Miki had not only changed Cecelia's life but also impacted her own, Bernadette lifted her glass, "I'll drink to that!"

On Thursday night, Clark was waiting by the visitors' spots when Bernadette arrived. He had already pulled his Corvette into one of the empty slots to save time. Bernadette parked, grabbed her bag, and hurried to the passenger side where Clark was waiting patiently to open and close the door for her. She noticed a blond eyeing her jealously as Clark jumped into the driver's seat, turned the ignition, and the engine began to purr. As they pulled out onto the street, the blond was still staring at them. "Jealous of the fat girl," Bernadette thought, and the image of her and Clark together was so ridiculous a smile broke out.

Glancing her way, Clark commented, "I'm glad you're happy after all about attending this."

Not wanting to share her thoughts, Bernadette put on her sun glasses and said, "Looking forward to it."

Adjusting the seat slightly back, she relaxed and enjoyed the ride over Lake Pontchartrain to the North Shore while viewing the setting sun.

They had been traveling on Interstate-10 East. Once they passed the last exit in Slidell, Clark began giving Bernadette detailed directions pointing out landmarks so she could find her way to the wedding easily. The route seemed very straight-forward so Bernadette opted not to take any notes. Once they crossed a tiny bridge over Bayou Lacombe, Clark took an immediate left, and Sacred Heart church was on the right. It would be hard for Bernadette not to find the church Saturday morning. Pulling into the parking lot, she was beginning to understand what Clark meant by his family doing everything in a big way. The number of cars present was more indicative of the wedding day than just a rehearsal.

When they entered the door of the church, Bernadette wondered if she suddenly became invisible because, as fat as she was, it would be kind of hard not to see her. That entire night, some of the women completely ignored the fact she and Clark were together. Did being fat automatically discount you as a significant other in the minds of these skinny chicks?

"Clark! Clark! Over here!"

Both Bernadette and Clark turned to the left to see a petite girl hobbling towards Clark as fast as she safely could on six inch heels. As the lady threw her arms around him and planting a kiss on his check that left bright pink lip marks, Bernadette could tell he not only had no clue who she was but was also not comfortable with the outrageous display of affection. That didn't stop this lady though.

"I'm Linda! I know it's been years." She slapped Clark's lower arm gently chiding him for not remembering her and gave him her widest smile. "I'm Cher's best friend from high school. Remember? You used to drive us to cheer leading practice?"

Bernadette wanted to puke.

Even if he didn't remember Linda, Clark was polite and did a good job of pretending the light bulb clicked.

"Wow! Look at you – all grown up." Trying to put some distance between them, Clark responded as if he was pleasantly surprised as he pushed her backwards an arm's length under the pretense he was trying to see her better.

Bernadette picked up a church bulletin and pretended to be reading it though she was using it to hide the smirk on her face. No wonder he wanted her here – a bit of sanity amidst the chaos he would have to endure.

"I'm the maid of honor so we might get to walk down the aisle together."

It was clear Linda was excited about the probability.

"Not a chance," said an elegant looking older woman walking up. She hooked Clark's arm in hers and reached slightly up to kiss his cheek. "As the matron of honor, that will be my privilege."

"By tradition, the MATRON of honor walks alone," Linda retorted.

Making it clear the emphasis on the word matron was not appreciated, the woman scowled at Linda and replied, "The Laurents make their own traditions."

Seeing the expression on the woman's face, Linda took the hint and retreated quickly into the church.

"Hi, sis." Clark leaned down and returned the kiss, "Thanks for saving me." Turning with their arms still locked, he introduced the woman. "This is my friend, Bernadette. Bernadette, this is my second eldest sister, Constance."

The woman's face changed from the scowl to a welcoming smile, "Just call me Connie. Everyone else does. I'm his favorite sister but... don't tell the others." Connie winked at Bernadette, "Come this way. I'll introduce you to the family."

Dropping Clark's arms and grabbing Bernadette's, she started leading her to the section of the church where the ladies were gathered while pointing out to Clark the section where the men were meeting with the director receiving their instructions.

As they approached the group, Constance yelled to everybody that Bernadette was Clark's girlfriend. Then she started calling out everyone's names so quickly, Bernadette didn't have time to correct her. What shocked Bernadette more than the announcement was the group's reaction – no one seemed upset that Clark was dating an overweight person. When Connie completed pointing out everyone in the group, Bernadette clarified that she was only Clark's escort for the wedding – just friends, not romantically involved. They all listened, but Bernadette doubted her comments really registered by the smirks on their faces.

Bernadette took a seat in one of the pews with others not involved in the ceremony and watched the rehearsal. Afterwards, the cars heading from the church to Clark's aunt's house resembled a wagon train. When they arrived at his aunt's estate, Bernadette could see why his sister wanted to hold the reception there. The house had to be sitting on at least two acres of land, and the grounds were beautiful that time of year. Azalea bushes of every hue were in full bloom. Seeing the array of colors was breath taking: violet, red, white, pink, and rose. Purple wisteria vines ran along the fence. The fragrance of jasmine and gardenia bushes was heady. The scent of blossoms from citrus tress also filled the air. Workers were still setting up a dance floor, huge tents, and lighting next to her rose garden but an adequate area was already completed to welcome those that had attended the rehearsal dinner. Dinner had been catered and was set up buffet style so everything could flow smoothly. A gentleman was carving a turkey, ham, and a beef roast. You served the sides yourself choosing from a jambalaya pasta, Brussels sprouts, and a carrot soufflé. Pre-served saucers of Caesar salad had been laid out. Family members had pitched in and made a variety of desserts. A chocolate fountain was in the middle of the dessert table surrounded by fresh fruits. A gentleman had also been hired to serve as a bartender and mixed any drink you could imagine from memory.

Bernadette and Clark sat at a table with his older sisters over dinner while his younger sister Cher sat at a table with her fiancé and their parents. Each older sister enjoyed showing off pictures of their baby brother at different stages. They pulled out their wallets, compared photos, and handed them to Bernadette to see. Then they started telling stories about Clark when they were growing up. At first, Clark was laughing at the shenanigans they shared as he remembered those times as well. He grew serious and began fidgeting when Corinne brought up the girls' dating years. Being closest to him of his six siblings, Connie was the only one that noticed the mood swing.

"Bernadette, Clark was all of our chaperones." Corinne started providing details.

"Chaperones?" Bernadette indicated she didn't understand.

"When we wanted to start dating, my Dad would not let any of us go out alone with a boy. Not until we were at least nineteen. He would say, 'You can go only if you take your lil' brother with you!' My Dad gave him his own show fare and concession money to accompany us. We all fought over Clark to get out the house."

Colleen contributed, "But sometimes he got us in trouble. Being so young, he didn't understand everything he saw and would say the wrong thing sometimes in front of our Dad."

Clark's eyes shifted to the left and he bit the bottom part of his lower lip. He happened to glance at Connie and both their faces broke into a grin. They knew the incident Colleen remembered, and Clark had known exactly what he was doing. Their faces tried to turn serious again as the sisters continued their tales to Bernadette.

"After a couple of years, he got smart and started charging the guys we dated," Catherine recanted.

"Charging?" Bernadette was confused again until Catherine clarified.

"He wanted a new bike, and Mom and Dad said, 'No,' because it was so close to Christmas. They probably were planning to get it as his Christmas present. That didn't dawn on Clark because he wanted it right then and didn't want to wait two more months. So, he refused to accompany us on a date unless the guy paid him three dollars. Even if we double dated, which we had to do sometimes to get a slot on the calendar, each guy would have to pay him three dollars."

Bernadette turned smiling at Clark, but the expression on her face said more, "You charged your sisters?"

"Hey, I was an entrepreneur at a young age…. And, I didn't charge my sisters; I charged the guy," he argued, but Connie saw he was fidgeting even more. That's the first time she ever heard him trying to defend his actions to a date.

Candace then recalled, "But he charged based on how much he liked the guy. Three dollars was just the standard if the guy didn't impress him either way. When I went out with Paul, Clark only charged him one dollar; but if I wanted to go out with Gary, Clark charged him five. So, Gary couldn't take me out as often as Paul could."

When Candace started whining, Clark responded with a biting remark, "Paul was the one you married. You have two kids for him so he must be doing something right."

When Bernadette turned to stare at Clark a second time to chide him, he turned his face from her and pretended to concentrate on eating his meal again.

"Wow," thought Connie. She had never seen any woman silence her baby brother and with just a look?

"They're twins so only one pregnancy," Candace reminded Clark. "But, yes, he is so sweet," Candace added before looking lovingly towards the gym set where Paul was patiently watching over Sara and Seth. They were the only two children that attended the rehearsal since they would be serving as the flower girl and ring bearer for Cher and Cedric.

Bernadette finally got a chance to make a comment on everything the sisters had shared, "So, Clark learned about relationships from going on dates with you all? Being your chaperone, he learned exactly how to treat a lady based on your experiences?"

The remark was lost on four of the sisters but not on Connie. Connie had remained silent during the entire exchange choosing instead to study the interactions between her baby brother and Bernadette. As soon as Bernadette made that comment, she recognized the same reaction from Clark he had demonstrated since he was three years old, a reaction she knew well. It was the one he displayed each time one of his parents caught him doing something he shouldn't, and he was trying to think of how to get out the situation and avoid being punished.

"You little cad," Connie thought. "Your cover just got blown." Clark's eyes moved to the left and shifted downward. He started biting at the left side of his lower lip. If he was still three, she'd spank him herself. When Clark glanced at Connie, observed her crossed arms, and saw her expression, the smirk he gave her indicated he knew the impact of Bernadette's words had not fallen on deaf ears. His other four sisters were still chattering away completely oblivious and Clark was doing just what he had done when he chaperoned their dates: sitting still, listening, observing.

In fact, he would sit so quietly on the car's back seat they sometimes forgot he was there. Connie remembered that even when they got home, they didn't think about the silent little boy who never interrupted their stories. Sitting in their parents' den, the sisters chattered among themselves sharing everything that had gone right or wrong on the date. They would discuss what the boy did that they liked and what the boy did that made them so mad that they'd never see him again. Five older sisters with different personalities, different temperaments, different hopes and dreams were enough templates for him to piece together the perfect approach for any woman he met within a matter of minutes.

Connie had to laugh because the little rogue was handsome. Tanned skin, dark wavy hair, deep set eyes, high cheek bones, and the trimmed moustache and goatee created a combination women found hard to resist. Though she was eight years older, she had single friends that still inquired about him, asked if he was married yet, and making it very clear they would not mind going out with a younger man. With those muscles, she knew he still worked out. Over six feet two tall, he had inherited the best genes from both of their parents. His looks alone served him well. On top of all of the physical God given gifts, he was intelligent, kind, generous to a fault, and well-mannered. He could never enter a room without the ladies noticing. Having grown up with seven women in the house, he had learned to ignore the ladies. The looks he got always went unnoticed on Clark's part until he initiated the hunt and his eyes locked with another pair. Connie imagined he had to learn to ignore them all being the only boy. Her father had learned to ignore the seven females in the house too. Without being able to tune them out, the two guys wouldn't have survived.

Connie remembered their Dad leading Clark by example: opening the car door for their mother as he still did, carrying her packages, remembering her birthday in some special way, knowing her favorite color and sending her favorite flowers just because. Besides their father's example, Clark also had five older sisters that didn't realize they had taught their baby brother how to be suave. "We created him," she thought, "No wonder women don't stand a chance against his charms.

She suddenly felt sorry for him. With Cher getting married, he would be the only single one left of the siblings. She thought back to an incident that had happened when he was three.

Chapter Fifteen

Clark had been enrolled in nursery school to give their grandmother a break from the mischievous tot always seeming to get into something. Surprisingly, he had adjusted well to the discipline of the day nursery run by nuns and established for the purpose of helping working parents. His behavior had been exemplary until Valentine's Day came. Her Dad had brought home a dozen American Beauty roses for their Mom who was busy preparing dinner for the family of eight. She turned, kissed him softly on the cheek, thanked him, and went back to caramelizing onions. The six children were all seated around the dining room table doing their homework, and Connie was helping Clark complete his preschool assignment. Her Dad also had bought a single rose for each of his daughters. He walked over delivering a rose to each of them and giving each of them a kiss on the cheek. Then he walked back to the stove and cut off the burner her Mom was using.

"Calvin, I'm trying to finish supper."

"I'll finish preparing dinner tonight. You're going to rest. Open your card." He spoke the words so sternly that she exhaled but obliged. As she slit the envelop open, a diamond tennis bracelet fell onto the countertop.

Her mother gasped, "Oh, Calvin! It's beautiful!"

Her Dad smiled, reached down, picked up the bracelet, and circled it around her mother's wrist and fastened the clasp.

Her Mom turned her wrist to watch the diamonds catch the light before flinging herself into his arms and kissing him more passionately. Clark's face was intense as he watched the scene play out.

Turning to Connie, Clark said with determination, "I'm going to get me a wife so I can kiss her on the lips."

The other four sisters giggled at his comment and he stared at them his feelings obviously hurt. To soothe things over, Connie told him, "Do you see Mommy is wearing a ring?"

He looked towards their mother and then turned back to Connie before replying, "Yes."

"How are you going to get a wife if you can't buy her a ring? Do you have money? The ring means she's married."

"I have some money in my piggybank."

"It takes more than that to buy a ring."

He thought about that for a moment and realizing he probably didn't have enough money, he frowned. Knowing she had caused his unhappiness, Connie told him, "Come with me."

He followed her to her bedroom where she dug a ring out of her jewelry box. Turning to Clark, she said, "You can have this ring. I was lucky and got it out a bubble gum machine when I was five."

Clark's face brightened and mimicking their mother's reaction, he smiled at her and said, "Oh, Connie! It's beautiful!" He turned and ran to his bedroom to store his treasure.

Little did Connie know how much trouble a simple, bubble gum ring would start...

The next day, the nun who served as the principal of the nursery school phoned the house, and to Clark's misfortune, their Dad was home and took the call. He contacted their Mom and said he would be picking Clark up because he had to meet with the principal and discuss a behavior issue. How long he stayed in conference with the nun Connie didn't know, but it was far after the rest of them got home that their Dad marched Clark into the house and straight to the study he used as his home office holding him firmly by the upper arm. When they finally emerged, he told Clark sternly, "You are still punished. Go to your room and stay there until your Mother calls you for dinner."

Clark immediately obeyed and when he had disappeared up the stairway and they heard his bedroom door close, their Dad walked over, grabbed one of the carrots Connie had cleaned and took a bite before sitting on the stool by the counter where her mother was chopping seasonings.

"Did you spank him?" Her mother knew a strong father figure was essential but she set limits. It still broke her heart whenever Calvin disciplined one of her babies.

"No. It wouldn't have done any good in this case…. We talked all the way home, but I wasn't getting through to him. Besides, that nun had already taken it upon herself to administer corporal punishment. I'm never going to punish our child twice for the same offense."

Connie could tell by the aggravated way her father spoke that he was not pleased with the turn of events. Her father was strict but fair. Any punishment he doled out was always appropriate based on the age of the child and the seriousness of the transgression. She had never seen him give Clark more than three controlled slaps on his bottom. She got the impression her father felt the nun had gone too far.

"What happened? He's done fine all year. Why she did call you to the school?"

"Clark had some ring and gave it to a little girl named Kayloni."

Connie froze.

"I asked him where he got the ring, and he said it was a bubble gum machine ring."

Connie looked out the corner of her eye, but her father made no move or indication he knew she was the one that had given Clark the ring. He had told the truth but only enough of it to satisfy their father's demand. No sense in both of them being in trouble. He's learning. She sighed with relief!

"So, what's wrong with that?" Her mother asked perturbed.

"Apparently, he thinks he and Kayloni are now married so he's been kissing her on the lips all day."

Her Mom smiled and said, "Ooohhhh, his first love…"

"His first love? That's why the nun was appalled by his behavior. Heck, they're three years old and giving each other a little peck. It's not like they're high school students caught having sex in an empty classroom or something."

Connie froze again. Her best friend Kathleen's sister had been expelled for exactly that reason. Kathleen was nothing like her sister, but she was afraid if her father found out that he might restrict the time she could spend with Kathleen and especially at Kathleen's house."

"I guess she feels if you don't nip it in the bud at an early age, that's where the behavior will end up. So, where do we go from here?"

"Clark sat in the chair with his arms crossed and adamant he's never divorcing Kayloni because marriage is forever."

Their mother chuckled at the thought. "Well Calvin… You always said we must lead by example. I wonder where he learned that one?"

Her father ignored the slight and seemed exasperated, "I tried different appeals but only one seemed to work."

"Which is?"

"Well, I tried to explain to him that kissing isn't appropriate at school. It's best saved for at home. For example, like when I kissed you yesterday for Valentine's Day…. He thought about that for a while. It looks like he understands, but now he wants to invite Kayloni to spend the weekend."

"So, no more kissing at school?"

"Just pray because I think it's in God's hands now…."

"You wanted a son and, now that you've finally got one, it's clear he's going to be a hand full."

Her Dad reached over and playfully swatted her Mom's bottom, "You gave him to me."

They kissed and said a silent prayer that tomorrow would be back to a normal day.

The next day, Connie went with her Mom to pick up Clark from the nursery school. When he climbed into the back seat next to her, she had never seen him look so sad.

"Clark, what's wrong?"

He looked up at her and a tear rolled down his left cheek. He unclenched his right hand and handed the ring back to Connie, "Kayloni's Mom made her give me the ring back. Kayloni said, 'No more kissing!' I'm divorced." He was silent the rest of the way home and only picked at his dinner that night.

Eyeing her baby brother again, she sighed remembering his first heartbreak. She still had that bubble gum ring in her jewelry box. Connie remembered his second as well, the one with Rebecca. He had called Connie and asked her to lunch. He poured his heart out telling her all about the break-up. She had to fight hard to hide her elation. From the moment she had met Rebecca, she knew she wasn't the right one for him. To her knowledge, she and their cousin Clay were the only two who knew how serious he had become about Rebecca and how quickly the relationship had fallen apart.

Maybe the third time will be the charm for him. She was sorry she had planted the seed about buying the ring when he was so young and impressionable. The moment he finished college and got started on his career path, he took whatever lady he was dating to nothing but the best restaurants in town and showered her with lavish gifts: necklaces, bracelets, watches, and earrings. The majority of them were not deserving of the money he spent on them, especially Rebecca.

Through the years, Connie had never seen him give anyone else a ring. She wondered how deep the incident had scarred him because he hadn't gone through the expense of buying Rebecca an engagement ring yet. It seems he wasn't about to give out another ring lightly. The lesson he learned at a young age still burned in his subconscious.

"Odd," Connie thought, "He's been looking for a wife since he was three and he's the only sibling that hadn't found the right person yet." Her grandmother use to say, "Some people can't see what's right in front of their own nose." She was so little when she first heard her grandmother say that, she didn't understand what she meant and took the expression literally. She had gone to her bedroom and put an open book right in front of her nose. Her eyes crossed, she got dizzy, and she couldn't read a thing. She laughed at herself remembering her attempts to prove her grandmother wrong, but it was true literally and metaphorically. Was that Clark's problem? Was he too close to the situation to see what he had? As Connie pondered her grandmother's words, she began studying Clark and Bernadette's interactions more closely.

Chapter Sixteen

A tired Paul walked up and began a conversation with Candace about their plans for the kids at the wedding. Trying to control two bouncing bundles of energy, Bernadette could tell Paul was tired and ready to call it a night. Candace, however, was enjoying the conversation with her siblings and wasn't indicating she was ready to leave. As the conversation between Candace and Paul heated, Connie observed Clark once again. His body straightened in the chair. He was on full alert. His head didn't move but his eyes stared to the right towards the couple. He was listening intently, observing their reactions, and learning all about what it takes to have a successful marriage. All the do's and don'ts of a committed relationship were being played before him at each family gathering, and he soaked it all in like a sponge. "Some things never change," Connie thought. 'We're still teaching him."

Their aunt's announcement broke up the tirade.

"I have 'to go' boxes out now. Please don't leave all of this food behind, or I won't have room for what's being delivered tomorrow to prepare for the wedding Saturday."

Connie stood first rushing to Paul's rescue.

"Let me take the kids while you and Candace pack up. These two have been playing the entire time and you know they'll want to eat the minute you get home. You best fill up on the macaroni and cheese and grab some of those chocolate chip cookies I made."

Paul appeared grateful to have a break as Connie took Sara and Seth by the hand and marched them over to her parents. Her mother Camille saw her coming and discretely moved in their direction to meet her. They observed Bernadette and Clark at the buffet table. Bernadette was filling 'to go' boxes based on Clark's direction. She'd pick something up and wait for his nod indicating yes or no before adding the item.

"Someone else to spoil him?" his mother asked prompting Connie's feedback. "What do you think of this one?"

Based on the interactions she had observed, Connie filled her mother in.

"Yes, she will spoil him, but she'll also keep him in line. She's not the usual type he has brought to family events before.... It seems they've been together for a while."

"She doesn't appear to be a girl interested in just a physical relationship." Camille looked at Bernadette more intently.

"When I first introduced her, she said she was not a girlfriend per se but just a friend. This one is intelligent, friendly, a good conversationalist. Seeing them together, I believe her. Clark doesn't treat her like the others. He treats her like a worn pair of shoes. He's at ease with her. There's no pretense between them. It's as if she's one of the guys but just happens to be a girl. I know they're NOT having sex."

As Camille continued to observe the way her son acted with Bernadette, she questioned Connie further.

"I wonder how they met. She's a pretty girl but not the type that has attracted Clark in the past."

"She is overweight so I think instead of being attracted to just a physical appearance, my baby brother has finally met someone that appealed to the right head this time."

Camille and Connie both laughed at Connie's crude remark.

"So, what do you rate her overall?"

"Mom, I'd be disappointed if this one didn't stay around. I like her. I like her a lot. She fits in with our family and she's good for him. Clark just doesn't realize yet how good they do work together."

Camille spotted Cher and Cedric going over the music for the wedding with the disc jockey. She looked at Connie and said, "I like her too so we need to make sure we DO see her again."

Camille tilted her chin slightly upward and towards the table where Cher was sitting.

Connie understood the unspoken message and replied, "I'll talk to Cher and Cedric."

Camille took her grandkids off Connie's hands so the plot they were scheming could thicken.

Chapter Seventeen

On the day of the wedding, Clark felt a chill when he woke that morning. He didn't relate it to any omen but to his nervousness hoping everything would go well for his baby sister that day. The chill ran through him a second time. Glancing at the setting of the central system's vents, he attributed the chill to the air conditioning. Eyeing the tuxedo he had to wear hanging on the door of the closet, he wondered if he would ever find the right person to take that same step. Since he hadn't yet, he was grateful Bernadette would be there to help out. Sometimes his family was overbearing, especially being around six sisters. He took comfort knowing his friend would be providing her support. He was beginning to feel he would always be able to count on Bernadette being there for him.

Taking advantage of his aunt's invitation, Bernadette parked at her house and rode to the church with Clark's family so they arrived about forty minutes before the wedding was scheduled to begin. She had a wonderful time at the rehearsal dinner Thursday night so was looking forward to seeing his parents and sisters again. It would also be nice to meet the rest of Clark's nieces and nephews. Having seen the gym set, she was tempted to bring Miki along knowing Miki, Sara, and Seth would have a grand time together but she also didn't want to distract from her commitment to Clark. He had asked her to attend because he needed her there for him.

Though Clark's aunt wanted her to sit with the family, Bernadette didn't sit in the reserved section. She selected a center aisle seat about midway between the entrance door and the altar on the bride's side of the church instead. She was hoping to get to talk to Clark before the wedding started and the seat granted her a view of all entrance doors. About fifteen minutes before the wedding march was scheduled to begin, she spotted Clark entering the church through the side door on the bride's side. As soon as he began moving down the aisle, he was accosted.

First, a tall lady with her hair dyed a reddish-brown stood and stepped into the aisle in front of him forcing him to stop. Bernadette saw him force a smile as he leaned down and planted the expected kiss on her cheek. When she began fingering the ruffles on his tuxedo shirt, Clark reached up, took both of her hands in his, planted a second kiss on the back of her right hand, uttered some excuse, and moved away quickly without releasing her hands until he was out of grab range again.

As he moved forward down the side aisle, a brunette stood and waved. He smiled, waved back and kept walking pretending he didn't understand her signal to come over. With two people sitting between her and the aisle, the brunette didn't make it to the aisle in time before Clark passed their row.

Bernadette was beginning to feel a little jealous by the time Clark spotted her. When he did, his eyes brightened, and he selected a nearly empty row to cross towards the center aisle to greet her.

She stood so they could speak discretely.

"Thanks for coming. Is my tie ok?"

Bernadette reached up and tightened the clip slightly so the knot lay perfectly centered and finished with a light pat against his chest.

"It's just right now, but you look exhausted."

"I've been up since three this morning helping finish everything Cher wanted. Me, my Dad, two of my brother-in-laws and three uncles have been grilling, putting drinks on ice, and boiling seafood. I wish she would have let us cater today too, but she whined that the caterer didn't season things like Daddy does and his barbequed ribs weren't tender enough. Of course, my Dad gave in to the brat."

Without thinking, Bernadette caressed his hand.

"It'll be over soon and you have all day tomorrow to recoup."

"I plan to crash on the lanai and not move the entire day. You may have to come over tomorrow afternoon and poke me to make sure I'm not dead."

They laughed together, but the red head, the brunette, and others watching were not laughing at all. Neither was Camille who had entered the back of the church and was observing the loving way Bernadette looked at her son and hung on his every word. Connie walked up at that point, stood beside her mother, and immediately locked in on them as well.

"All set?" Camille questioned not taking her eyes off the couple.

"You know Cher couldn't resist the opportunity."

A chill hit Clark again. He shrugged his shoulders trying to shake it off. In doing so, he noticed his mother at the back of the church.

"See you after the ceremony. I need to walk my Mom down the aisle to her seat."

"Okay," Bernadette winked to let him know all would be fine before taking her seat again.

Bernadette failed to notice the women who didn't miss a second of their exchange. Glancing around the church checking who had attended, Connie didn't and thought, "We better make sure Bernadette doesn't go to the restroom alone."

Bernadette had never seen or imagined such a beautiful wedding. Cher wanted a rainbow wedding, but instead of the ladies wearing the same dress in different shades, they all wore white eyelet gowns with pastel colored sashes at the waist. The sash, the ribbon on their wide brimmed white hats, and the flowers each carried matched the color the bridesmaid was assigned. Colleen was the first to be escorted down the aisle. Her sash, hat ribbon, and flowers were a pale pink. Corinne was next and had a pale peach. Catherine followed in yellow. Candace wore a mint green. Cher's best friend Linda was in baby blue. Connie ended the line of bridesmaids wearing a pale violet. Watching Clark take his sister's arm and escort her towards her spot by the altar, all Bernadette could think about was how great he looked in a tuxedo. She was forgetting to turn back to see Sara and Seth until the traditional "Here Comes the Bride" march sounded from the organ in the choir loft.

All the guests stood as Calvin proudly escorted Cher down the aisle. Another one of Clark's aunts that Bernadette had met at the rehearsal dinner had chosen to sit behind her so she could also be on the aisle and positioned to snap pictures. She leaned forward and whispered, "She's wearing her mother's gown."

"A family so similar to her own," Bernadette thought. "A family that was close... A family that supported each other... A family that valued tradition...." She knew this was a demanding day for Clark but hoped he realized how lucky he was to be surrounded by so much love.

After the ceremony, as people were scurrying outside the church to retrieve their cars and line up behind the Bride's limousine, Clark approached Bernadette and shoved the keys for his Corvette into her hand.

"My aunt said you drove over with them?"

"Yes, I'm parked at her house."

"Great! Turns out I need to ride in the limousine for more pictures on the way so please drive my car over."

"Clark, I've never driven a car that expensive!"

He laughed before responding, "They all work the same way. You'll be fine."

Clark was so grateful Bernadette was there to drive the Corvette for him that, without thinking, he grabbed Bernadette's upper arms and planted a kiss on her lips.

"Thanks. Got to go!" He turned and sprinted toward the open limousine door.

The fact he had kissed her for the first time didn't register to Bernadette. She was too upset he had dumped the responsibility for his Corvette in her lap. The thought of driving a sports car with an engine that powerful made her nervous. She got more upset when she realized he hadn't even told her where he parked it. She started to call out to him, but the door of the limousine was closed and it was already pulling off. Turning, she began searching for Clark's car. When she found it parked on the side of the church under a tree and clicked the keys for the door to unlock, the same sets of eyes that had watched the exchange in church and their kiss were still on her.

After what seemed to be a million flashes of light, the pictures were all taken and the reception was in full swing. Bernadette had one of the reserved seats at the table with the families and the wedding party. Clark plopped down next to her and loosened his tie.

"I'm done." He told her before slouching in the chair exhausted.

Bernadette handed him a glass of bourbon over rocks. His eyes lit up.

"Thanks... I need that right now."

"Want anything to eat?"

"Nay. I tasted enough helping with the cooking this morning. It was one of the ways I stayed awake."

"Your family is so much like my own. I feel like I've known them all for years."

"They do have their bright moments just not often enough."

"Same with mine."

Bernadette looked at Clark, and they laughed together. Seeing that exchange, the pairs of eyes that had been staring at them finally shifted to other prey.

When Connie appeared at Bernadette's chair, Bernadette thought it was just to say hi, but Connie indicated with her thumb Bernadette needed to follow her.

"Where?" Bernadette questioned.

"It's time for Cher to throw the bouquet, and all single gals need to be on the floor. Let's go."

Bernadette looked at Clark pleadingly with an expression that said, "Please save me!"

When Clark saw the expression on Connie's face daring him to intervene, he shook his two hands and laid them on his knees. He started laughing before looking at Bernadette and responding to her expression.

"You ladies have a good time out there."

Bernadette had no choice but to follow Connie to the dance floor. She moved toward the far left corner of the staged area trying to get as far out of range of the bouquet as she could and also out of camera range. Clark's sisters flanked her on all sides. Seeing his married sisters remain on the dance floor for a tradition for single ladies only was clearly signs of a set-up materializing. When the time came for Cher to throw the bouquet, Cher turned around to assess who was standing where and another family tradition kicked in as if on cue. Clark's sisters use to tease about not wanting to catch the bouquet and be the next one to wed so, in unison, they would start retreating slowly as soon as the bride turned her back so they would avoid catching the bouquet. With all of them being married now, their interest in being part of the activity was all about Bernadette.

Clark watched the five slowly retreating and creating a circle where Bernadette was the only one in the area. When he saw they blocked any other single lady from getting near her, Clark's initial guess was confirmed instantly. It was a set-up.

Poor Bernadette looked like a prisoner with his sisters surrounding her on the dance floor waiting for Cher to toss the bouquet. She didn't have a choice when it came flying her way. She had to catch it to keep the beautiful floral arrangement from crashing to the floor.

While the seat next to him was empty, Clark's mother had walked over and sat down. Camille was the type of woman who favored a direct approach and didn't want to leave anything to chance. She wanted to ensure her son knew how she felt. Placing her right hand on his left, she patted it gently. In response to the loving gesture, Clark placed his right hand over hers.

"I like this one Clark," Camille spoke the words softly so only Clark could hear.

Clark leaned towards his mother, shaking his head in disgust.

"Mom, Bernadette's just a friend I met purely by accident. We just hang out. We have common interests. We both enjoy fine dining and trying out new recipes. We catch movies, especially foreign films. Sometimes, on a weekend, we may check out a local festival or a play."

Camille locked in on the recipe comment. Maybe Connie's assessment was wrong. If Bernadette was at Clark's apartment cooking, then maybe they were having sex.

"So, the two of you cook together?

"Sometimes... It's relaxing standing over a stove with the scent of seasonings filling the condo. Makes it seem like home. She's like one of my best buddies right now...."

Seeing her son's face as he stated the last sentence, Camille knew Connie was right. Clark thought about Bernadette as one of the guys. There was no romance here yet....

Clark patted his mother's hand recalling the scents of her cooking in the kitchen when he was a child. Camille could detect that far-away look, the one that longed for the comfort of family, but it was time for him to have a family of his own.

"How long ago did you meet her?" Camille was determined to push things along, and she knew the best way to plant the seed with Clark.

Though Clark's eyes were following every move his sisters were making on poor Bernadette, his mother's eyes were focused only on her son's face.

"Oh, it was right before Glenn moved to Europe," he responded absent mindedly keeping his eyes on Bernadette. "That was around Labor Day... I guess we first met in August so I'd say about eight months roughly."

"Clark," his mother spoke his name in the tone he had learned early as a child, the one that commanded eye contact and his undivided attention.

Camille knew to get through to him she had to hit below the belt. As he turned, her gaze was intent as she spoke, "Are you seeing anyone else, son?"

A shock wave went through Clark. He felt as if all the blood in his upper body was draining to his knees. He could only stare blindly at his mother. Her words seem to keep echoing in his head, *"Are you seeing anyone else? .... Are you seeing anyone else? ... Are you seeing anyone else?"* Slowly, he turned and looked at Bernadette again trying to gather his thoughts. Clark felt like he couldn't think clearly.

Had it actually been over eight months since he had sex? With Bernadette in his life, it was so complete he hadn't even thought about the physical side of a relationship. Had it been that long since he caressed the soft skin of a woman lying beside him in his bed, had the pleasure of a woman's body beneath his, and woke to the scent of a woman's perfume lingering on his pillow? His head was drumming with his mother's words. As his sisters gathered around Bernadette congratulating her on catching the bouquet and the lights from cameras began flashing once again, Clark swallowed hard before answering his mother emphatically, "NO!"

Rather than continue to lean forward with his arms resting on the table, Clark fell backwards into the chair shocked by the realization.

His mother placed her right hand on top of Clark's left again but this time squeezed hard. She whispered softly to him.

"Your father and I started out the same way, son. We were best friends and here we are married almost fifty years now. Think it about, my heart.... I LIKE this one, Clark."

She squeezed his hand one final time before rising as Bernadette arrived back at the table. Camille congratulated her on catching the bouquet before returning to her own seat.

"Clark, is everything okay?" Bernadette could tell he was distracted as she took her seat next to him. She had learned his moods well, but this is one she had never seen.

Clark didn't respond. He lowered his head, closed his eyes, and was massaging his forehead with his fingers when Cedric placed his hands on Clark's shoulder.

"Hey, you're my best man. You have to get out there and at least pretend you want to catch the garter."

"I'm coming," Clark responded barely loud enough for Cedric to hear, and Bernadette could tell he was agitated. He stood muttering something about "eight months."

At the rehearsal dinner, Bernadette had felt an immediate rapport with Camille. Everything about her indicated she was as perfect as a mother could be. What possibly could she and Clark have discussed that caused this mood change? Bernadette tried to focus on the wedding activities again but glanced at Camille occasionally. A sense of protectiveness grew inside of her. How dare she upset Clark on a day that should be all about celebrating and happiness? He'd been up since the middle of the night barbecuing and working for the event. Did she demand something else of him? How unfair? Maybe he was just getting tired. After all, it had been a long day for him. Every time she glanced Camille's way, Camille smiled back but it was hard for Bernadette to return it. She was too concerned over her friend.

Clark purposely stayed to the far right side of the dance floor expecting the groom to throw the garter straight back. Though he remained in camera range, he was a good five feet from the nearest competitor. Clark was watching the other single guys in attendance pushing and shoving each other, trying to get the ideal spot when the garter skimmed his cheek. Looking down, the white circle of lace with a pale blue bow and ribbon lay at his feet. The crowd started cheering and the photographer's camera was zooming in on him so he had no choice but to pick it up and pretend to be happy about it. Glancing at Cedric, he could tell from the smirk on his face that the throw was targeted.

"I'll never forgive you for this one old friend but just wait...," Clark thought before waving the garter to the crowd and returning to his seat next to Bernadette, "You deserve to be married to Cher." That thought gave Clark a slight bit of satisfaction.

Bernadette stuck with the bride's bouquet and Clark stuck with the garter made them some of the select group of people at the reception that were not happy. Of course, the only other unhappy guests were the women who had approached Clark earlier and had hoped to catch the bouquet.

Sensing their feelings were in tune, Bernadette leaned towards Clark and whispered, "What time does the reception end?"

Whispering back so no one else could hear, Clark responded, "Things will get worse before they get better.... We have to dance."

Bernadette turned and glared at Clark. He felt her eyes like daggers so he didn't return the gaze.

"What did you just say?" Bernadette's volume rose slightly.

"I said we have to dance," Clark murmured back indicating she needed to bring her voice back to a whisper but spoke the words emphatically. It was a simple sentence and Bernadette was an intelligent woman. What part of that didn't she understand?

"Clark, I am not getting on any dance floor. What are you talking about?"

"It's a tradition in my family. Whoever catches the bouquet dances with whoever catches the garter. They expect us to lead the next dance."

Bernadette felt her mouth open, but she couldn't close it.

"You've got to be kidding! Clark, I have never danced in my life and I'm not about to have my first dance lesson in front of an entire wedding reception. Besides, fat people should not go on dance floors and be jiggling around like a bowl of gelatin. There is no way I'm going up there! Maybe I'll just sneak out and leave quietly now...."

"First of all, the last time I checked, there are about six cars blocking the Corvette, and your car is even more blocked in than that. We're not going anywhere for a while.... Sneaking you out is not an option I can pull off.... You need to get a more positive image of yourself. You're an attractive lady, and you're not THAT big! Why do you think you shouldn't be on a dance floor?"

"THAT big! THAT big?"

Turning and seeing Bernadette's expression, Clark knew he had emphasized the wrong word. She was getting pissed at his family and him. He tried to salvage the moment, "Bernadette, as long as we've been friends, you KNOW I didn't mean it that way...." Clark lifted his shoulders and extended his arms slightly outward with his fingers fanned apologetically. "I'm saying you're NOT that big. There's no reason you shouldn't be dancing."

"That's NOT the way you said it.... Let me make my meaning clear, Clark. I'm drawing a line. Put friendship aside. I am NOT doing this! You said you needed an escort for the wedding. Then I ended up at the rehearsal dinner. Then I end up driving your sports car. Then I'm stuck on a dance floor with a bouquet of flowers in my hand. Now this? Look, I like your family. I've had a nice time. But, enough is enough! You didn't say anything about dancing. Dancing was not part of the deal."

When a spotlight shown on the two of them waiting for the couple to rise and move to the dance floor, Clark whispered to Bernadette, "You don't have a choice in this."

With all eyes turned to them, it seemed Clark was right. There was no way to avoid the dance without making a scene. Clark stood and pulled Bernadette's chair back though she was holding the sides and pushed her heels down trying to prevent it. Pretending to help her rise, he grabbed her right upper arm with his left hand nearly lifting her out the chair, and he almost dragged her as he led her towards the dance floor.

When they reached the center of the staged area, Clark whispered, "I'm sure this will be a slow dance. Just place both your arms up around my shoulders and let me guide you. Nothing fancy.... You just need to move your feet as we sway to the music...."

"You owe me another dinner at Blaine's for this one."

"Anything you want, my heart." Clark unwittingly used the term of endearment his mother had spoken to him. He was so angry his family would do this that he didn't even notice the slip. His protective instinct was in high gear. As soon as the song began, it removed all doubts from his mind. This was a set-up. It was one thing for his sisters to play their games on him but he felt he could never forgive them for subjecting Bernadette, his friend, to their tricks. The song was the one he had recommended to Cher and Cedric for the bride's and groom's dance. The version was by his favorite local artist Aaron Neville. That proved Cher had selected it and planned the reception music with him and Bernadette in mind. The family gathering in a circle around them with cameras was the final proof he needed. Everyone knew the goal of the game but him. For once, they had all actually kept a secret. Even Connie, the one he was closest to, hadn't warned him but had played a part in the plot. All he could do at this stage was to comfort Bernadette and help her through this.

"Arms around my neck," he looked down into her eyes and whispered softly.

Bernadette was fighting to hold back the tears. There were over three hundred guests watching them. She had never danced before and that made things even more embarrassing. This was not the time to learn. Memories of the incident with Greg and Kevin flooded her mind. Was this a joke? Was she going to be used as the entertainment? Did everyone want to laugh at the fat girl getting to dance with the hunk? Was this intended to be the funny part of the wedding activities, a bit of light-heartedness among the more serious aspects of the day? After meeting Clark's family at the rehearsal dinner, she didn't think they would be that cruel. One tear drop fell to her cheek, but her mind refocused as soon as Clark moved her arms to around his neck, placed his hands at her waist, and pulled her against him. Refocus is a mild description of her body's reaction.

"Just follow my lead," Clark's mouth was close to her ear.

Clark pulled Bernadette even closer as the lyrics were sung, so close she could feel his manhood. The sensations that flowed through Bernadette were nothing she had ever experienced or imagined. Her vaginal area constricted. She felt light-headed, her knees weakened, and an audible gasp escaped. Clark took her reaction for nervousness so pulled her even tighter against him as the first verse began.

By the time the instrumental interlude began, Bernadette and Clark had entered their own world. Bernadette felt comforted in Clark's arms. The scent of his cologne was calming. It drew her towards him. Her face soon snuggled against his neck as he held her closer. Feeling his body against hers triggered such pleasant sensations, she was no longer fearful of him holding her. Swaying together on the floor began to feel so natural, so perfect for the two of them. Her body was relaxing. She wondered why she was ever apprehensive about a simple dance. Clark was right. All she had to do was just follow his lead. She was completely lost to anything around them. Only his presence mattered.

Taking Bernadette in his arms felt so right. Clark's hands soon began wandering slowly up and down her back. It felt so good to have a woman in his arms again. Her powdery perfume wasn't intended to be sensual but it was. His fingers caressed her soft curves. Pulling her tighter seemed the natural thing to do. After all, he needed to protect her. By the time the last lyrics were playing, Clark's cheek was resting on Bernadette's.

Neither Clark nor Bernadette noticed Clark's family encouraging the other guests to join the couple on the dance floor. They also didn't notice Cher going to the disc jockey and changing her instructions. The song was immediately followed, with no break in the music, by another similar love song. When Michael Jackson's *Thriller* blared through the sound system, Bernadette and Clark were startled. The music was so loud they separated, by instinct, and their eyes focused on the teenagers gathering to join the dance routine that had become as famous as the song. Grabbing Bernadette's hand, Clark led her the shortest distance back to their reserved table.

After taking their seats, both were entertained by the *Thriller* crowd on the dance floor and fell easily back into their old comfort zone. Clark's family members that had participated in the plot continued to watch them. They all knew differently. Their love was clear to everyone but the two of them. Camille watched them on and off during the remainder of the reception. She wondered, "What was it going to take to open his eyes?"

Chapter Eighteen

Two weeks after the wedding reception, Clark called Bernadette on her cellular phone speaking excitedly.

"A package came in the mail yesterday! I know it's the DVD of Cher and Cedric's wedding. Doing anything Friday night? Want to come over? I'll order in and we can watch it together."

"Sure, I'd love to," Bernadette responded eagerly. "Chinese?"

"Yep. Order the usual?"

"Sounds good. 7:00 ok?"

"Perfect. See you then."

The conversation between them had become routine to the point the two of them could speak while busily sorting through, deleting, and filing E-mails. It was a routine that even Faye didn't bother to ease drop on anymore. When nothing of interest was playing at the local theaters, they often just hung out at Clark's condo and opted to order an old classic on a pay per view cable channel. Sometimes they would sit on the lanai having a drink and watch the sun set. The latter proved such a restful way to wind down from the stressfulness of the work week, it was becoming their activity of choice more and more often. Adrian no longer looked surprised when Bernadette entered the lobby. He even called her by name, and Clark had set up a special code for her to access the elevators on her own.

When Friday morning came, Clark woke shivering. He couldn't imagine this being an omen on such an ordinary day so was glad whatever bug he may be coming down with had hit on the weekend. His agenda at work was too aggressive, and he couldn't afford to miss a single day. As soon as he and Bernadette called it a night, he planned to rest the entire weekend.

Arriving at the front door to the condo, Bernadette punched in her special access code, listened for the lock to click, and opened the door. A bell chiming signaled that someone had entered. "I'm in the kitchen," Clark yelled down. The scent of popcorn cooking and butter melting filled the air. Bernadette climbed the stairway, dropped her purse on a side table, and joined Clark in the kitchen.

"I didn't have time for lunch today so that popcorn smells heavenly."

"Just started," Clark replied. "I already ordered the Chinese food. It won't be here probably until after we view the video. Maybe we could eat on the lanai."

Bernadette watched Clark pour the melted butter over the bowl of hot popcorn he had prepared. He handed the bowl to her while he grabbed two root beers out of the refrigerator. As Bernadette walked towards the sofa, she picked up the roll of paper towels. It was a routine they had developed while watching movies at his condo. Bernadette took her spot on the left side of the sofa and propped her feet up on an ottoman. Clark took the right side which converted to a lounge chair. He pressed the start button on the remote, and both of them sat back picking popcorn puffs from the bowl on the cushion between them.

The video began with clips of Cher and Cedric when they were little.

"How cute!" Bernadette exclaimed. "I thought it would just be the wedding."

"This photographer has done the weddings for each of my sisters. He is really good at making it into a memory of their lives instead of just filming the event."

They watched clips from the rehearsal at the church and the dinner at Clark's aunts.

"It was a fun time," Bernadette stated looking at Clark lovingly when the camera caught the two of them laughing hysterically at the stories his sisters were sharing.

Both of their moods changed when a scene of Camille and Connie having a serious discussion popped up. Bernadette sensed the discussion was about her. She wondered if the kindness Clark's family had shown was just a front. It looked as if they didn't like her after all. Clark recognized the strategy discussion about the plot. He didn't realize before that Connie and his Mother were the ones that had planned it. It was upsetting to see the two women he trusted most in the family were the ones that had pulled the trick on Bernadette. All this time he had been blaming Cher.

Scenes from the wedding lightened their mood again. Seeing his sisters in their bridesmaids' dresses and the twins preceding Cher and Clark's father down the aisle elicited oohs from Bernadette. The photographer had even shot scenes of the couple being bombarded with rice and bubbles blowing as they stepped out the church for the first time. The camera continued rolling capturing guests offering their congratulations and getting into their vehicles to create the wedding procession. Sounds of the sirens from the motorcycles of the state troopers who would escort the cars to the reception started blaring.

When the next scene rolled, Bernadette froze. She was actually watching Clark kiss her on the lips. She tried to recall when that happened. She crossed her legs at the ankle on the ottoman, a sign of protecting herself, and leaned backwards into her cushion. It was just a quick peck, but why didn't she remember that happening? She didn't appear distraught over it.

Out of the corner of his eye, Clark saw Bernadette cross her legs. He couldn't look her way. He wanted desperately to hit the rewind button and confirm what he had just seen but would have to wait and review the video again when Bernadette was not present. The action on the screen looked so natural but he had never kissed her before that he could recall. He wondered what possessed him to do something that impulsive. He shrugged it off as excitement over the wedding and being glad the ceremony was over and none of his sisters fell down during the procession wearing those ridiculous heels Cher had selected. When he first saw the size of the heel on the shoes, it was a miracle they appeared to glide over the floor. Even Linda made it down the aisle without looking like she was balancing on stilts.

Shifting his head slightly to the left, he noticed Bernadette was still eating popcorn but purposely not turning her head towards him. Maybe he should have looked at the video before asking her over, but it was too late to back out of the situation now. He prayed the Chinese food would be delivered early.

The rest of the scenes restored a sense of normality. Clark and Bernadette began chatting about the scenes they liked the most. Bernadette had even uncrossed her ankles again.

When the disc jockey announced it was time for the single gals to get on the dance floor so the bride could throw the bouquet, Bernadette had to comment.

"Did you know they were setting me up that day?"

"Not until they started crawfishing!" Clark laughed.

Bernadette laughed as well, not just at the trick they had played on her but also at the local term Clark had used that represented people walking backwards.

When the scene of Bernadette and Clark dancing together started playing, Bernadette was tempted to grab the remote and hit the stop button. She crossed her legs at the ankle again shocked at her behavior. She was hanging all over the man. Bernadette was doing what her father called that old belly rubbing dancing. She couldn't believe how brazen she was acting in the open public with over three hundred guests watching her. No wonder Clark's mother and his sister had that expression earlier. They were anticipating the kind of girl she was. She tried to remember how many drinks she had at that point. Knowing she had to drive back across Lake Pontchartrain to New Orleans, she had not consumed more than two so she couldn't blame her actions on the alcohol.

Bernadette wished she had something stronger than a root beer right then. She didn't remember laying her head on Clark's shoulder, but there it was on film. She looked like she was trying to make love to the man. Instinctively, her right hand moved upward to cover her face. She was so embarrassed! How would she ever be able to face him again? She glanced to the left assessing how far the stairway was from the sofa. Maybe she should just make a run for it and leave but that would be too childish. Besides, with all the security codes you had to press in this building, she wouldn't get far if Clark followed her. She kept waiting for the song to end. Bernadette felt she was having a heart attack when a second song followed. The pounding in her chest can't be natural. How long was this going to go on? How long were they out there? They should have taken their seats after the first dance because nothing forced them to stay on the floor for another. She began wondering if this was an edited film. What she was seeing was too incomprehensible.

Bernadette's reaction was mild compared to Clark's. He was oblivious to the film's effect on his friend. Clark had pulled the lever to get the lounger back to an upright position. He placed his hands together in a prayer-like position and hooked his chin on the tops of his thumbs as he leaned forward, resting his elbows on his knees while he studied the film. The scene between his mother and Connie at the rehearsal dinner made sense to him now. They had picked up on something between him and Bernadette Clark had never realized. He watched the way his hands were moving across her back caressing her. It wasn't sensual. It was an act of love. The way he looked at her and slowly laid his cheek against hers. He thought that anyone seeing only this clip from the video would assume they were the bride and groom. Their bodies were swaying in tune with each other. Had they really danced to two songs? After the initial nervousness surrounding the set-up had subsided, it looked like neither of them wanted the music to end. Even when the Thriller music kicked in, Clark watched the way they laughed together as the song jumped from a slow dance to rock. He focused in on the way he took Bernadette's hand to lead her back to their seats. All of their actions signified they were a couple who were romantically involved and had deep feelings for each other. "What the hell are you seeing, man?" he thought, "What does this mean?" Standing, he walked out to the lanai.

Clark paced back and forth replaying in his mind the conversation he and his Mother had at the reception. He remembered her posing what should have been a simple question.

"Clark, are you seeing anyone else, son?"

He remembered the thoughts that started plaguing him.

Had it been that long since he caressed the soft skin of a woman lying beside him in his bed, had the pleasure of a woman's body beneath his, and woke to the scent of a woman's perfume lingering on his pillow?

His Mother's comments were coming through clearly to him now, *"Your father and I started out the same way, son. We were best friends and here we are married almost fifty years now. Think it about, my heart.... I like this one, Clark!"*

Had he actually fallen in love? Is Bernadette the woman he had been seeking all these years? Had he finally found the right person by accident in a greasy spoon dive? Had their relationship actually started as the result of an argument over oatmeal cookies and a stupid bet that followed? He fell into one of the Adirondack chairs. Clark interlocked his fingers and moved his palms to rest on the crown of his head, elbows extended. He was no longer replaying the video in his mind but had leaned back in the lounger and was staring at the sky. His Mother and sister knew him better than he knew himself and that thought as well as others started passing through his mind.

"Damn!" he finally uttered loud enough for Bernadette to hear though he made no move to change his position or to stop gazing at the sky. He started recapping everything that had happened between him and Bernadette since that first meeting at Joe's. It was like movie clips of their time together flashing through his mind. Not a single negative image was coming to him: laughing at herself when the sauce fell on her chin after biting into a crawfish pie at Chef Blaine's place, the scared look on her face and hesitation before she took the first bite of alligator sausage,   the look of satisfaction she gave him knowing they had impressed his boss with the dinner they prepared together, and the concern over him being so tired when they met in the church for Cher's wedding. All of these different emotions they had shared. He thought about them cooking in his kitchen side by side, popping popcorn and watching movies together. So many routines had developed in their relationship. Relationship? Add sex and a marriage license and they would be the same as any of the married couples he knew....

Clark didn't respond when Adrian announced via the intercom that the delivery boy from the Chinese restaurant had arrived. He was lost in his thoughts and the images flashing through his brain.

When Adrian's voice came across the intercom, Bernadette slipped off the sofa as quietly as she could, grabbed her purse, stepped down the stairs as if she walking on eggshells, punched in the security code, and slipped out the front door closing it as gently as possible. She stopped by the security station and paid the delivery boy. She had never lied like this before in her life but felt she didn't have a choice.

"Adrian, Clark is dead asleep. Could you just keep the food here until he wakes up and rings for it?" She slipped a bill to him and smiled the way Joe had taught her.

"No problem, Miss Bernadette. I have a refrigerator close by. I'll handle it for you."

Bernadette walked out the leaded glass entrance door for what she was sure would be the last time.

Clark's reverie was broken by the noise signaling static on the television screen as the tape ended. Walking back to the living area, he grabbed the remote and pressed the off button. Looking at the empty seat on his right, he knew Bernadette had gone.

"So what do we do now?" He spoke aloud though he was the only person present. "Where do we go from here?"

Clark sat on the sofa and reviewed some of the scenes again. Why hadn't he seen it before? They had become like a pair of worn slippers. The only thing missing in their relationship was sex. His feelings were now clear, but what were Bernadette's? Why had she left without saying anything? What did she want? Maybe they both should take the weekend to think things over. If he still felt the same, he would call her first thing Monday morning and find out if the feeling was mutual.

Chapter Nineteen

Bernadette was coming back from getting a cup of coffee when she heard her cellular phone ring and saw Faye pick it up.

"Give me that!" she ordered pulling the phone from Faye's hand. The look she gave her made her retreat to her cubicle, but she knew Faye was listening.

Glancing down, she saw Clark's number and that Faye had already pressed the accept key. He had already waited longer than normal for a response calling out hello a second time.

"Hi...." Bernadette acknowledged she was there, but the words she had practiced all weekend just couldn't flow knowing Faye was listening.

"Can you meet me tonight? There's something I want to talk about, and I don't want to do it over the phone."

Bernadette caught Faye's face peeking around the corner of the desk. Bernadette definitely did not want to hold any conversation about their relationship over the phone either, not while she was in the office at least.

"If it's about the wedding video, then dinner tonight would be best."

"Great! Meet for seven at Blaine's?"

"That will work for me."

"See you then...."

As Bernadette flipped her cellular phone closed, Faye stood up and leaned into her cubicle.

"Wedding video? You're getting married?"

"No! And quit listening to my conversations." Bernadette turned her back to Faye and started working at the computer. She could hear her grunt before taking her own seat and getting to work.

Clark was waiting for Bernadette in the booth the hostess had begun referring to as 'their usual.' Bernadette let another couple be seated first allowing her time to remember the speech she had practiced all weekend. When the hostess returned to seat her, she thought she had it just right. Before Clark went to speak, she put her palm up.

"Don't say a word, please. I just have to get this off my chest; and, if you say something, I won' get through it."

She was keeping her face averted from Clark's. After taking a sip of her favorite cocktail Clark had already ordered for her, she started her speech.

"We've been friends a long time now and I don't want to do anything to destroy that relationship. I'm sorry I left without speaking Friday night but seeing the way I was dancing was too embarrassing. My father calls that the 'old belly rubbing' dancing. "

Bernadette rolled her eyes before continuing, "That wouldn't be appropriate even if we were a couple and we're just friends. I am so sorry. Can you please forgive me? I just want to put that video behind us and forget that ever happened. I don't want what I saw to change anything between us."

"Whoa!" Clark thought, "Changing the relationship to something more is not what she wants." He remembered what his mother said, *"Your father and I started out the same way, son. We were best friends... "* Recalling that his parents dated five years before they married, maybe he was going too fast. He was disappointed, but he'd just have to give their relationship a little more time. He'd have to watch for a sign Bernadette was ready for more.

Bernadette reached her hand over the table to him, "Still friends?"

She was looking straight into his eyes now, and her apprehension clearly showed.

Clark forced a smile and, though he was thinking, "'No," took her hand and responded, "Sure…."

Bernadette sighed in relief, put her napkin on her lap, and questioned, "So, what did you want to talk about?"

Disappointed by the turn of events, Clark offered a simplistic explanation, "I was going to apologize to you for my family tricking us into dancing."

"No need to. It was all in fun. They know we are just friends so they'll be laughing about that video for years. It would be nice if you could happen to erase that section accidentally though."

Bernadette was settling into their old routine, but Clark was having difficulty doing the same. It wasn't long before Bernadette sensed he wasn't comfortable.

"Clark, I could tell something is bothering you. What were you really planning to tell me? Were you going to break off our friendship after seeing that? Did it completely disgust you? I would understand if you did."

"No, trust me. It did not disgust me. I swear that's the last thing I thought…. Um, the Tennessee Williams festival is this weekend. Is it too soon to do something else? If we go Saturday night, we can catch a play."

"I'd love to. I've lived here all my life and have never gone. Clark, that sounds great."

"Ok…. I'll check on the tickets and give you a call to confirm the time."

"How to dress? Do I need to get fancied up? It's casual day at the office. I may need to bring a change."

"No, you don't need anything fancy. The theater we're going to is an off-off-Broadway type of establishment so wear your tennis. We can just meet at the condo…. Then we can walk along the levee to get there."

"Sounds good." Bernadette picked up the menu and starting talking about the specials for the day. Clark tried to be as enthusiastic about dinner, but he didn't feel hungry anymore.

Saturday night, Bernadette parked at Clark's condo and they walked down to the French Quarter. The doors weren't open yet so they joined the other patrons in the area by the cocktail bar to kill time. Clark opened a tab against their reservation.

"I've never had one of those," Bernadette commented as she pointed to a picture of a famous New Orleans' concoction which was the special for the night.

 "Care to try one tonight?" he offered.

"Why not?"

Clark ordered two and they sipped them slowly, not talking, waiting for the doors to open.

"I didn't know it was only a fruit punch," Bernadette commented.

Clark was about to explain that the drink had a pretty strong alcohol base, and one was more than most people could handle. Most recipes are made with just rum, but he had watched the bartender. The ones they ordered were blended with light rum, dark rum, vodka, gin, and amaretto liqueur. It was quite a combination, and the type of sweet drink that sneaks up on you before you realize it. The doors to the theater opened, and the usher announced they were now seating before he got the words out. Patrons starting moving towards the door, and he and Bernadette were separated temporarily. By the time they were rejoined, half of her drink had been consumed.

During the intermission, Clark excused himself and stepped out to the lobby to speak with an old friend he had seen in the audience. He told Bernadette he hadn't seen the guy since they were on a junior bowling league when he was ten. When he returned, Bernadette had finished her first and the waitress had bought her a second she was sipping happily. As the final curtain rose, the waitress bent down and asked Bernadette a question before walking away softly.

Clark whispered, "Was she asking about the bill? I thought anything we ordered would be automatically charged to the same credit card I used to purchase the tickets. It should be on file. Is there a problem?"

Bernadette whispered back though other patrons were beginning to stare at them talking during the final scene. "No problem. You don't have to sign anything. She was just taking last call orders so I got a punch to go."

"You what?" Clark spoke too loudly and everyone around them turned to stare.

"Shhhhhhhhhhhhhhh...." Bernadette slurred back to him.

As the play ended, the waitress delivered the last drink. Clark reached over and took it before Bernadette got her mouth on the straw and whispered, "I think I better carry that for you."

"Thank you.... That's... shweet," Bernadette responded her head rolling to the left as she smiled at Clark.

"Let's take a cab back to the condo, ok?"

"You... don't ... want... to walk... along the river... like... we usually ...do?"

"No, sweetheart. It's too muggy outside. I think we need to ride."

"Ok!" Bernadette slurred back reaching for her drink.

"Let me hold it until we get in the cab, ok?"

"OK!"

There were a line of cabs outside and the theater was not very large so it only took about five minutes for Clark and Bernadette to secure one. Once in the cab, Bernadette began slurping her punch again. She looked up at Clark.

"These... are... so good! You... want sh'ome?"

Bernadette shoved the straw towards Clark's lips.

"No, I'm fine, sweetheart."

When they got to the condo, Clark kept his hand around her waist and supported her as they walked across the lobby. About midway there, Bernadette turned towards the security desk and yelled out.

"Good... n-i-g-h-t, A-dri-an!"

Adrian only waved in response and quickly pressed for an elevator to descend. As Clark punched the code into the panel of his condo, Bernadette slurred, "I need ...to get... to the... bathroom." Seeing her eyes roll and Bernadette's color fading, Clark surmised correctly the drinks finally had her stomach churning. Opening the door, he saw the cleaning lady's cart in the hallway. "Damn!" Clark thought. As they approached, he saw Esmeralda had been mopping and the floor was still wet in the guest bath. Taking one look at Bernadette, he picked her up easily and carried her to his master suite. Placing her close to the commode, he closed the door to provide her privacy. Esmeralda had followed him.

"I'm sorry, Señor Clark. I had a doctor's appointment yesterday so I had to come today to do the cleaning." Hearing Bernadette gagging in Clark's master bath, she offered, "Does your lady friend need anything?"

"No, thank you, Esmeralda. I think we got here just in time."

"I'll leave now and come back in the morning to finish."

"Don't worry about it, Esmeralda. Tomorrow's Sunday."

"I have to come anyway. A new tenant is moving in, and I have to prepare their apartment for Monday."

"In that case, if you insist.... Good night."

"Buenas noches."

Clark sat in the arm chair, picked up a magazine, and flipped through it while waiting for Bernadette to come out. When the door finally did open, she just leaned against the sill.

"Clark...."

Looking at her face, he dropped the magazine and rushed to her.

"I feel dizzy."

She started to droop but he caught her in his arms and carried her to the bed. After laying her down, he propped a pillow under her head and went to the bathroom. Soaking a wash cloth in cold water, he returned to the bedroom and pressed it against her eyes.

"Is that better?"

"Yes," Bernadette murmured before drifting away.

Clark removed her tennis shoes and started to return to the armchair. Glancing at the clock, he thought a short nap before Bernadette woke wouldn't be bad. He removed his shoes as well, and as he was placing them into the built in bin under the bed, he grabbed hers and shoved them into the bin, not wanting her to trip over anything in case she needed to make another quick pit stop. Using the dimmer switch, he lowered the lights to a soft glow before going to the opposite side of the king sized bed. Laying as close to the edge as he could to give Bernadette as much space as feasible, he cupped his hands under his head and drifted to sleep.

The next morning, Esmeralda rolled her cleaning cart to the door of Clark's condo, punched in her code and entered the hallway to finish the cleaning she had started the day before. She rolled the cart down the hall absentmindedly checking the appearance of everything as she normally does. When she got to the top of the stair that descended downward into Clark's bedroom, she pulled out her mini cleaning tray and her feather duster. She dusted the banister on the left as she descended before turning to the left into the alcove Clark used as his home office. She dusted, emptied the trash, and tidied up in general stacking his papers neatly before walking out to clean the bedroom.

As soon as Esmeralda stepped out of the alcove, she started screaming, "Lo siento! Lo siento! Lo siento!" She ran up to the top of the stairs shoving the mini cleaning tray into its position on the cart before quickly exiting down the hall and back out of the condo. She screamed, "Lo siento!" repeatedly the entire time.

Clark and Bernadette had been sound asleep when Esmeralda started the tirade. Bernadette was laying on her left side facing the wall where doors led to a series of closets and the master bath. Clark's body was molded against hers. His right arm was across Bernadette's midriff but bent at the elbow allowing Bernadette's right hand to be on top of his. Their hands were clutching. Bernadette's right leg was bent at the knee with her lower leg extending outward allowing Clark's right leg and thigh to mold against her resting along her left leg.

Hearing Esmeralda's screams, the couple shifted slightly. Spanish lessons from her high school days drifted to Bernadette, and she turned her head a little to the right but without opening her eyes and whispered to Clark, "Why does she keep screaming she's sorry?"

Clark exhaled, and without opening his eyes, grumbled, "I don't know, but we'll deal with her later...."

Bernadette called out, "De Nada!" winning a chuckle from Clark before they snuggled closer and drifted back to sleep.

Chapter Twenty

There was too much sunlight in the room.

"Had her mother come in and open the blinds in her bedroom?" Bernadette wondered as she blinked and tried to assess why the room was so bright. She was facing a wall of doors. Her body grew stiff when she realized there was a body not just in the same bed but intertwined with hers. She looked to her right and recognized the short flight of stairs that descended from the entrance hallway to his master suite.

"Oh, my God! Had she spent the night with Clark?"

Bernadette just remained laying as still as she could but she was frightened. She didn't know what to do. She listened to his even breathing and knew he was still asleep. When his leg shifted, his manhood pressed against her buttocks. In a panic, Bernadette pushed his arm aside and moved into a sitting position. The sudden movement startled Clark. He rolled over onto his back and then to his right side. Glaring at the amount of sunshine, he wondered what time it was. The answer came soon as the sounds of Bernadette closing closet doors and muttering, "Where's my shoes?" registered.

Turning his head cautiously to the left, he saw Bernadette searching for her shoes. Recalling the night before, Clark realized they had both fallen asleep and were so tired that they had slept through the night. At least, he was tired. Bernadette was tipsy from the three concoctions she swallowed down like water.

"Good morning," Clark called out to her nonchalantly. He yawned and stretched his arms first upward then outward.

"How is this a good morning?" Bernadette screamed back, picked up a pillow, and tossed it towards him.

Seeing how upset she was, Clark rose, walked over to the stair, and leaned against the railing trying to figure out the scene playing in front of him.

Bernadette had opened every door along the wall on the left side of the bed. Although they were three closets, none of them housed a single pair of shoes.

She turned to Clark distraught and demanded, "Where are my shoes? I've got to get out of here... I'm going straight to hell!"

Hearing the last sentence, Clark questioned innocently, "Why do you think you're going to hell?"

"Because I just spent the night with a man, and we're not married!" Bernadette screamed back at him and asked again, "WHERE ARE MY SHOES?"

Bernadette was turning from one side to the other looking around his bedroom trying to figure out where shoes would possibly be. Her face was so distraught Clark advised, "There's a slide out drawer below the bed that was built especially for shoes. Just pull the lower drawer out, and your tennis should be there."

Bernadette followed his instructions, pulled out the tennis, slammed the drawer shut, sat back on the bed, and kept muttering she was going to hell.

Clark commented nonchalantly, "Nothing happened between us. We didn't have sex. All we did was sleep.... If something had happened, let me assure you, you would not be waking up fully clothed. Sweetheart, the only suit you'd be wearing is the one you were born in."

She glanced towards him, and he could see tears streaming down her face as she cried out to him, "Clark, just sleeping together is enough! I have now spent the night in the bed of a man I'm not married to!"

Clark folded his arms, turned his head, and started replying, "Damn, Bernadette, you're acting like...." He stopped midsentence before the words he was thinking were spoken, "a fourteen years old virgin. You're acting like Helena!"

A pain shot through his chest causing him to exhale sharply as he remembered Helena and what had happened between them when he was fifteen….

One of his father's comrades from his basic training days had made the military his career and was stationed at the base in Algiers. The family had been invited to his daughter Helena's fourteenth birthday celebration. The minute Clark saw her, he had fallen in love. He knew by the shy smile she gave him she felt the same. No one in either of their families seemed cognizant of the blossoming love between the two of them, and one day they had been left alone for too long. A stolen kiss quickly became an act of passion. That was the only time Clark ever recalled having unprotected sex. Thank God Helena didn't get pregnant. Afterwards, the Catholic values that had been drilled into her came into play. Despite his declarations of love and promises to marry her as soon as they were older and he could support her, she couldn't stand to look at him. She refused to see him or even accept his phone calls. She was so guilt ridden over what had happened. About three months later, her father's orders changed and her family had to move on. He never saw her again. When she was twenty-four, he found out from a cousin of hers that she had married a widower fifteen years her senior and was helping him raise his three kids. He often wondered, "Had she fallen in love, or was she committing to a lifetime of penance for her perceived mortal sin?"

"Damn," he muttered under his breath. Was a similar scene playing out before him? He leaned back against the railing allowing this new knowledge about Bernadette to sink in and knowing she was feeling just as guilty as Helena, but this time, it was over nothing! A virgin! No wonder she responded that way to the wedding video and the two of them dancing. Thinking of comments she had made, Clark realized she had never had a boyfriend. Bernadette started sobbing, "What am I going to tell my parents?" It was like reveille to Clark.

His mind went to his sister Corinne, the one the siblings had labeled the good girl because she was the one that always did exactly what their parents expected of her. One time she had gone to bed without brushing her teeth. She came running into the breakfast nook the next morning confessing her transgression. Corinne could write a twelve page essay on the importance of good dental hygiene. He recognized the similarities between Corinne and Bernadette. He thought about how his father would have reacted had one of his sisters not come home at all after a date. He shuddered at the thought of him finding out they had spent the night at some guy's apartment. He would have been furious and that was an extreme understatement. Even his mother wouldn't have been able to control his Dad's reaction. Realizing now why Bernadette wouldn't accept this so casually, he needed her to calm down before she left the apartment. His mind went into rewind. Learn from the past, Clark. What to tell her? He knew he couldn't let her drive in that state. He'd have to do something, anything, to get her rational.

He could watch Bernadette in a different light now. Here was a sophisticated, professional woman who was competent in her field and in her personal affairs except for sex. In that area, she was at the same stage of development as a girl of about fourteen years old.

His mind kept rewinding and fast-forwarding through his past experiences. "Think, Clark, think. What to do, what to say! Then it paused as he remembered Julia…." That memory triggered others and a template began to form. In less than a minute, action steps he needed to take had formulated: listen to validate her perceived problem, support, distract from the current situation, present a logical alternative, and force defense of a different position. That was it! He needed her to shift her focus to something more important to her than her own predicament.

Clark walked softly until he stood in front of the closets facing Bernadette. She looked up at him, her face stained with tears. She hadn't even tried to put on her tennis. She was too busy berating herself.

"Oh, Clark. I don't know how I could disappoint my parents this way. They don't deserve to be hurt again. I can't believe I did this…. Spending the night with a man and not being married."

With those words, he knew this was about more than her spending the night at his condo. He also knew this was not the time to pry. Whatever was in the past would come to light soon enough if it was meant for him to know.

Bernadette looked down at the tangled strings on her tennis and clasped her hands together covering her nose and mouth sniffling. Clark walked to the nightstand, grabbed a box of tissue and laid it on the bed next to her. Sitting down on the carpet before her, he understood why she was spending more time crying and chiding herself instead of performing the simple task of putting on a pair of tennis. She had no experience in dealing with the situation and no clue how to even begin.

"Let me help," he said so softly Bernadette had to stop crying to hear him.

Clark started untangling the laces, restringing the shoes and tying them for her. Bernadette was still distraught so he looked up while working on her shoes and gave her a simple command.

"Sweetheart, please do this for me…. You know when you go to the doctor's and he tells you to take a deep breath?"

Hearing something safe and familiar, Bernadette was listening. She nodded in affirmation.

"I need you to do that now." Clark was looking in her face and coaching her through it. "Deep breath…. Hold it…. Let it out slowly…. Again… Deep breath… Hold it…. Let it out slowly… One more time, please. Deep breath… Hold it… Let it out slowly….."

When he saw her calming down and a little heady from the extra oxygen, he tightened each lace and sat back on the floor his legs crossed beneath him. The first question he asked shifted Bernadette's thoughts.

"Isn't your friend Valerie from Mississippi?"

Bernadette was caught off guard by the strange, seemingly unrelated question, "Yes?"

"You said she stayed in the college's dorm, right?"

"Yes..."

"Ever spent the night in her dorm?"

"Yes, all the time," Bernadette answered but in a stronger voice this time folding her arms and knowing where Clark's logic was going.

"And you told me you did STOP by Valerie's place before we met up, didn't you? So, it would not have been odd based on your history with her that you may have stayed there for the night? And, if anyone asked where you were, you could honestly respond, 'I stopped by Valerie's.'"

The seed he was planting started to fertilize as he continued, "I don't understand why you feel you did anything wrong? It's no different staying here than staying at Valerie's. Nothing happened between us so you didn't commit any sin."

"The difference is we're not the same sex, Clark."

Clark waited a minute letting her think the argument was closed before continuing.

"Ever evacuated for a hurricane?"

"Sure. Lots of times. I've lived in New Orleans my entire life." Bernadette got a little indignant that Clark insinuated she didn't know about emergency procedures.

"So, where did you go, and where did you sleep?"

Bernadette knew where that was going too and that wasn't the same either. She turned her head towards the stair and pretended she wasn't listening as Clark continued.

"I know when my family evacuates because of a hurricane threatening, we usually go by my uncle's place in Ville Platte. Nine of us plus they may be housing other families too. We're sleeping all over the place.... Lots of us in one room together in sleeping bags or on makeshift beds of quilts and blankets. Fathers, mothers, brothers, sisters, cousins. Lots of folks all sleeping in the same room for the night. No sex.... No sin.... "

Bernadette took a breath, and her face indicated it was still not quite the same.

"Your family never had to do that? It was like a big slumber party. It was fun."

"Of course we've done that!"

She looked back at Clark her facial expression this time saying, "Don't be stupid."

Bernadette saw Clark's face changed. His brows crinkled and he seemed hurt. He spoke so low, Bernadette had to strain to hear him as he seemed to be trying to figure something out.

"So, it's me.... It's ME! Okay to sleep by Valerie's.... Okay to sleep in a room with other males.... It's just not okay to sleep by MY place.... I guess I was thinking more of our relationship than you do."

Clark looked into Bernadette's face, and she could tell how much he felt hurt by the way she had acted. The tone of his voice indicated such as he continued.

"I'm sorry, Bernadette.... We've been hanging out so often that I took for granted you considered me a close friend.... But I understand now! After all, I do things at the office with my coworkers.... We have luncheons for special occasions, and we all go out and eat together at times. I'd feel strange too if I had to SLEEP in the SAME ROOM as one of my coworkers…. Thinking about it from that standpoint, I KNOW HOW YOU FEEL!" His voice lowered a notch and was shaky as he said, "I'm sorry…. I jumped the gun, and in my mind, I thought we had developed a closer relationship than THAT." Clark had turned his face to the side so he wasn't looking into Bernadette's anymore before he continued speaking in an even softer tone of voice, "Now I know I was wrong, and I understand…. I understand…. Well, you have your shoes…. Pardon me if I don't see you out."

He stood keeping his face turned away from hers and walked towards the window. He kept his back to the room, folded his arms, and just stared out the window.

Bernadette turned on the bed and watched him for a few minutes beginning to feel embarrassed that the way she acted had hurt his feelings. She got up and walked towards him. When she got to the window, she stood on his left side, leaned against him, and started massaging his right shoulder with her right hand. When she started talking, Clark turned his head to the right away from hers.

 "I'm sorry the way I acted. Clark, please forgive me…. Of course, we are friends…. I think a lot of our relationship. It's very important to me. I don't think of you as a coworker. We've grown close, and your friendship is just as valuable to me as Valerie's."

Clark glanced at her, grimaced, and turned his head quickly to the right again indicating he wasn't convinced she truly meant what she said; he felt she was only patronizing him.

"Clark, I meant every word. Let me make it up to you…. P-l-e-a-s-e…. "

Clark kept his face turned to the right and took a deep breath. Bernadette put her other arm around him so she was encircling his waist. She hugged him tight.

"I know. How about breakfast together at the café you love down the street, the one with the almond filled croissants? Let me treat this time."

Clark turned and scowled at Bernadette. "That wasn't fair. You know those croissants are my weak point.... You knew I wasn't going to refuse that offer."

"So you'll go and let me make it up to you?"

Clark smiled, yielding in to her request, "Y-e-e-e-s-s-s!"

Bernadette was smiling as well, happy she was able to convince her friend to agree to her suggestion. She forgot how the tension between them had started. She glanced at the clock on his nightstand.

"Let's hurry. I don't have much time. I need to get home in time to go to the ten o'clock mass with my family." She walked quickly to the nightstand to grab her purse.

"I just need to grab my wallet and shoes."

"You don't need a wallet. My treat. Remember?"

"I'm sorry. I'm not getting anything right this morning, am I?" Clark appeared frustrated with himself.

After he slipped on his shoes, Bernadette walked over, put her arm around his waist, and started guiding him towards the stairs.

"That's o---k—a---y!"

She reached up and kissed him on the cheek.

As Clark and Bernadette walked across the lobby to the entrance doors, Adrian checked his log. He remembered them coming in the night before. He checked videos, too. He saw them enter the condo door and the cleaning lady for the condo leaving shortly after. He saw her enter the condo again this morning and leave in a hurry shortly afterwards. The logs, the alarms, and the videos all indicated Clark's front door did not open again until the two of them just left. "The first time he allowed a woman to stay the entire night?" Adrian thought and understood what that meant. He picked up the want-ads. Adrian needed another means of supplementing his income. He knew his well with Clark had dried up.

Over breakfast, Bernadette and Clark chatted away about the Tennessee Williams festival and the play they had seen. By the time they walked back to the condo and Bernadette got in her car, they were finalizing their plans for Friday night. Clark felt confident she would be focused when she drove now but to take one more precaution, he leaned inside the driver's window, grabbed Bernadette's left hand, pulled it to his mouth, placed a soft quick kiss on the back of it, and told her, "Thank you for your friendship."

Bernadette smiled as she backed out the parking space and waved as she drove off.

Chapter Twenty-One

On Monday morning, Clark felt a chill so turned to his left in the bed away from the vent and pulled a cover around his shoulders. The scent of Bernadette's perfume lingering on the pillow was pleasant causing him to dream of her beside him. The dream had no sexual connotations. They were intertwined just as Esmeralda had seen them, and he was enjoying the warmth of her body, the comfort of having her at his side. He pulled her close to him, and they snuggled together enjoying the quiet moment of just feeling and knowing you were loved. The peacefulness was short lived. A chubby toddler and an energetic kindergartner came running down the stairs, jumped on the bed, and began bouncing up and down on the mattress screaming, "Mommy! Daddy! We want pancakes."

Clark was startled out of his dream. He glanced around the empty bedroom hearing the little voices echoing in his mind. He looked at the empty bed beside him, and in that instant, he made a decision.

"Sorry, Bernadette, but even if it costs me our friendship, I need more."

He laid on his back contemplating how to approach her and move the relationship forward.

When Friday night arrived, Bernadette parked at Clark's condo. He met her in the lobby, and they walked together into the French Quarter. A new restaurant had opened on the riverfront, and the menu on the web sounded eclectic so they were both excited to give it a try.

Bernadette was chattering away about events that had happened at work that week but Clark wasn't hearing a single sound. Every time he thought of a way to approach her about changing their relationship, it just didn't seem right. There were none. He had never felt this way about anyone. The closest was his relationship with Rebecca, and he didn't want to copy any part of that history. There was nothing in his past to relate to. Clark was growing more and more frustrated as the night progressed. The words he needed were not coming to him.

As the waiter was removing their entrées, Bernadette saw Clark had barely touched his.

"Would you like a 'to go' box, sir?"

Clark was waving him off, but Bernadette answered, "Yes. Please pack his dinner."

If Clark didn't want it, she did. That steak had melted in her mouth. She was not about to let one just like it get dumped in the garbage. She sat watching his facial expressions. Something was bothering him. At one point, the fingers of his right hand started tapping softly but rhythmically on the tabletop. He was trying to figure something out.

"Can I help?"

Her words seem to pull him back from whatever realm he had entered. He glanced at the table confused as the waiter placed the bill in the empty space in front of him.

"We finished dinner?" Looking at Bernadette for the first time since he had entered whatever world he was in, he asked, "Did you want anything else?"

"No, I'm fine," she replied but Bernadette was worried that Clark wasn't.

He paid the bill and asked if she was ready to go. As they walked from their seats, he placed his left hand at the small of her back. Arriving across from Jackson Square, Clark took Bernadette's right hand into his left. At first, she thought it was to give her extra support as they climbed the steps of the Moonwalk. As they walked along the levee, he didn't release her hand. When they finally arrived at her parking spot, she pulled her hand out of his so she could dig through her purse for her car keys. Finding her keys, she opened the rear passenger door, tossed in her purse and the 'to go' box, and turned to tell him good night.

Clark had an expression she had never seen. He had finally given up on creating a template from his past but was not going to let her leave without expressing what he felt.

"Forgive me, Bernadette."

"For what?" she was looking up at him confused.

"For this...." Clark's voice was so deep and sensuous. His left hand slipped behind her waist holding her against him as his right index finger caught that little indentation in the 'V' the bones made right under the chin that allowed him to easily and fully control her head as he tilted it up to him so his mouth covered hers. When his tongue invaded her mouth, Bernadette tried to pull away from him but Clark easily maintained total control. Confused and in disbelief at the power of a single finger strategically placed, she squirmed as he pressed his manhood against her; but Clark continued the assault until a wave came across her body, and she melted in his arms.

Gasping for breath, she looked up at him in shock. His hands released her, and the full weight of her body rested against her car. He placed his hands on either side of her, resting them on the car as he leaned down and spoke to her.

"If this ruins our friendship and you never want to see me again, I'm sorry. But the regret is all for myself. I know I've fallen in love with you and I can't settle for being just friends anymore. I know this is unexpected, and I know you need time to think about it. But, Bernadette, I've been thinking of nothing else since Sunday morning. Sweetheart, I want you in my life, but I can't be this close to you from now on and not have something more. If our friendship can't move to the next stage, it has to end. I can't settle for only what we have now.... Not anymore.... I love you, Bernadette."

Clark stepped back from her car, turned his head at that point, and didn't look at her as he completed his thoughts.

"Why don't we meet here next Friday at 7:00 and go to Blaine's? That's where our relationship started. If your decision is 'no,' it seems it would be appropriate for us to end it there. Do you think you'll have an answer for me by then?"

Bernadette's entire body was still trembling, but she choked out, "Yes."

"Until then...." Clark walked away quickly not looking back.

Bernadette just stood for a moment shaken. Hearing a sound nearby, she opened the car door, got inside, closed it back, and locked it quickly. She just sat in the driver's seat until she stopped feeling jittery and thought she could drive.

Faye plopped her butt on the end of Bernadette's desk but even that caused no reaction. She had played her radio loud. She had pulled Bernadette's top drawer open and taken a candy bar without asking permission. She had grabbed her stapler and brought it to her own desk without returning it. She had reached across Bernadette, bumping her on the head to borrow her dictionary which was also not returned. She had done everything she could think of to get a rise out of Bernadette and no reaction. Her butt on her desk was the ultimate thing Bernadette hated her doing and that got no admonishment.

"Bernadette!" Faye started snapping her fingers right in front of her eyes.

Bernadette grabbed her hand and moved it away from her face.

"What is it, Faye?"

"You need to make a doctor's appointment. You haven't been yourself any day this week. You're not here. You're in la-la land."

"Not just days," Bernadette thought. "She hasn't been able to sleep nights." As soon as her head touches the pillow, all she could think about was Clark's request. One night, she had dreamt he was holding her and kissing her just like he had last Friday, and she woke breathing hard as sensations throbbed through her body. But the week was also plagued by how they first met and what had happened between her and Greg.

"Bernadette! Bernadette! There you go off again! Something is wrong with you…. Good thing today is Friday. You'll have the weekend to recuperate from whatever you have."

"It's Friday," Bernadette moaned.

"Need me to drive you home?" Faye looked at her concerned.

"No, Faye, I'll be fine."

As she pulled her car into the one of the visitors' spots at the condo, she saw Clark had parked the Corvette in the same area and was waiting for her. He was leaned back against the hood, his arms folded, and his face looked like he had gotten even less sleep that week than she had.

As Bernadette walked towards him, she started picturing all the wonderful times they had experienced together. They were so comfortable hanging out they had started feeding each other when they went out to dinner. If she had ordered something that Clark hadn't, she would scoop up a spoonful using her right hand and place her left hand under the spoon to catch any drippings as she guided the sample to his mouth. She would hold the utensil just right until he took the bite. He'd do the same. She remembered him grabbing her hand and the two of them running for cover when a sudden storm broke at a festival. She remembered him taking off his sport jacket and putting it around her shoulders as they walked across the levee one night after seeing her rub her arms with her hands because of the night air. She remembered him placing a bag on the table when she joined him for dinner one Friday and opening it to find the bracelet she had admired in the flea market. She also remembered how nice it felt when he held her hand and slipped it on her wrist. She thought about them shopping and cooking together for Robert and Angela and their antics in the kitchen as they prepared the meal. She remembered the proud look that was on his face that night when he introduced her. She remembered a lot of things as she stood before him except what she was going to say.

Turning her head up, she kissed him gently on the lips. Clark's arms encircled her and he pulled her against him as he kissed her back passionately. When he finally released her, he smiled.

"I like that answer. Let's go celebrate."

Chapter Twenty-Two

Valerie wondered what Bernadette was searching for in her purse. She kept digging and shoving things around, checking different sections. Finally she gave up and looked at Valerie pleadingly.

"It's that time of the month, and I didn't bring enough with me. May I use a couple of your pads?"

Valerie shifted her head downward slightly and gazed at Bernadette over her glasses, "All I have in there right now is tampons, girl. I don't think those and your virgin booty are going to get along too well. But, if you want to try one, you can. If not, you know the other option. You're going to just have to bunch enough toilet tissue into your panties until we run down the street to the drug store."

"Today is a heavy day. I might still have an accident before we get back despite how much I bunch in. Where are they?" Bernadette sighed.

"Top shelf in the cabinet under the sink. Look in the back on the left side." Valerie picked up the remote and pressed stop instead of pause. She knew they would be making a trip to the store soon so why bother letting the movie they were watching kick back on in their absence.

Shortly, Bernadette returned, sat calmly on the sofa, and was waiting for Valerie to turn the movie back on. Glancing her way, Valerie questioned, "We're going to the store?"

"No. The tampon worked fine. It just slid right in...."

Valerie turned and spoke to Bernadette accusingly, "Girl, you done did the nasty with that hunk I met? You've been holding out on me! I know you know the date too. When did it happen? A girl won't forget her first time.... You have got to tell me everything! When did you start? Don't leave anything out. I want to hear it all."

Valerie turned to Bernadette and waited impatiently for the tale to start. Bernadette blushed. A lot had been happening between her and Clark, and she felt the need to confide in someone about everything that had occurred. She had no one but Valerie she could tell. Sighing, she started at the beginning.

"Well, we had gone to the Tennessee Williams festival in the French Quarter. We even caught the play *A Streetcar Named Desire*. Based on a little incident, things started getting strained between us. So, one time we had gone out, Clark suddenly grabbed me in his arms, kissed me, and said he wanted more than for us to just be friends. We started seeing each other at least three times a week. Most weeks, we'd hook up four times. We'd go to a movie. We'd go to dinner at our favorite restaurant or cook at his condo. We might catch a festival, but we always end up at his place after. We spend at least one of our dates each week just hanging out at his condo looking at movies."

Bernadette hesitated, but Valerie coaxed her on, "Hurry up, girl, so you get to the good parts!"

Blushing, Bernadette tried to continue but hesitated. If she couldn't tell Valerie, then who could she tell, but something held her back. She couldn't voice out loud the most intimate moments that had happened between them even to Valerie.

She started recalling how quickly their relationship had progressed. It seemed to start out so innocently with Clark putting his left arm around her shoulder. He'd put his right hand on her left side by her waist and pull her towards him and kiss her passionately. Then he would pull her down beside him on the sofa. As they were kissing, his right hand would lightly stroke her side from her upper thigh to her breast. It was a calming effect, and she had begun to yearn for the comfort of his arms.

One night, she hadn't even felt or known when it had happened but, as she lay pinned between his body and the back cushions of the sofa, her blouse was unbuttoned and her bra was loosened. He slipped her bra to the side and started a trail of kisses down her neckline until his mouth captured her breast. She gasped and started to protest but went silent in shock as his hand slid across her thigh, and he began massaging her between her legs. Suddenly, a wave came across her entire body, and she went weak in his arms. Feeling her climax, he stopped the assault and started kissing her lips softly again as he held her gently against him.

Each date, it seemed he began attacking her senses in a way he hadn't before. She closed her eyes thinking of how he would tease her first by placing soft kisses along her neck, tickling her with his tongue his breath light as a feather over her chest and nipples. She didn't realize her facial expressions were changing, and she had crossed her arms as she thought about how skillful he was in giving her pleasures.

She remembered the day she had been forced to take a conference call at her desk and her headset was causing feedback on the line so had spent over an hour with the phone cradled in her neck. By the time she reached Clark's, she had a headache and stiff neck.

"Have any pain killers?"

"Why do you need those?" he asked her with obvious concern in his voice.

"My neck is killing me, and I have a headache."

"Let's try this first."

He had stood behind her as she sat on the sofa and asked her to drop her head towards her chest. Then he placed his hands on her shoulders and started using a circular motion with his thumbs expertly massaging her deltoids and moving inward towards her neck, then upward to the base of her skull. By the time he had finished the massage, she was totally relaxed, her neck felt great, and it dawned on her the headache was gone.

"Better?"

"Yes!" She turned her neck without pain and had looked upward at him amazed.

The next time she had a headache, she had asked if he could give her another neck massage. Looking at the pressed blouse she was wearing, he frowned.

"What's wrong?"

"I have a spearmint-scented body oil that's a great stress reliever, but I don't want to get you wrinkled or to chance ruining your blouse... Why don't you take your clothes off?"

Bernadette's eyes had widened. She started to tell him, "Maybe the women you're accustomed to dating shed their clothes on command, but you're in a different league now." He acted as if he didn't notice her reaction and continued, "There's a robe in my bathroom you can use."

Hearing he meant for her to just slip into something different, she still hesitated at first when he began walking from the living area. She had reluctantly followed him to the master suite where he showed her where the robe was hung. She had undressed, hung up her clothes, and slipped the robe over her underwear. By the time she emerged, Clark had the oil warming on the night stand. After massaging her neck, he told her to lay flat on the bed. She grew nervous when his hands grabbed the collar of the robe and then slid it down to her waist. When he unsnapped her bra, she panicked at first; but recalling scenes of massages she had seen on television, she stayed motionless. It didn't take long for her to be fully relaxed once he started an upper body massage... From then on, they had begun making out in his bedroom.

"Well?" Valerie's irritated voice interrupted her train of thought.

Bernadette started to speak but choked on the words thinking of last Friday. The massages hadn't stopped there and that activity had progressed as quickly as the other lovemaking between them. She and Clark both took off from work and spent the day at his condo. When she walked in, he invited her to breakfast on the lanai. They nibbled on fresh fruits and buttered almond croissants with imported preserves. Then they drank café au lait and watched the ships on the Mississippi.

When it started getting too hot outside, Clark told her to give him a few minutes and then meet him in his bedroom. When she followed, he was lighting the last of an array of votive candles. Body oils were warming on the nightstand, and the most sensual incense filled the air.

"Candles in the daylight?" she had questioned thinking the scene would be beautiful if it was night.

"Not for long."

Clark walked to the side of his bed next to the window, tapped a cover and it popped open. He touched a button inside, and Bernadette heard a soft whirring. Glancing towards the ceiling, a panel had opened above them, and a room darkening screen was slowly descending covering the windows. The room was soon in complete darkness except for the light from the candles.

"Better?"

Bernadette responded by smiling, going over to the bed, and excitedly removing her clothes. Thinking about last Friday, she couldn't admit to Valerie she had gotten totally nude in front of him of her own accord, had lain face down in his bed, let Clark pour the warm oils over her body, and give her a full body massage. He had her so relaxed she had fallen to sleep. The lovemaking came later....

The amount of clothes Clark wore had changed gradually as well. It started with him just leaving the top buttons of his shirt undone. Then he had the entire shirt open. One night, after he had pleased her and pulled her towards his body, he was nude from the waist up. That was the first time their nude bodies had touched.

Bernadette didn't realize as she recalled the last event, she had exhaled sharply. When she glanced at Valerie, her friend had this blank stare, and her mouth was wide open.

Valerie fell backwards on the sofa and called out dramatically throwing her arms wide, "Take me, Clark! Just take me!"

Bernadette leaned over and slapped her hard on the knee, "Don't say that!"

"Ouch!" Valerie looked at Bernadette surprised she had hit her so hard. "Girlfriend, you're getting possessive of your man, huh?"

Bernadette kind of liked the sound of 'her man' even if she was embarrassed by the words Valerie spoke. Valerie had been like that since college, and she accepted her just the way she was. She knew Valerie would probably never change.

"You better be possessive. You don't have to tell me a thing. Just watching you, I already see that plenty has been happening between the two of you. I know that man is skilled, girl! The minute I saw him, he came across as competent and confident. I knew he would know what he was doing. You weren't going to get no fumbling loving when you crawl into his bed."

"Valerie, it's more than just the physical attraction I have for him. When he looks at me, he makes me feel that he wants me as much as I want him. Me, the pink elephant!"

"Girl, you still haven't got over that? I apologized..."

"I feel adored when I'm with him. When we go out to eat and ladies are trying to catch his eye, it's as if they don't exist to him. His eyes are only on ME – wanting to hear how my day at work went, wanting to hear how I'm feeling, wanting to hear about my dreams and my aspirations." Bernadette's voice grew more passionate, "I'll tell you this much. I've been completely nude in front of him, and he's never said a single derogatory comment about by body or my weight. Instead, he looks at me as if I'm a goddess! He touches me and holds me like I'm a treasured piece of fine porcelain.... He makes me feel loved! Growing up, everything was always about Cecelia.... Anytime we went anywhere, people would comment on how cute Cecelia was dressed and how cute Cecelia looked. Then, as an afterthought, they would add, 'You look nice too, Bernadette.' Clark makes me feel beautiful. He makes me feel good about me, and that's something I haven't felt in a long time.."

Bernadette lowered her head and took a deep breath tears welling in her eyes. Valerie gave her time to calm down. When she thought her emotions had settled, she said in almost a whisper, "So, when did you do the nasty?"

Bernadette finally held her head up again and turned towards Valerie, "What do you mean, the nasty?"

Valerie got off the sofa, walked over to a plant, and pulled a key from behind it. Unlocking a cabinet next to her entertainment unit, she glanced over the DVD titles and finally pulled two out. Popping the cases open, she tossed the cases on the sofa next to Bernadette and plugged the two discs into her player. Glancing at the cases, Bernadette didn't know that many 'Xs' existed in movie ratings. She looked up at the screen when Valerie started punching in buttons.

"I know exactly where this scene is so I'm fast forwarding...."

The camera lens showed a women's face before gradually scanning down the length of her nude body. Her lover appeared in the scene also nude at the foot of the bed. At the site of the man's erect penis, Bernadette turned her head quickly and stopped watching. Seeing her reaction, Valerie rewound to a clear shot of the male organ and hit pause.

Bernadette couldn't conceal her reaction, "They can put that on film? I thought only doctors would see that."

"Girl, don't tell me you ain't seen one before?"

Bernadette just kept her head down.

"Well, I guess you don't have to see it as long as you're feeling it, right? That's right.... You only have that one sibling and she's a girl too! You've never changed a baby boy's diaper?"

Bernadette squealed out a soft, "No."

"That man is still keeping his clothes on for you?"

Valerie let her sit quietly for a while. When she saw Bernadette finally move her head, it was to the left, further out of view of the screen.

"Girl, you better take a good look and get used to seeing one. Your man doesn't look like one that wants to be all bound up. I bet that man sleeps nude. I'd bet my new car on it so it won't be long before you're seeing his. And, I checked out his crotch that first time I met him. I'm sure he's is bigger than what this poor boy on this screen has!"

Bernadette took another glance but was visibly embarrassed.

"Enough of wonder boy," Valerie thought. She punched some numbers in, and the system switched to the other DVD. This time a woman was in command of the love scene. She was caressing the man much the same way Clark caresses her. Bernadette turned away again.

"I've never touched Clark back!"

Valerie turned and stared at her. "What do you mean? How can you not touch a man if you're in bed with him?"

"I mean I've never touched him like that. We hug but the caressing and all…. I've never done that."

"You just lay there, let that man do all the work, and enjoy yourself?"

Bernadette felt not only ashamed but selfish. She watched the way the lady in the film was massaging the man.

"Now that I've seen this, I'll try some of those touches next time but ONLY above his waist," she looked at Valerie and clarified.

"So, when did he do it?"

"Do what?"

Valerie took the remote, switched to the other DVD, and kept replaying the man mounting the woman over and over again.

"When did he do that? When did he take his thing and stick it up you?"

"He hasn't!" Bernadette looked at her in shock.

Seeing her reaction, Valerie got upset.

"I thought we were being honest with each other. Why can't you tell me when you did the nasty? If you didn't do the nasty, all you've been doing is foreplay. Girl, you gonna tell me all you've been doing is foreplay for weeks?"

Bernadette touched Valerie's arm. When Valerie turned and eyed her expression, Bernadette's face was so sincere that Valerie believed her when she repeated again, "We haven't!"

Valerie fast forwarded the movie to a point where it showed a man ejaculating. Reaching across to Bernadette, she started running her fingers up her thigh from the knee.

"That man hasn't stuck his thing up you yet and let those little critters start swimming upstream?"

"Valerie, I'm not going to embarrass my parents again by their only other daughter getting pregnant. No, we haven't!" Bernadette was emphatic.

Valerie believed what Bernadette was saying but was confused. If they hadn't had sex, why was she able to slip in the tampon and not feel any discomfort? She thought about an erotic book she had read once about concubines in the Orient. When a virgin was scheduled to have sex for the first time, an elder would prepare her body. Every night, he would go to her bed with raw egg white. The elder would massage her using the egg white, but each night his finger would move further in. Then he would repeat the process using two fingers. He massaged the girl until he knew she would experience her first time with very little pain. Remembering what she read, Valerie turned back to Bernadette.

"He's been sticking his fingers up there!"

When Bernadette turned away, Valerie knew she was right. Bernadette didn't have to answer her and Valerie also knew Bernadette had no clue where the relationship stood and that it was about to change in a big way.

"Bernadette, that man is a saint to treat you the way he has, but you're in trouble, girl!"

Hearing that comment, Bernadette turned to Valerie showing she was ready to listen, "Why?"

Valerie took her fingers and started running them up her thigh again, "Because it won't be long before those little critters are inside you."

Bernadette pushed Valerie's hand away, but Valerie saw she was worried. She sought to comfort her.

"That man loves you, girl! How long has this been going on? Right after the festival? So, it's been over five weeks? Girl, men don't act like that with women even if they do love them. I've never seen or heard of a man having this kind of devotion to a woman! He's been preparing you for over a month so he doesn't hurt you and you enjoy the first time just as much as he does."

 Bernadette appeared to calm down a little.

"He has any kids?"

"He's never mentioned any."

"That's because he's smart. I could tell he's not one of those my baby's mama types. That man knows better not to plan! He ain't gonna get hooked up with some hussy for the rest of his life, stuck in a bad relationship just because she opened her legs to him. Since he's smart, you don't have to worry about those critters. That man is going to use protection."

 Valerie realized the falseness in what she had just said. Turning to Bernadette, she spoke in an agitated tone, "Bernadette, if you don't want no baby, you are going to have to protect yourself, girlfriend! That man doesn't care if you get pregnant."

Bernadette was getting frustrated and confused and Valerie could understand why. She had just contradicted herself.

"That man isn't just in love, he's blind. Girl, you can get anything you want out that man. He ain't gonna let you go. The way he's been treating you…. Don't you see what I mean, Bernadette?"

Valerie could tell she was trying.

"Listen, he's been moving real slowly with you… If he puts his thigh between your legs, the next time he's going to take both of those steel thighs of his, separate yours, and girl those little critters are going to be swimming. And, if you're not ready for that, don't touch the man!"

"Why not?"

"Ever took a can of soda when you were little, shake it up, and then pop it open?"

"Only if you want to get splattered?"

"And, girlfriend, you're about to get splattered."

Valerie looked at Bernadette with pity. It didn't take long when she first met Bernadette to know the girl had been raised like a nun, especially when she showed up for classes in that pink waitress' uniform. She should have started schooling her on sex, and not just fashion, back then. Valerie tried to relate where Bernadette was in her relationship with Clark to something she could understand.

"That man's body is just like that can of shaken soda. Girlfriend, after five weeks, he is ready to explode. That man has nerves of steel as well as patience. You'll never find a man like this again! I didn't think they existed…. I don't know any man that could be that patient for that long but he has to be getting close. He can't keep it bottled up much longer. Girlfriend, he has to be on the edge. His nerves must be shot. If you start touching him like in that movie and not ready to give it up, that would just be cruel, Bernadette…. That would just be cruel! Think you can tell him, 'no'? Think, if he pulls you underneath him, you can tell him to stop?"

Bernadette thought about all the times her emotions were completely out of control, yielding to Clark and willing to let him do whatever he pleased to her. She felt guilty she had been so hard on Cecelia because she understood now how easily a woman could have intercourse with a man she loved.

"No...."

"Bernadette, you have to protect yourself. This man is in it for the long haul so he doesn't care if you get pregnant. He has everything he wants in life – a fine car, luxury condo, successful career. All he's missing right now is a family, and at his age, he's probably ready for one. And, girlfriend, I know he done already picked you to carry it for him. He might not use protection. Based on what you've told me, it won't be like with your sister. That man will be by your side, but if you don't want a baby before he puts a ring on your finger, you have to control this situation, Bernadette!"

"So, what do I do?"

Valerie started digging through her purse. She found a business card and handed it to Bernadette. You call my doctor! Don't go to the one your Mama's been bringing you to since you were little. Use my address and contact number so letters aren't going to your house. When this man asks you questions, be honest with him. Don't hide anything. Tell him you're there to get birth control pills. Remember, when one of Clark's thighs goes between yours, it's time."

Bernadette took the card but looked guilty.

"He's already done that, hasn't he?"

Bernadette remembered the massage last Friday and how intertwined their bodies were as they napped.

"Yes...."

"When are you seeing him again?"

"With it being my time…. Not until Saturday."

"You want him to?"

Bernadette was embarrassed to admit it, but she did, "Yes."

"Pills don't work that fast. We need to get you something to use."

Valerie thought awhile, "We're making a drug store run. We'll get something even your lil' virgin mind can do right. And we're going shopping and picking you up a negligee. When you get to his condo Saturday, change first, and follow the instructions on the package right then. You hear me, girl! Make sure you use whatever we pick up as soon as you get there, Bernadette, because as suave as that man is, you are not going to remember once he starts touching you…. Before we go shopping, I need a drink! You want one?"

Bernadette's nerves were beginning to get on edge. She didn't realize how close she had come to repeating Cecelia's mistake. Her parents would have been devastated. She was thankful her period had come a couple of days early. Otherwise, instead of watching a movie at Valerie's that afternoon, she would have been at Clark's.

"Yes, please!" She answered Valerie praying the alcohol would help her nerves settle down.

"You drink only a glass of wine still?"

"I'll take a Tequila Sunrise if you have the mixings."

Valerie turned in shock. "When did you learn about any Mexican suns rising?"

Feeling more relaxed now that she had bypassed spilling her guts but had confided in Valerie despite of it, Bernadette began speaking freely, "Clark mixes all kinds of things for me to try. At first, everything he gave me tasted just like different kinds of fruit punch. They'd be so good,

Valerie, I would usually have two, sometimes three drinks, before we started making out."

"Damn, that man is smooth. He could seduce a nun, and she would walk away not even realizing he had had her," Valerie thought to herself before saying out loud to Bernadette, "So how often have you been dragging your Catholic ass to confession?"

Bernadette was relaxed now that her sex lesson was over and started speaking openly to Valerie.

"Did I ever mention Clark used to be an altar boy?"

"No, not that I recall," Valerie responded over her shoulder as she stood at the bar pouring tequila into two cocktail glasses.

"Well…. Having been one, he has spoken a lot with priests over the years so he knows so much more than the average layperson about our Catholic religion and the rules. We have spent hours discussing issues. If I'd share how I'm feeling with him especially when I'm feeling guilty about things he's doing to me, Clark is able to elaborate on teachings and passages on the subject…. He even has a Bible."

Valerie turned and said, "So the Gideons make house calls? I know the man is good, but to the point they heard of his place and made a private condo stop?"

Bernadette was giving Valerie a confused look indicating, "Why are you interrupting my story, and what gibberish are you talking about now?"

Valerie thought it best not to explain that joke so took her right hand and waved it downward towards her waist indicating Bernadette should just forget it and continue her story.

"He keeps the Bible in a glass case in his living area. It's been handed down for five generations now on his father's side and has his father's lineage recorded in it. The tradition is to give it to the first-born son when he makes twenty-five. Since Clark has that on display, I know how much he must have studied that Bible because he can quote passages I never read or heard of, and he interprets them for me. He presents things to me so logically that I don't understand why I didn't see concepts that way before. He reminded me how religion class was. You just had to memorize things and got graded on if you could regurgitate the words. There wasn't a lot of discussion and debate like he had with priests all those years he served as an altar boy. I grew up just memorizing answers, but now I can understand things better seeing them through his eyes. When we first started making out, I use to get so upset and feel what we were doing was so wrong that I'd be going straight to hell. But, after Clark reinterpreted some things I had learned in religion classes for me, my conscious is clear…. I don't know the last time I went to confession."

Valerie turned from the bar where she had been mixing their cocktails. Her mouth opened wide as she eyed Bernadette. She thought Bernadette was just messing with her. The girl had to be joking. When she observed the serious though somewhat blank look on Bernadette's face and could tell she had truly believed whatever Clark must had told her, she turned back to the bar and had to hold the edge with both of her hands to keep herself from falling flat on the floor as she bent her knees and began laughing. Valerie then pulled herself up, let go of the bar, and started dancing in a circle, slapping her knees as she laughed hysterically and screamed, "Damn, that man is good!" over and over again.

Bernadette rose from the sofa, and as she passed Valerie, she slapped her hard in the center of the back and yelled, "I'll fix my own drink."

Clark had warned her not to talk about things they discussed between them with Valerie. He had said, "By Valerie not being Catholic, she won't understand." Looking at Valerie, she knew Clark was right. How could Valerie be dancing around like that and laughing over something as serious as confession? Clark was so right once again.

As they drove to the shopping center later that day to pick up the birth control and lingerie for Bernadette, traffic was bottlenecked with everyone trying to take advantage of the Pre-Memorial Day weekend sales. They were in the far left lane trying to bypass the folks fighting to get into the strip mall across from the indoor mall. Bernadette and Valerie were so busy chatting that Bernadette didn't notice Clark's Corvette parked outside the jewelry store on her right.

The cashier's hand was trembling as she handed a Mount Blanc pen to Clark to sign his approval for the ring to be sized. She worked on commission and had never sold anything in this price range before.

"When did you say it'll be ready?

"I promise you that you have not only my personal guarantee but the owner's as well. This ring will be ready for you no later than noon on Friday, Mr. Laurent."

"That would be great. I don't need it until Saturday night, but I have a cousin flying in Friday afternoon to spend the holiday weekend with me so I'll pick it up on the way to the airport."

Clark sat down and took the ring out the case one more time.

"You're sure she'll like it?"

"Mr. Laurent, in this price range, jewelry items come with a 100% satisfaction guarantee. If she doesn't like the ring, just bring it back within ninety days. There are no questions asked if you want to change it to something else, but I can't imagine any lady not being VERY pleased with what you've selected. If not, I promise we will work with her until she's happy."

Clark looked at the ring at different angles. He had paid special attention to the jewelry Bernadette wore and to jewelry she admired the times they were at the flea market in the French Quarter. He felt he had selected a ring that matched her taste, but he wanted Saturday night to be perfect. "Think about the fact you're being paid to make critical decisions every day and stop second guessing yourself," he thought.

Clark looked at the saleslady and said, "Size it," before shaking her hand and then stuffing the paperwork into his pocket. As he exited the store, he thought he saw Bernadette and Valerie passing in Valerie's car. He wondered what the two of them were up to....

Chapter Twenty-Three

Arriving at the airport, Clark parked on the upper level waiting for his cousin Clay to arrive. As soon as he spotted him in the crowd of passengers, he waved him over. No words were spoken between them. They looked in each other's eyes and a bear hug followed. When they released, Clark popped the doors on the Corvette and Clay dumped the weekend case he had brought behind the seats before getting it on the passenger's side. As they pulled away from the terminal, Clay began filling Clark in on everything that had happened since Clark attended his college graduation two weeks before.

When they arrived at Blaine's, Clark introduced Clay to the chef. When Blaine heard Clark had invited Clay for the Memorial weekend to celebrate his graduation, he told them all drinks that night were on the house.

As the discussion surrounding Clay and his future plans came to a close, Clark reached into his pocket and pulled out the ring he had purchased for Bernadette. He handed it to Clay. When Clay opened the case, he dropped the ring on the table, got up, and hugged Clark as he rose as well. They sat back down and Clark slipped the ring back into his pocket as the waiter delivered another round of drinks.

"I'm happy for you, Clark! When's the big day?"

"I'm hoping it'll be Sunday."

Clay tilted his head and eyed Clark questioningly.

"I'm bringing her to dinner here tomorrow night. This is where we had our very first date. I'm planning to pop the question then. If she agrees, she and I will be getting on a plane to Vegas when I drop you off Sunday to catch yours back to Texas."

"If I didn't have to wrap things up at my apartment and vacate before my lease expires June 1, I'd come serve as a witness."

"I can't wait for you to meet her on Sunday. She's a wonderful lady, Clay. I never imagined I'd be this lucky."

A cloud came over Clay's face. Clark raised the subject reluctantly.

"You still think about CeeCee?"

"It's rare for a day to go by that I don't, especially now that I'll have a decent job and can take care of them. " Clay exhaled sharply before continuing, "Them! I don't even know if she had the baby. If she did, I'm still hoping I'll find her one day and we can be a family. If she didn't, Clark, I pray I'll never find her. I loved her so much, but if she was the type of girl that would abort my child, I'd feel I had her all wrong. I'd feel I didn't really know her. Do you understand what I mean?"

"I think I do…. I know I do."

"CeeCee Detiege… I can't stop thinking about her."

As the waitress delivered the entrées, their conversation drifted to more pleasant subjects.

Having stayed up most of the night talking and recalling fun times they had in the past, Clark and Clay slept late Saturday morning. A sudden chill woke Clark. He smiled knowing this day would be life changing. It's the day he would ask Bernadette to marry him. When Clay woke, they took a run on the levee together. After they returned to the condo to shower, they headed to Joe's. As they were driving to Joe's, Clark warned Clay they may run into his college buddies, Willy and Michael. He shared stories about his college days with Clay. Clay could tell Clark's fondest memories were the stories he told involving Glenn.

As they entered the restaurant, Clark introduced Clay as his cousin to the owner Joe. When Clark told him Clay was in town for the weekend celebrating graduating from college, Joe personally showed them to a booth and then brought out a hot assortment of mini muffins on the house. He poured them each a cup of coffee and told them to enjoy the muffins while they decided what to order.

Clay's fingers were popping the mini muffins into his mouth, his eyes locked on the menu as Clark pointed out the dishes he enjoyed the most at Joe's place. Until she asked if they were ready to order, neither had paid attention to the waitress who approached, pulling out her pad to take their order. Once Clay shook his head at Clark indicating he'd go with Clark's last recommendation, he looked up to give the waitress his order.

"CeeCee," he uttered.

Clark watched as the blood drained from Clay's face and that of the waitress. The waitress dropped everything – her tray, pad, pencil – and walked quickly towards the owner.

Not letting his gaze lose sight of her, Clay jumped out of the booth and followed. Patrons had turned to stare at the commotion.

Clark couldn't believe the girl had been right under his nose. He had seen her often on his visits to Joe's but she always worked the section nearest the kitchen. He had no idea what her name was. Glancing towards the waitress stand, Clark saw the exchange between Clay and CeeCee was getting heated. He got up and walked over right when CeeCee ran out the front door into the parking lot. He grabbed Clay's arm to prevent him from following her.

"Clay, let me talk to her first. Let me calm her down. You need a time out as well. Take a moment to gather your thoughts before you talk to her. OK?"

Clay shook his head in agreement. "Thanks, Clark."

Saturday morning, Bernadette was taking care of Miki, as usual, for Cecelia to work the breakfast and lunch shifts. She had started playing CDs, and she was swinging Miki around the room dancing to the music.

Her niece was giggling and begging for more as soon as Bernadette put her down.

"You're happy today, Aunt Ber'dette!"

"From the mouth of babes," Bernadette thought before answering, "Yes, Miki, I am!"

"You're as happy as I was when I made three. I had the best party. I want one just like it when I make four."

"We'll see. By the time you're four, you may change your mind and want something different."

"No, I love pizza. You have to get me pizza again, Aunt Ber'dette."

"I promise, Miki, to make sure you always have pizza at your party."

The tyke smiled, and Bernadette's attention shifted as the doorbell rang.

"I'll get it!" Miki screamed running to the front door. Bernadette scurried behind her in fear she might actually open the door on her own before Bernadette knew who was on the other side.

When they peeked through the window, Bernadette saw a postal delivery truck parked in front of their house. Opening the door, the postal carrier showed her a package and stated someone needed to sign for it. After signing for it, Bernadette studied the envelope.

"Miki, this is for Mommy, and it's from the college. I think it's her admission kit because it's too big to be a reject letter so I know this is something that's going to make Mommy very happy. What do you say we ride over to Joe's and give it to Mommy?"

"Can we get ice cream too?"

"Sure, we can."

"Then yes!"

Bernadette followed the same route to Joe's her Uncle Aaron had used when he first brought her to meet him. Bernadette thought about the different milestones in her life that were now tied to Joe's place. It was her first job. It was the cause of her meeting Valerie who she still considered her best friend. Thinking about the lingerie hidden in her trunk and the other supplies she had bought with Valerie, the most pleasant milestone was that it was the place she met Clark. She couldn't wait to surprise him tonight by wearing the outfit. She and Valerie had fought over style and color. They both had finally fallen in love with a midnight blue gown that complemented Bernadette's skin tone and figure perfectly. Bernadette was so in love and happy as she thought about the word Miki had used and peeked in the rear view mirror to check on her niece.

"Not much further, Miki. Just two more traffic lights," she called seeing her beginning to twitch in the car seat.

As the light turned green, Bernadette drove forward slowly. Joe's would be on the left at the next light. At this time of day, she was certain she could get a spot in the parking lot so she would need to turn left when they reached the light.

 As she concentrated on finding an opening in the traffic, Miki yelled, "There's Mommy!"

"Yes, Miki. That's where Mommy works, but Mommy will be inside waiting tables. You won't see her until we park and go in."

"Mommy's outside. She's right there, Aunt Ber'dette!"

Bernadette was still in the right lane. She pulled into the parking lane and glanced towards Joe's place. She could see Cecelia in the lot but she wasn't alone. She was in the parking lot at Joe's arguing with Clark. Before they saw her car, Bernadette made a quick right turn and drove away.

"My ice cream! Aunt Ber'dette, what about my ice cream?" Miki called.

Bernadette didn't respond and soon the tyke was crying as well as screaming for ice cream. She remembered an ice cream parlor on Carrollton Ave. and started driving towards it. When she had purchased a cone and Miki was happily licking the sweet, creamy concoction, it gave Bernadette time to sit and think about what she had just seen.

All kinds of thoughts were swirling through her mind but the prominent one was the one she didn't want to believe. The interaction between Cecelia and Clark was not a waitress-patron type of discussion. Bernadette had no doubts the conversation was personal. She stared at her niece as if she was seeing the child for the first time. Suddenly, it clicked. She had met Clark's father briefly the night of the wedding rehearsal. Though she had met at least thirty of his relatives that night, Bernadette remembered his father's looks vividly because of the circumstances. If it wasn't for the obvious age difference among the two gentlemen, his younger brother standing next to him would have been mistaken for his twin. She remembered Clark introducing him as the uncle they stayed with in Ville Platte. The resemblance was now clearly there for her to see and the pieces fit. Miki was a feminine version of Clark's father. Cecelia and Clark were arguing because this is Clark's child. She remembered the conversation last weekend between her and Valerie.

"He has any kids?"

"He's never mentioned any..."

"That's because he's smart. I could tell he's not what of those my baby's mama types. That man knows better not to plan! He ain't gonna get hooked up with some hussy for the rest of his life stuck in a bad relationship just because she opened her legs to him. Since he's smart, you don't have to worry about those critters. That man is going to use protection."

Studying her niece again, Bernadette thought, "The next time she saw Valerie, she would have to tell her. There's at least one time he didn't use any protection! His baby's mama is my sister!"

When they got back home, it was time for Miki's nap. After her niece drifted to sleep, Bernadette just sat on the edge of the bed and stared at her. As sick as it sounded, it seems knowing she was Clark's child made her want to love her more. She could never take this out on Miki, an innocent child, but she had to get out of the room Miki shared with her mother. Bernadette had to get out of that bedroom. She couldn't stand being in Cecelia's space. Cecelia had always been a spoiled brat but now she had had sex with the man Bernadette loved. That was more than she could ever forgive. A voice seemed to speak to her reminding her that Cecelia had him first. Bernadette was the second choice. Pinky - shaped like a round chimney, the pink elephant, the fat cow was his second choice. Bernadette was in tears by the time she sat on her own bed.

Recalling her plans for the night, she was sickened by the thought that she was going to wear that beautiful gown and lay in the same bed where Cecelia and Clark might have made love. She knew Clark hadn't lived a celibate lifestyle, but she was sickened by the thought he had sex with a minor. That was more than she could bear. Having witnessed their lovers' quarrel, she was sickened by the thought Clark and her sister may still be making love. Was he banging Cecelia on his lunch hour and then seeing Bernadette at night? Had he restrained from going all the way with her because he loved her or because he didn't have anything left in him by the time Bernadette got there? Maybe eating together was the only value she played in his life. Based on Miki's age, she knew Clark would have had the finances to support the child, but he hadn't. She was sickened by the thought he was the type of man that would walk away from his responsibilities. The list kept growing the more she thought about it. It wasn't long before she was sickened, in general, over anything associated with Mr. Clark Laurent.

When Bernadette heard a door slam, she went to check on Miki. Cecelia was on the bed sobbing hysterically.

"YOU'RE GOING TO WAKE YOUR BABY!" Bernadette spat out at her.

"Bernadette, PLEASE just leave me alone. I just got in an argument with her father. I can't deal with anything else right now. Could you please just get out of my room, close the door, and leave me alone?"

"GLADLY," Bernadette hissed before going back to her own bedroom. Hearing Cecelia speak the words validated what she had seen in the parking lot at Joe's. Looking at the time, she still had several hours before she met Clark at Blaine's.

Bernadette sat and watched the clock as everything she had concluded kept playing over and over in her head. By the time she was leaving to meet Clark at Blaine's, she was also sickened by the thought of him ever touching her again, and she couldn't wait to tell him.

Chapter Twenty-Four

As soon as Clark walked into Blaine's that night, he knew his face was looking worse. The hostess was obviously taken aback by his appearance, but she tried to ask him in an upbeat tone if he wanted his usual booth for two. He followed the hostess, but when he took his seat, the events of the day proved too much for him. He slouched in the booth, leaned his head against the top cushion, and closed his eyes.

He opened his eyes when he heard Chef Blaine's voice, "You got hit by a truck?"

Opening his eyes, Chef Blaine was standing next to the booth and chuckling, "Is your lady friend coming tonight?"

Clark used his hands to help move his bruised torso into a more erect position.

"She should be here any minute."

"Man, you look like you need to be home in bed. I haven't seen a shiner like that one since I retired from the police force. How did the other guy look? I hope you fought back."

"Fight back? Not this time! I'm not a man that backs down but I couldn't fight back under these circumstances…. I probably wouldn't be here tonight if I had. I'm sure I'd be in central lock-up and the keys to my cell would be lost. This damage is from one of your buddies."

"One of my buddies?" Understanding what Clark must have meant, Chef Blaine questioned, "A cop?"

"Man, it's a strange story." Clark's breath seemed labored, and Chef Blaine could tell he was struggling to stay awake. The man looked exhausted.

"Did he punch you?"

"That and more," Clark pulled a handkerchief out his pocket and patted away a little drainage from the area under his left eye.

Chef Blaine had taken the seat opposite Clark and was inspecting his face. "If it wasn't by your cheekbone, the blow probably wouldn't have broken your skin. How many stitches?"

"I think the ER physician said twelve."

"Twelve? For a cut that size? They must be very fine stitches. That's good. That many stitches should help reduce any scarring."

"Thanks for the positive," Clark shook his head and reached for the bourbon the bartender had brought over.

"Man, you can't drink with a head injury. They didn't tell you that?" Chef Blaine pulled the liquor out of Clark's reach before continuing, "I've seen a bunch of those during my thirty-five years on the force. That's a closed head injury meaning, in your case, your face connected with someone's fist. "

Chef Blaine couldn't help but laugh a little. When Clark looked up in obvious pain, he felt bad he had made fun of the situation and got serious again.

"Listen – no drinking for at least two days, and take the pain medication they recommended. Trust me! You need to be on it now. If that headache gets worse or you start vomiting, get back to the ER. I'm going make you an ice pack. Didn't they tell you that you should apply it every hour? When's the last time you put it on?"

"I haven't used one at all yet. After I got out the ER, I didn't have time to do anything but stop by my place long enough to clean up and come straight here."

"Instead of staying home and applying an ice pack like they told you," Chef Blaine was speaking with the authority of a police officer now. After today's experience, Clark knew that tone well.

Clark just shrugged his shoulders.

"Why? Your lady friend seems real nice. Does she know what happened? Would she get that upset if you broke the date?"

Clark spoke softly and with a slight slur. He felt so exhausted. "She has no idea yet."

"She will the minute she takes one look at you!" Chef Blaine couldn't help laughing again. "I'm sorry, man. I appreciate your business but you really need to be in bed. I thought I'd seen everything in my thirty five years on the force, but this is one for the books."

"This is a special night." Clark eased his hand into his trouser pocket and pulled out a jewelry case. He handed it to Chef Blaine. "I picked that up yesterday."

"How many years it's going to take you to pay for this one?"

"Against the advice of my financial advisor, I sold some stocks and paid cash. That size is considered an investment, and it should go up in value. I figured I should pay at least half as much as I did for my car if it's for something that lasts forever. Diamonds are forever, right?"

"That's real nice, real nice. You did good. Look, when she says 'yes,' signal the bartender. I'll tell him to watch out for you, and when he sees you signal, he'll bring over champagne for her and sparkling grape juice for you. We keep that on hand for the minors. And, man, anything you order tonight is on the house. I mean anything. My treat! Congratulations from me to one of my best customers."

"Thank you, man," Clark managed to lift his arm, and they exchanged a high five. The hostess had just sat a couple in the adjacent booth. Seeing the jewelry case and the sparkling of the diamonds, she came over, took it from Chef Blaine, and began admiring the ring.

Chef Blaine told Clark, "Did you know this is my daughter Megan?"

Clark held out his hand to shake the young lady's before responding he didn't.

"Yeah! She goes to college but is helping me out now that school is out for the summer. I have a niece that helps me out as well. She's handling the kitchen for me tonight. In fact, my niece and I are going into business together. Since I'm doing so well here, I'm going to partner with her and open a restaurant in New Orleans East. She wants to call it Chez Jolie. It'll be one of those fusion style places. I'll let you know when the Grand Opening party is so you two can come – everything will be free that night to let future customers sample the menu."

Chef Blaine's daughter was still admiring the ring. "If she doesn't accept it, I'll take it."

Chef Blaine scowled at his daughter, took the ring case from her, and handed it back to Clark before saying in an admonishing tone, "You better get back to that hostess stand."

Megan looked towards the front door and saw a line had formed. Seeing Bernadette among the patrons, she advised Clark, "You girl friend is here now. I'll bring her right over."

Chef Blaine rose and shook Clark's hand one last time. "Good luck," he said before walking to the bar area.

Clark quickly slipped the ring back into his trousers' pocket.

As Bernadette followed the hostess to the table, she immediately sensed something was wrong. By now, Clark would have been standing and would not have sat down until she was seated. Already upset over the topic she had to raise, the lack of the usual gentlemanly courtesy didn't help her mood. She tossed her purse onto the seat and sat across from him in the booth. Glancing at him, she noticed the bandage on his cheek and the bruising. She wanted to inquire what happened, but she had pondered what she saw in the parking lot for hours now. Instead she thought, "It's good he's hurting. I wonder if he feels as bad as I do right now."

Having just discussed his face with Chef Blaine, the fact Bernadette didn't ask about his appearance didn't register at all. The anesthesia from the stitches was beginning to wear off so the cut on Clark's face began throbbing. His attention was focused on that and the increasing swelling which was making it hard to see clearly out his left eye. He was also feeling slightly nauseous. He tried to pull himself into a more upright position. He had planned this too long. He wanted to propose Memorial Day weekend. He shifted and pain shot across his forehead. "Then I'm going straight home," he thought.

The waiter had brought Bernadette her usual drink without even being prompted to do so. But she hadn't taken a sip. He looked at Bernadette confused as to why she wasn't drinking and why she was not looking at the menu either. They both knew the standard menu well, but Chef Blaine always advertised specials based on seasonal prices and availability. They typically at least checked those out. When he saw the expression on her face, he knew she was upset and it was serious.

"Oh, Lord, what now?" Clark uttered right when Chef Blaine was approaching.

Chef Blaine heard the comment and started chuckling again. He turned to Bernadette and shook her hand, "Hey... How ya' doing tonight? It's nice to see you again."

Then the chef turned to Clark. He shook his head a couple of times and laughed some more before handing him the makeshift ice bag he had put together. Clark uttered his thanks before taking the clean kitchen towel filled with ice cubes into his left hand and holding it against his left eye.

Bernadette was beginning to feel torn between the subject she wanted to raise and concern over what had happened to him. Picturing Clark and Cecelia in the parking lot again, all the images she had conjured since flooded back. She could imagine Clark and Cecelia in his king sized bed at the condo making love. She got more irritated wondering if Cecelia got pregnant in the same bed she and Clark had been using.

Bernadette wondered if he was still seeing Cecelia. Was he having sex with Cecelia at the same time he was with Bernadette? She was so embarrassed and disgusted at the idea that she might be sharing a man with her sister, the anger in her voice was clear. She wanted to hear him admit it. She needed him to admit it and remove any doubt.

"Clark, I saw you and Cecelia arguing in the parking lot at Joe's today. Are you responsible for my sister getting pregnant?"

The color drained from Clark's face. The throbbing in his head grew worse but not due to the cut. His chest was heaving. He dropped the ice pack onto the table and slouched back against the cushion again. He stared at Bernadette in disbelief. It seems he heard her voice through a fog angrily repeating the question.

"His reaction said it all," Bernadette thought. She hissed at him, "I couldn't believe what I was seeing so I drove off before you saw me."

"CeeCee... is... Cecelia? CeeCee... is... your... sister. You don't look anything alike...." He was trying to process the information Bernadette just shared, but his mind was refusing to believe it. "You can't be.... Lord Jesus, help me if you are.... What are the odds?"

So, is that his excuse Bernadette thought for making out with both of us? So cheating, apparently, is OK with Mr. Clark Laurent, but he just wouldn't cheat with sisters? Is that his point? With sisters, the odds of him getting caught are too high? But should she forgive him since he didn't know because we don't resemble? Bernadette was fuming at the implication.

"Yes, you're right! We don't resemble! My Uncle Aaron got her the job at Joe's when she got pregnant just like he got one for me when I graduated from high school. Funny that's where she ended up and you met me, isn't it?"

Clark moaned and sighed, "Uncle Aaron is then your uncle too.... Oh, Lord.... Oh, Lord! Have I been that bad in my past? Help me, Jesus."

Bernadette got more upset with Clark's apparent negative reaction to her comments about her uncle. Uncle Aaron had done a good thing by getting them both jobs. She also thought, "Why am I discussing family genes and my family at all? What's the point? She's still my sister and the man she thought she knew well, the man she thought she loved, and the man she had planned to lose her virginity to that very night was the man that had got a teen-aged kid pregnant right before she made sixteen!" She was growing angrier each minute. She wanted to hear him admit it.

"Clark, just answer me. Are you responsible for my sister getting pregnant? YES or NO!"

Clark thought about the question. He thought about the day's events. He thought about that summer almost four years ago when his cousin Clay stayed with him at the apartment he had in New Orleans East. Then he thought about the yes or no answer she was demanding. That's the second time today he was guilty until proven innocent. He pondered the events of that summer.

Clark was dating Rebecca and didn't plan on Clay coming in town for school. Clay had wanted to earn additional college credits so he could fast track to graduation. Since Clark only had a one bedroom apartment, he especially had no idea Clay would want to stay with him so had planned a four day get-a-way to the Caribbean for himself and Rebecca. After spending day and night together for that length of time, Clark felt he would know for sure whether she was the one. He had second thoughts about still taking the trip, but Clay wasn't a minor anymore so he didn't cancel.

The trip turned out to be a fiasco. Rebecca spent two hours getting ready whenever he wanted to do anything. She was a beautiful woman, and he didn't feel she needed any makeup at all and had told her so often. Despite his efforts, she was constantly applying or retouching her makeup. On their dates, it had not been to the extent he had noticed it.

Now he understood that when she said she had to powder her nose, she meant it literally. If they were planning to go to the beach, she had a moisturizer with SPF. If they were going to dinner, she had brought along a special mirror that simulated candlelight so she'd get her makeup perfect for that setting. She had a lipstick and eye shadow for each outfit she had brought along, and if they changed, she had to redo parts of her makeup if she didn't cleanse her face completely and start over. She had brought a small suitcase along just for her makeup. Each bottle or tube had a special place in the suitcase and each had to be lined up a special way on the bathroom counter. The day they were leaving, the cab was waiting, and Clark was getting concerned they would miss their flight. He mentioned those facts and Rebecca was calmly and meticulously continuing to put on mascara. If they missed that flight, another was not going to be available for two days meaning Clark would also miss a meeting at work that was critical for him getting a promotion. After four days of makeup dominating their time together and knowing what he had at risk at work, Clark lost his patience. Using one arm, he swept all the makeup into the case, slammed it shut, and told Rebecca, "We are leaving now!"

On the flight home, Rebecca talked about nothing but her makeup. She had taken the case on board and was using both Clark's drop down tray as well as her own to resort everything. She kept chattering about how inconsiderate it was of Clark to behave in such a Neanderthal manner. After all, she only did these things to be beautiful for him. By the time the plane landed, the relationship was over. Clark never regretted it. Unknown to him, the company's CEO was in attendance during his presentation. He was so impressed that he had Clark placed in an executive fast track program. After being given various assignments to test his leadership and decision making skills, he was promoted whenever a vacancy occurred. He was now financially sound. The meeting he would have missed had he and Rebecca skipped that flight was the turning point that had skyrocketed his career.

Clay picked him up at the airport and asked about Rebecca when he didn't see her. He told Clay he had paid for a cab to take her home.

Clark was so upset his holiday plans crashed, he didn't think to ask Clay how his holiday had gone. When Clark got home and went into the bedroom to unpack, it dawned on him how clean and neat the apartment had appeared. When he had walked through the living room, there was no empty beer can or half eaten chip bags on the table. This was odd for a college kid that had spent the entire weekend alone. The cleaning lady wasn't due until Thursday. Suspicious, he pulled back the sheets allowing a flowery scent to waft up to his nose. Freshly washed sheets? He looked up at Clay, and the guilt he saw in Clay's face was so clear that Clark didn't have to ask what he'd been doing that weekend. He knew.

Looking at Bernadette once again, he chided himself. Every night over dinner, all Clay had talked about was CeeCee. Clark knew Clay was enamored, and he also knew Clay came from a very strict, traditional upbringing. All Clay would have learned regarding birth control was abstinence. If he hadn't canceled the trip, he should have at least sat him down and talked with him about protecting not only himself but the girl as well before he got on that plane. If he tried to explain that holiday to Bernadette, would she realize how important the trip was to him? He was thinking about asking a woman to marry him. That was such a significant milestone in his life. Could he get her to understand that, or would she just see it as Clark being irresponsible? Would she feel he had gone off for a weekend of daiquiris and sex on the beach while her baby sister was in an unsupervised environment?

"Clark, did you know she was only sixteen when she had that baby? She was in a Catholic school and got kicked out. She didn't even graduate from high school. Not only her dreams but mine died as well when she got pregnant. My plans had to go on hold to help her take care of that baby! You know... To help us remember the difference in the symbols for the sexes, a high school teacher once emphasized in a class I took that the symbol for the male was the arrow. It signified he was free and clear to move on. The symbol for the woman was the cross. She told us, 'Remember that, girls. You will be the one carrying that baby, and most likely, you'll be caring for it alone.' How right she was. Women are the only ones that suffer due to unwanted pregnancies. "

Bernadette was seething. How many times had she asked him the same question now? She had lost count, and he still hadn't admitted anything. She had picked up her purse indicating she was about to walk out on him. The stitches by his eye were throbbing and the swelling was getting worse. After the events of the day, he conceded even though it was Bernadette. To try to present something logically was going to take more effort than he was able to put out at this stage of the game because, when he looked into Bernadette's eyes, he could see that the verdict was already in. For the second time that day, without the privilege of a trial, he was guilty as charged.

"Clark, this is your last chance to answer me. Are you responsible?"

Clark felt like the fist that had struck his face that morning had slammed through his chest, grabbed his heart, and was squeezing it. He could feel his heart constricting, and the pain was getting unbearable. Clark wouldn't consider himself a man if he didn't answer her. He also knew the minute he did, it was over between them. He couldn't lie about it, especially to Bernadette. He had given the young couple the means. He had given them the opportunity. He had failed to coach Clay on preventing CeeCee from getting pregnant. Three strikes? You're out! He lifted his hands slightly into the air with his fingers fanned then dropped them into his lap. Shaking his head, he responded, "Yes….," before hanging his head slightly.

Bernadette stood saying emphatically, "I don't EVER want to see YOU again!"

Clark didn't watch Bernadette as she stormed out the restaurant. Instead, he picked up the icepack and held it against his left eye which was almost completely closed. A few seconds later, Chef Blaine was at his side chuckling again.

"Looks like that went well."

With blurred vision, Clark placed the icepack on the table and started fumbling with his wallet to pull out his credit card. Handing it to Chef Blaine, he said, "If you can get me my check, please. No offense but I'm ready to pay and get the hell out of here."

"Save that. Everything is on me tonight."

As Clark saved the credit card and started fumbling in his pocket for his car keys, Chef Blaine signaled to his daughter. As soon as Megan arrived at the booth, the chef questioned Clark.

"What kind of car do you have?"

Clark answered hesitantly wondering why but was not about to question the ex-officer. He had learned that lesson well too. "A black Corvette coupe...."

The chef turned to his daughter and barked instructions. "Tell one of the waiters to watch the hostess stand for you. Go get our family car and follow me. I'm driving this guy home."

"But Dad, he has a Corvette! Let me drive him home while you follow!"

Chef Blaine didn't entertain that suggestion at all and impatiently responded, "Go do what I told you!"

Turning back to Clark, he took the keys from his hand. "You shouldn't be driving. I'm taking you home. What's your address?"

Chef Blaine was acting not only as a chef but also in his old role as a police officer. At the restaurant, he quickly cut off the alcohol supply, called a cab, and paid the fare for anyone that appeared to be getting intoxicated. That practice had endeared him to his patrons, and his clientele had increased to the point his restaurant was typically packed nightly.

The motto of the New Orleans Police Department is "to serve and protect." Clark could tell Chef Blaine had been a dedicated officer that took that motto seriously. He was not about to let a person that appeared to have reduced use of his faculties drive himself. After today's events, Clark was so deflated, he was not about to argue. Clark wrote his address on a small pad the chef provided.

Seeing where Clark's condo was, the chef advised, "I know exactly where this is. I used to work in that precinct. Let's go, buddy."

The patrons overhearing the exchange were visibly impressed with the restaurant owner's actions. Though he was acting with no intent of gaining personally from it, Chef Blaine won additional, faithful advocates for his business that night, something no amount of advertising could buy.

Hearing the alarm system disarming, Clay exited from the guest bedroom to check on Clark.

"How did it go, man?"

Without returning his gaze, Clark murmured, "It didn't…. We broke up."

Clay began following Clark down the hall towards his bedroom inquiring, "Can I get you anything?"

Clark turned and gasped, "No offense, but all I need right now is to hit the sack. This has been a day straight from hell!"

Clay understood what he was asking of him. Clark needed him to back off; he wanted to be alone.

Clay didn't press the issue but silently watched Clark retreat to his master suite before returning to the guest bedroom.

Chapter Twenty-Five

When Clay woke Sunday morning, his first thought was to check on Clark. When Clark returned home the night before, Clay had never seen a man look so downtrodden. Quietly stepping to the top of the stair and observing Clark in bed, Clay was sorry he had entered his room. He felt totally responsible for what he saw. Clark had stripped down to a pair of briefs and had lain across the top of the comforter but the physical damage from the day before didn't allow him any position he could rest. It seemed he kept fretting into another sleep position. He finally shifted to lay flat on his back, a position he knew Clark hated.

"All for me," Clay thought. He was still acting in the role of a big brother and Clark had always spoiled him rotten. Anything Clay wanted, he tried to get for him.

When they were sitting in the emergency room the night before waiting for the results of the x-rays, Clark got visibly upset that Clay didn't understand why things had played out the way they did.

"Clay, listen. When a cop arrives on a scene, the first thing he needs to know is that he has control of the situation. If he doesn't, the safety of citizens is at risk as well as his own. I'm telling you to keep your mouth shut and just do what he says. Once he knows everything is under control, he will take out that pad they all seem to carry, and he'll come to you and ask you for your side of the story. Until then, keep your mouth shut and just follow his orders. If you remain calm, things won't escalate. Show him respect, and he'll show you respect. At the end, he'll even apologize to you for the inconvenience."

"But, Clark, we didn't do anything!"

"Clay, everything that cop did was well within his rights and how he had been trained as an officer. Keep in mind too that this was not just a regular citizen but his niece. I'm thinking about it from his perspective. Out of all my nieces and nephews, Sara is my little princess. Clay, I'm telling you that his reaction was mild compared to the one I would have had if I caught anyone in that situation with Sara."

"But, Clark, why did he act that way to you? When you screamed at me to stay down and put my hands behind my back, all the guy did was put his knee in my back and cuff me. You were on the ground and already handcuffed. I don't understand why he took that billy club and hit you like that. I don't know how you kept your cool after that blow…. Poor Joe was trying to stop him but it was a good thing the second police car arrived then and that cop Tyrone knew you. When Tyrone ran over and got between the two of you, he finally backed off."

"I didn't know Tyrone was a police officer. His wife Myra works at our firm. She used to be in the administrative pool. Whenever I sent any work down there, hers was always perfect. I got her promoted to our area when one of the ladies who worked for my boss retired. I've met Tyrone bunches of times at company functions but never knew his career path. I was lucky he was the one that showed up and started vouching for us. That's the only thing that made CeeCee's uncle start listening."

"At least he let Tyrone drive you to the emergency room while he interrogated me. But it didn't make sense for him to attack you like that. He had punched you out when he first got there, and you didn't fight him back."

"I did after that!"

"When, man?"

"Clay, your mind was only on CeeCee. When CeeCee closed that car door and you turned to go after her, the man called out to you to stop and you were completely ignoring him. When he pulled that billy club and aimed for you, I jumped between the two of you to block it using my upper right arm and shoulder. My body knocked into him hard pushing him down and tripping you as well in the process. It would seem to him that I had attacked him. I interfered with a police officer performing his duty. He had to gain control of the scene again."

"You always did look out for me, Clark.... I'm glad Joe offered him to use his little office instead of dragging me to jail.... I thought Joe was nuts when he called my name and kept touching his pocket. Then I saw the cop's name tag, and I knew I was screwed. I didn't catch on at first. The man must have thought I was messing with him and trying to be funny. Can you imagine the odds of him and CeeCee having the same surname? I started swearing to him that was the name the girl had given me. I don't think he believed a word I said until I told him to pull out my wallet and check out the business card of the investigator you had hired that summer to find her. I told him I loved her and wanted to marry her, but we couldn't find her. The investigator said if I had a picture of her, it would have made a difference. He stepped out the room and must have called the guy because when he came back, his attitude was altogether different. He called Tyrone and told him to take the cuffs off you and get back to his beat. Then he let me tell my story one more time. He acted so differently after he believed me. I thought it was great that he and Joe offered to take me to see CeeCee and to meet her family."

"You know, Clay, you need to bring the job offers you've received with you tomorrow. If things go well, you and CeeCee need to discuss moving to Dallas before you accept the job offer."

"The offer in Dallas is better than anything I've seen. When I first applied, I didn't realize it was the same company where Glenn had started and works. Thanks for discussing me with Glenn. There were so many applicants.... I'm sure his name in the references made mine stand out. I hate to give it up if CeeCee doesn't agree to move."

The heart monitor started beeping erratically and Clark's breathing became labored again. Clark was trying hard not to start a conversation with Clay on why he had to accept the Dallas offer regardless of what CeeCee felt because of what it would mean to their future. The job market was too tight now. There was no way Clay should turn down an offer he knew spelled Glenn had a hand in! The offer was too good for someone straight out of college with Clay's limited experience. But, remembering the fiasco from the last time he advised Clay, he held back. This had to be their decision this time and theirs alone.

When the doctor came in to discuss the x-rays, the doctor appeared worried. He lit the screen so Clark could see them clearly as well.

"Mr. Laurent, your chest cavity is not filling with fluids but you do have a hairline fracture on your rib cage. That's the tiny white line you see here. It doesn't appear your lung is collapsed but, with your labored breathing, I prefer to keep you overnight for observation."

"No thank you," Clark responded adamantly. "I have an engagement tonight I can't break."

The doctor had looked at Clay pleadingly. "I can't retain him without his consent, but you understand discharging him is not in his best interest."

Clay took one look at Clark. He knew that look well. Having seen the ring he purchased and knowing Clark's plans for that night, Clay knew that nothing was going to convince Clark to stay.

Reluctantly, Clay shook the doctor's hand and said, "Thank you, doctor, but it's clear we're leaving."

The doctor started to approach Clark one more time and saw Clark had started looking at his watch.

He sighed and said, "The nurse will be in shortly with the release papers."

It was nearly six o'clock when the nurse finally came in to discuss the final orders. Clark wasn't listening to a word she said. His eyes were fixated on the wall clock in the room and it seemed he was counting the seconds. She finally drew impatient with him and spoke in a louder voice, "Mr. Laurent, do I need to repeat the instructions, sir?"

Clark turned and looked at her. Seeing the clipboard and papers she held, he took them from her, glanced quickly through the sheets and turned back to the nurse.

"If I sign each of these sheets where you've placed an 'X,' am I then free to leave?"

"Yes, sir."

Clark scribbled his name quickly on each of the designated spots and handed the clipboard back to the nurse. "You did a beautiful job explaining. There's no need to repeat anything. Thank you."

The nurse seemed agitated and concerned, but once the papers were signed admitting she had covered the doctor's orders and the patient understood, she had no choice but to leave when Clark dismissed her.

When he pulled his dress shirt out the plastic bag and saw the blood, grass, and dirt stains on it, he tossed it into the trash.

Turning to Clay, he commented, "It's a good thing I was wearing an undershirt this morning. I can imagine us getting pulled over because it appears I'm riding in a car nude. I'm sure there's some law on that."

He glanced at his watch again. Pulling on his slacks, he slipped his feet into his shoes, and without bothering to tie the strings said, "Let's get out of here!"

When Clark began coughing, Clay walked down the stairs and towards him. Clark sensed his presence and attempted to sit up. When pain shot throw his left side, Clay put his right hand out so Clark could grab it. After pulling him into a sitting position, Clark's breathing became less labored.

Clay initiated the conversation.

"It's clear you're feeling worse. Want to go back to the ER?"

Clark glanced at the clock on the wall. "It's almost time for you to leave to meet Joe and CeeCee's uncle. I'll be fine. I'm just sore. I haven't had bruises like this since I was fourteen."

Remembering an incident at Clark's house, Clay questioned, "Your father?"

"Yes...."

"That's why I quit staying with you."

Clark turned to Clay, and his confusion was clear.

"What do you mean?"

"I had begged my mom to let me spend the Christmas holidays with you. I was only four years old at the time so you were about eleven. Your parents were throwing a big party in their den, and you snuck into your Dad's study to taste his bourbon. I kept begging you to please give me some and that was one time it looked like you just were NOT going to give in to me. I kept begging to the point I started crying. When I started crying, you broke down. You finally gave in and told me only one teeny, tiny sip. You were going to hold the glass yourself to make sure I didn't drink more. You had just put the glass to my lips when your Dad walked in and caught us. He grabbed me, put me over his knee, and spanked my bottom three times. Then he put me on the sofa crying and turned towards you. Man, it was like slow motion.... I remember him unbuckling and pulling off that wide leather belt he used to wear. He said, 'You are giving hard liquor to a four years old baby?' When he started walloping you, I started crying louder because I knew it was my fault you were getting a whipping. Connie heard and came in. When she saw what he was doing, she ran out crying and went to get your Mom. When your Mom came, she told him, 'Calvin, that's enough!' You weren't even crying but, after I saw the way he started beating you, I knew not to get caught doing something wrong at your house. When my mother would ask me if I wanted to spend time by you, I would tell her, 'No, make Clark come here!'"

Clark smiled and started laughing but winced when the pain shot through him and stopped before replying, "I remember that.... I knew you never wanted to come back and stay any length of time, but I never knew why."

"From then on, I only stayed overnight if my own parents were with me. I wasn't taking any chances with you father. He was harsh. He bruised you like that when you were fourteen? Do you hate him, Clark? Treating you like that all those years."

Clark looked straight into Clay's eyes.

"Hate him? No way…. My Dad and I are cool. He had NEVER been that harsh with me before. He did have a firm hand but that was not the way he treated me. I did suffer under that strap until I was twelve. After that, he treated me like he did my sisters. If you did something wrong, he would march you into his office and sit you at a chair across from him at his desk. What he would have you do is write in a composition book what you had done wrong, why it was wrong, and how your behavior would be different in the future. Then, he'd read your composition. Sometimes you had to write more. When he was satisfied, he would give you a lecture, and you would have to sign your name at the bottom of the composition as your contract with him that you wouldn't do it again."

Clark started laughing causing him to wince again.

"What's funny?"

"After everyone was in bed for the night, I would sneak into his office and take one of my sister's books. I'd slip it inside a magazine and go back to my bedroom to read it. I'd be laughing my head off at some of the things they had written and thinking this is what fathers expect of their little girls. Then I'd sneak back down and save it. I always used something to mark the spot in his file cabinet so I kept everything in the right order, and he wouldn't catch me."

"If you started writing compositions at twelve, how did you get bruises at fourteen?"

"I asked him to."

"Come on, Clark. You asked for an ass whipping?"

They both started laughing so hard, Clark had to place his hand against his side to act as a brace, but the laughter was good. It provided an emotional healing from his ordeals the day before though his rib cage wasn't ready for it.

"I was dating Marlene at the time and I got caught using his car."

"You can't get a driver's license at fourteen…." Clay looked confused.

"Starting to understand better now?"

Clay shook his head in disbelief, folded his arms and listened.

"My Dad had worked really hard to be successful. He got in on the insurance game right when they had started hiring more Afro-American agents. His first accounts were his former military comrades and their families. As corporations began opening their doors to more black professionals due to legislation on Equal Employment Opportunities, those professionals, in turn, were the ones that gave them no choice but to increase the representation. They wanted black agents. My Dad ended up opening his own office and business boomed for him. He was able to buy the house where they are living now and my Mom could stop working. He was most proud the day he was able to buy himself a top of the line Lexus. No one was allowed to touch that car except my Mom. And no one needed to. If you were responsible, he would buy you a car as soon as you qualified for a driver's license. Since we only had a two car garage, he had added a carport on the right side of the house for the kids' cars. That was a shorter distance for my Mom to unload groceries so she started parking her SUV in the carport. With her sewing room and the kitchen on that side of the house, my Mom would stay there all day long. If I pulled out that garage, it was a clean get-a-way."

"Clark, tell me you didn't!"

"I thought it was worth the risk. Marlene was four years older than me. She was a classmate of Cathy's. I had escorted Cathy to a dance and she introduced us. Marlene took for granted I was Cathy's older brother because of my height. Marlene's the one that taught me almost everything I know to please a woman in bed. She would go into her parents' bedroom when they were out and watch their adult video collection. When we hooked up, she wanted to practice, and we would try different things she had seen. One Saturday night, her parents were out when I called her. She had her own phone so she could talk about anything and not risk them hearing her. That night, she told me to call her back on the main line because she was looking at a movie in their room and would pick up the phone there.... Clay, she started describing everything she saw on the film so I knew exactly what we'd be doing the next time I took her out. I was getting really wound up right when my Mom picked up the line. We both heard the click and stopped talking immediately, but the movie was still playing in the background. I know my Mom must have heard some of it before Marlene pressed stop. Then we heard the click that she had hung up. I knew I needed to get off so I asked Marlene if we could hook up for the 7:15 pm movie the next night."

"So did you Mom come up to your room?"

"No, she didn't come into my room that night, and she never said anything until the next day. That Sunday was the day of our church's annual fundraiser. My Mom served on the committee so my parents went every year, and they never got home before eleven thirty. My Dad had called that morning and said his plane was delayed so he wouldn't get home on time. I got scared my window of time was narrowing. When my Mom went into the kitchen to finish up her cake for the fund raiser, I knew I needed to slip out and do a condom run."

"Damn, Clark."

"I had the car back and the overhead door was closing when I spotted my Mom coming towards the garage. I jumped out the car, locked the door from the inside, and closed it as quietly as I could. Then I ran over to my bike and took it off the rack. When I heard her open the door to step into the garage, I lifted the bike back onto the rack and turned to face her acting surprised to see her there. She told me she was going to the pantry to get more powdered sugar and thought she heard the garage door open.   I told her it was just me coming in from a quick ride. She looked at the bike and told me it was nice I was getting exercise."

Clay shook his head in disbelief, "Clark, you never lied but you were always so good at pulling out parts of the story and telling just enough pieces of the truth that a person would draw a different conclusion on their own."

The two cousins enjoyed another hearty laugh….

"It's good that Lexus was so smooth. If I had used her SUV, the engine would have still been ticking from cooling down, and she would still be able to smell the exhaust fumes."

"So, how did you get caught?"

"Because my Mom almost caught me, I hadn't enough time to reset the trip meter. My Dad used to do mileage studies so he always reset the trip meter to zero. When the cab pulled up, he went straight into the garage and dumped his brief case into the front seat since he knew he wouldn't use it until work the next morning. His eyes happened to glance at the trip meter and saw it registered four miles. He came in, kissed my Mom, and asked her if she had used the Lexus. She said, 'No,' and they both turned to look at me. That's when she asked who I was on the phone with the night before and I answered just some girl I met at a dance. She whispered something to my father and he smirked before turning serious and ordering me to his office."

Clark paused remembering those years before continuing.

"I held the family record on compositions. Having read my sisters' and having done this for two years already, I could get in that office, write the composition, listen to the lecture, and be out in thirty minutes. It was five thirty so I felt good about wrapping things up, but I couldn't clear my head…. My eyes just kept watching the clock tick away and the only thoughts that kept coming to me were what Marlene had described the night before."

Clay was thinking of an analogy, "Can't focus on anything but the lady. Watching the clock ticking away.... Just like in the ER."

"That's when I started wishing I was younger. "

"You didn't. Clark, please tell me you didn't."

"I did. That girl had me so wound up, I couldn't think straight. I stood up, took the composition book, slammed it onto the desk in front of him, and started screaming at him.... I told him, 'I've been stealing that car for nearly a year now. I haven't put a scratch on it. I haven't been stopped by the police. I haven't even got a parking ticket. I've been really careful....' Then I said, 'I promised Marlene I would bring her to the 7:15 movie, and if we're late for the show, she's going to be really pissed. I need you and Mom to leave and go to your old people's thing at the church so I can drive out of here by 6:30. Why don't you just beat me like you used to do so we can get this over with? Then everything can stay on schedule instead of me having to do all this writing crap.'"

"So, that's when he whipped you?"

"No. My Dad was cool. He didn't say anything. He didn't move. He just watched my face and waited until it dawned on me I had just revealed my plans.... When my expression changed, he very calmly said, 'I'm happy to accommodate your request, son.' That's when he came around the desk and beat the crap out of me!"

"Where was your Mom? She would have stopped him."

"A few of the neighbors had donated cakes for the event so she had taken the SUV and was out picking them up. She didn't get back until it was all over. When she walked in, she knew something had happened, but I was not going to say a word. She asked, 'Calvin? Clark? Is everything alright?' My Dad stared at me as he answered her, 'It is now that Clark has a new respect for what rules mean.'"

"So, you stopped stealing his car?"

"I didn't steal it that night because then I had to write three compositions: the one about driving without a license, one on lying to your parents, and one on showing proper respect to your father. No way I could do everything with Marlene and finish three before he got home so I had to call her and cancel.... I learned that night it is never worth it to lose your cool, and I haven't lost mine since. If I feel my emotions taking over, I literally walk away and come back to the situation once I can approach it logically again. Remember that, Clay. Walk away if you have to, but don't let your emotions rule your reaction."

"Man, I don't know if I could have got over my Dad doing that to me..."

"I can't say there wasn't tension between us after that and you could sense it whenever we were together until about two years ago."

"You'd been gone from home for years by then so what caused the change?"

"It wasn't him, it was me. When I bought the condo, I went over and asked him to change my renter's insurance to coverage for the condo. I gave him the info, and he went into his home office. I had sat down while my Mom was about to fix me breakfast when he came back in and told me to come to the study. He pointed to the same chair I sat in when I was fourteen. He started asking me questions about the value of the condo, the value of the Corvette, my current salary, and things like that. Then, he looked at me and said, 'Son, what you need is an umbrella policy. It's going to cost you a lot more than what you're paying in insurance for that apartment right now but let me explain why it's the way you need to go.' At my age, my Dad was still looking out for me. He started talking about liability and how even your salary was subject to liens. That's when I understood why my Dad overreacted when I was fourteen."

Looking at Clay, Clark knew he would have to hold a similar discussion with Clay once he took his job. He didn't have a clue either. Clark knew he also needed to raise the subject with his friends, especially Glenn.

"You felt he was right in whipping you to a point you were bruised."

"You agree that what I told him showed he was not getting through to me?"

"Hell yeah! You're in his office for using a car he told you not to touch when you don't even have a driver's license and you're telling him you're doing it again as soon as he walks out the door. But, Clark, to the point he bruised you?"

"When my Dad started talking to me about some of the lawsuits his clients had filed against them, I realized he might have lost everything if I had caused an accident as a minor driving without a license. If I had seriously hurt someone, he would have been sued to the point that even an umbrella policy may not have covered the settlement. He could have been ruined. I might have ruined my own future too. The lawsuit could have filed for a portion of any potential earnings I received in the future as an adult. "

"Man, I hadn't thought about it from that perspective."

"When I realized how foolish I had behaved when I was young, I knew the risk was not worth it. I was pondering all of that when I heard him say in an aggravated tone, 'Clark, are you listening to me?' I turned and looked him straight in the eye and said, 'No, sir!' He looked at me surprised and said, 'Son, I thought this was something important to you?' I answered him, 'It is but I've been sitting here in this same chair you've been sitting me in since I was a kid and I was thinking about something that was more important…. It was more important to me when I was growing up to have a father that knew saying, 'do it because I said to,' was not the way to raise a child…. It was more important to have a father that recognized when a child was able to reason, you needed to sit down and have discussions with them helping them to see for themselves why it was right or why it was wrong and to walk you through that decision making process….   It was more important to have a father who knew that was the best way to mentor a child into adulthood. And, until we sat down today to discuss this policy, I didn't fully understand that…. Thank you for being that kind of father…."

"Clark, now I'm regretting a little bit that I didn't come over and let him whip my ass too."

The two cousins started laughing again until Clark had to grab his side. When he could catch his breath, he continued.

"I could tell he was getting choked up and I was too but there was one more thing I had to get off my chest. I said, 'Dad, I want to apologize to you…. I'm sorry for what happened when I was fourteen. I know now I was the one that pushed you beyond the limit…. I'm sorry I forced your hand! That girl had my mind so messed up, you didn't have a choice. You did what you had to. It didn't feel that way back then but I know now it was because you loved me. Thank you, Dad!' That was the only time I ever saw my father cry. He got up, came around the desk and we were hugging each other and I started crying too. My Mom walked in complaining that breakfast was getting cold. When she saw us, she asked, 'Calvin? Clark? Is everything alright?' I looked at my Dad and said let me answer this time. I turned and told her, 'Mom, everything is fine now that I have a new respect for what rules mean.' Then he and I started laughing and we walked with his arm around my shoulder to the breakfast nook. We had a great discussion over breakfast. There was no tension between us anymore. From then on, we could speak openly and honestly about anything. It feels good, Clay. We're so tight now and it feels good. He can still give me that look that makes me feel like crap for days but I welcome it now. It's a sign I better stop and rethink what I'm doing."

The two cousins sat in silence each pondering the past events that had brought them to this day and apprehensive about the future.

Glancing at the clock, Clay stated, "Clark, I've got to run. I promised Joe and CeeCee's uncle I'd meet them at Joe's by 9:45. Need anything, man?"

Clark didn't change his position but spoke softly, "No, I can always punch the intercom, and Adrian would be right up. I'll be fine…. I'm just praying things will go better for you than they did for me last night."

"At least, I'll find out her real name if nothing else."

Clark thought, "After last night, I know that well. It's Cecelia Julien." He didn't share what Bernadette had told him the night before because Clay had enough baggage going into the meeting with Cecelia and Bernadette's father. No sense in Clay carrying Clark's baggage in with him.

"Clay, stay close to Joe. If her uncle is that protective, I'm worried about this father so just stay close to Joe. He's a good man. He'll have your back!"

"I will, man. Thank you again!"

Clark thought to himself, "If anything happens to Clay, I don't care that you are a cop. Aaron, you and I are going to have a faceoff, one-on-one, in a dark alley, and I'll gladly sit in a jail cell after."

When Clay got to the top of the stairs, he looked back at the sound of a drawer closing before stepping into the hallway. Clark was bent over, his elbows were resting on his knees, and his hands were supporting his forehead. Clay noticed one thing more. The ring case had been removed from the top of the nightstand.

Chapter Twenty-Six

Sunday morning in the Julien's household did not begin with the usual routine. Cecelia came in and placed Miki into her booster seat unceremoniously. Bernadette was slamming the silverware down by each place setting. Her father was the first to question his daughters.

"Bernadette, it's a good thing you're not in charge of setting the china. Every plate we have would be broken if you laid them down the same way you're handling that silverware…. Cecelia, what's wrong with you this morning? You just plopped that child down like she was a sack of sweet potatoes!"

Audra had also been studying her daughters, "Cecelia, why are your eyes so red? Have you been crying?"

The doorbell rang before attention was drawn back to Bernadette.

"I'll get it," Bernadette offered and quickly raced from the dining room through the living room to their front door. As she opened the door, she was taken aback.

"Good morning, Uncle Aaron, Joe, and…." There was a stranger with them that looked familiar.

Uncle Aaron provided the introduction, "This is Clay Laurent. He's Miki's father."

"Miki's father?" Bernadette couldn't believe what Uncle Aaron had just said.

Joe spoke up quickly, "And we came along because, this time, Cecelia is going to listen to what this young man has to say."

Joe must be really upset Bernadette thought since he called Cecelia by her given name instead of the nickname he assigned her when she became a waitress.

Uncle Aaron didn't wait for an invitation inside. He walked past Bernadette leading Joe and Clay to the dining room. Having participated in countless meals at his sister's house, he knew the family's Sunday morning routine well. The time they choose to arrive was not an accident.

As Clay passed Bernadette, she studied him wondering who the man was. He was shorter than Clark but not by more than two inches. Clay had to be at least six feet. He was a fairer complexion and of a slimmer build. Unlike Clark's, Clay's face was clean shaven. His eyes were a light brown, and his hair was coarser than Clark's. She knew that hair well. She had combed a head of hair like that a thousand times if once. His hair was exactly the same as Miki's.

"Are you from Ville Platte?" Bernadette blurted out.

Clay turned and his spirits seem to pick up over her question, "Yes. So, CeeCee told you about me?"

"No," thought Bernadette, "But I've met you Dad. You look just like him and so does my niece."

Bernadette first heard her mother greeting her elder brother.

She heard the pride in his voice as Clay asked with a tone indicating he already knew, "This is my daughter?"

The statement was quickly followed by Cecelia screaming, "Don't touch her!"

Bernadette's father yelled, "Is this the man that got my baby girl pregnant?"

Uncle Aaron quickly and firmly ordered, "Sit down, Junior! We're going to have a civil conversation."

By the time Bernadette locked the front door and reached the dining room, Cecelia was holding Miki protectively in her arms and running towards their bedroom crying.

Clay started to follow her, but Uncle Aaron grabbed his arm and pointed to the seat farthest away from Bernadette's Dad stating, "You need to talk to her father first."

Bernadette had never seen her father so stoic. Her mother glanced at the men that had invaded their otherwise peaceful surroundings, and unsure what to do, she asked, "May I get anyone a cup of coffee?"

Uncle Aaron was taking the lead, "Audra, pull out that bottle of bourbon Junior keeps hidden in the pantry behind the sugar and some shot glasses. We all are going to need something stronger."

Audra turned to oblige. Bernadette took the alternate hallway to the bedrooms to check on Cecelia and Miki. When she got to the bedroom, Cecelia was lying on the bed, holding Miki tightly against her, crying hysterically. The men's tone and Cecelia's actions were scaring the toddler. Miki had begun crying as well. Audra came in, picked up her granddaughter and left holding her gently and cooing to her that everything would be okay. Glancing over her shoulder, she called to Bernadette that the men were still in the dining room talking and that she was taking Miki to her room to calm her down leaving Bernadette to sit with Cecelia.

Cecelia had smothered her face in the pillow. Bernadette could tell by the movement of her shoulders that a flood of tears were still pouring. Bernadette picked up the large envelope she had placed on Cecelia's desk the day before. It was still unopened.

"Did you see this package that came from the university?" Bernadette was trying to approach things calmly though her head was spinning. What she heard this morning was not matching what Clark told her last night. She was getting angrier every minute. Her own happiness was tied to all of this so it was time for Cecelia to stop acting like a spoiled brat and confide in her. She needed to know the truth.

"Oh, Bernadette. Could you please drop the preaching to me about getting an education for just one lousy day? I saw the envelope when I got home, but I can't deal with that right now."

Cecelia turned and smothered her face in the pillow again. Bernadette was not going to let the subject dropped.

"I asked about the envelope because when the bell rang yesterday and the postman needed someone to sign for it, I received it. Then I took Miki and we rode to Joe's to bring it to you."

Cecelia turned her face just enough that she could look at Bernadette as she continued her story.

"When I got to the intersection right before Joe's place, I could see you in the parking lot arguing with a guy, but it wasn't this Clay who's in the room talking to our Dad now."

"I don't know the other guy. I see him in the restaurant often, but I don't wait the section where he sits. He's always in Lisa's area because he knows her sister Myra. All I know about him is what Lisa has shared. He had to be the one that brought Clay to Joe's."

"I know him. His name is Clark Laurent. I know him because I've been dating him."

Cecelia's eyes were wide. She sat up on the bed.

"You've been dating him? Are they brothers?"

"They're not.... I've met Clark's family, and he is the only boy. This guy Clay has to be his cousin. When I saw the two of you arguing in the parking lot, I turned quickly at the corner before you would see me and drove away.... Cecelia, PLEASE tell me what happened yesterday.... I need to know."

Cecelia started crying again but her tears were more controlled this time. "Everything happened so fast, I'm not sure of it all.... Rhonda called out sick so Joe split her section between me and Lisa. I was in the kitchen area getting a tray when Joe seated Clay and the guy you said is named Clark in the area I had to cover. My back was to Clay when I served the plates so I didn't know he was there until I turned to take their order.... I haven't seen Clay since the day I told him I was pregnant.... I couldn't believe he was sitting right there in front of me.... I was so shocked to see him that I slammed the tray down on their table and walked away as fast as I could.... I could hear him telling that guy Clark, 'That's CeeCee!'

I went to Joe and told him I could not wait on that table. Joe was asking me why when I realized Clay was right behind me. He grabbed my arm and turned me to face him. I pulled away and screamed at him that I didn't want to talk to him. I started crying and I... I ran out into the parking lot."

Cecelia paused for a moment, blowing her nose before continuing.

"The guy Clark must have convinced Clay to let him approach me first because he was the one that came to meet me in the parking lot... He walked up to me and he was speaking so softly that I started calming down. Then he put his hands on my upper arms.... He wasn't hurting me at all, just trying to get my attention. His hands were firm but gentle. He was just trying to get me to look at him.... It worked. I looked up, and he had the kindest expression.... He kept saying things to me that were so soothing that we didn't break eye contact after that."

"Things like what?"

"He kept his eyes focused on mine. It was hypnotizing. He apologized first. He said he was sorry me and Clay met again like that. He said he knew it was a shock.... He talked about everything I was feeling at the moment. It's like he could read my mind. I couldn't help but stare into his eyes and nod in agreement with everything he said.... It finally got to a point I was calm, and then he started saying that Clay and I needed to sit down and talk.... When he said that, I got really upset and started crying again and screaming, 'Please don't make me! I don't want to.' I kept saying it over and over again.... That's when everything blew up."

"What do you mean?" Bernadette demanded remembering Clark's face.

Cecelia hung her head in shame. Now that she knew the relationship between Bernadette and Clark, she couldn't admit to her that she had called Uncle Aaron on her cell the minute she stepped outside. She had told him the guy who raped her was there. She was only hoping to get revenge on Clay for not marrying her. She hadn't anticipated that Clark would be caught in the middle.

Bernadette could sense Cecelia was disgusted with what she shared next.

"Uncle Aaron was working that day so he was driving into the parking lot ready to hit Joe up for his free lunch as always. I guess when he saw Clark's hands holding me and me screaming, he may have overreacted a little bit."

Bernadette closed her eyes before demanding, "How? How did he overreact?"

"Like I said, that's when things got really crazy…. Clark was focused only on me, but I saw the police car pull into the parking lot behind him. Uncle Aaron got out and was running towards us looking really angry. When my expression changed and my eyes diverted to him, Clark let go of my arms and started to turn. He looked like he was trying to protect me from whatever scared me…. But, as he started to turn, Uncle Aaron hit him so hard in the face that blood spurted and Clark fell to the ground."

Seeing Bernadette's reaction, Cecelia tried to make things sound less serious.

"Maybe he didn't fall because the blow was so hard but because he was also slightly off balance. Uncle Aaron hit him right at the point he was repositioning himself."

"So what happened next?"

"Uncle Aaron screamed at him to lay face down and put his hands behind his back. Then he handcuffed him."

"He handcuffed Clark?"

"Then he pulled him into a sitting position, but things got more chaotic. I was about to explain to Uncle Aaron that Clark was not the one, but Clay must have been watching. He came running out yelling at Uncle Aaron to leave Clark alone. I screamed to Uncle Aaron, 'That's Miki's father.

Keep him away from me!' Then Uncle Aaron said, 'He's the other guy that raped you?'"

Cecelia wiped the tears from her eyes and blew her nose. Then she looked at Bernadette and reluctantly admitted, "You should have seen the expression on Clark's face when he realized he was in handcuffs because the charge was rape…. He's really a nice guy. I felt so bad and I was so embarrassed, I didn't know what to do. I couldn't look at him anymore."

"His career would be over," Bernadette said, "A rape charge, especially of a minor, would ruin him."

Bernadette remembered the lie Cecelia told when she couldn't hide the pregnancy anymore. She had claimed two men had forced her into the janitor's closet in an isolated wing of the university's library. No one believed her story, and after four months, anything would be difficult to prove. Being Catholic and at the stage she was in the pregnancy, her parents were resigned to the fact she was going to have a child. When Cecelia was adamant she would not give the baby up for adoption, everyone was even more skeptical of her initial story. Everyone that is, except Uncle Aaron, who swore he'd work with the district attorney's office and have them throw the book at the guys if he ever caught them. He'd have them charged with everything he possibly could.

"Did you explain? Did he let Clark go?"

"I didn't have time! Clay started walking towards us with an angry look on his face. Uncle Aaron stepped between us so I turned and walked towards my car in the back of the lot. I got in, closed the door, and was just going to drive away."

"And then?"

"I'm not sure. Since my back had been to them…. I know Joe and Lisa had come out because I heard Joe screaming at Uncle Aaron to leave the guys alone. Uncle Aaron was screaming at Clay to turn and put his hands behind his back. Clark was screaming at Clay to stop arguing and just do

what the cop said. I think I heard Lisa on the phone calling for Myra's
husband."

"Why would she call her brother-in-law?"

"Myra's husband Tyrone works for Uncle Aaron. He's a cop too and he
knows Clark well from events their company has held. I guess she
thought Tyrone might help since Clark was the one that got Myra her
promotion.... I just wanted to leave and get away from all of it and Clay.
When I closed my car door, Clay must have realized I was leaving and he
screamed at me, 'CeeCee, don't you run away from me again!' I saw him
break out in a run towards me. Joe tried to stop Uncle Aaron but he
pulled out that billy club and started after Clay. When Clark saw him do
that, he ran too and caught up with them. Right when Uncle Aaron was
about to hit Clay, Clark pushed himself in between and blocked the hit
but I know the club caught his right shoulder. All three of them went
flying to the ground. Uncle Aaron got really mad then! He put his knee in
Clay's back and handcuffed him. Then he took that billy club and went to
whack Clark with it. He looked like he was going for his head, but Clark
twisted and he hit him in the side instead. It sounded so loud, I
screamed. Then Joe was grabbing Uncle Aaron's arm trying to keep him
from hitting Clark again. Customers were coming out the restaurant to
watch. It seems everyone was screaming at someone all at the same
time. Then Tyrone drove his squad car into the parking lot with the siren
and lights blaring. Lisa started pointing the direction out to him. Tyrone
got out and came rushing through the parking lot with Lisa behind him
screaming at him to get Uncle Aaron to stop. I just drove out the back
driveway as fast as I could and came home."

Bernadette tried to hold her emotions in check when she asked, "So, you
don't know if Uncle Aaron ever actually arrested them and had them
charged on the books?"

"I don't know.... But he must have let them go. How else would Clay be
here and not in jail?"

Bernadette thought, "With the Laurents' money, they would have easily posted bail." She exhaled sharply. Bernadette remembered Uncle Aaron turning red faced when he had learned Cecelia was pregnant. He had always been as protective of Bernadette and Cecelia as their parents.

Cecelia turned to Bernadette with a concerned look on her face. They reached for each other at the same time and embraced. They sat holding each other until Bernadette remembered what Clark told her at Blaine's. Letting her sister go, she turned and propped her leg on top of the bed so she could face her better.

"Cecelia, Clark and I were at dinner last night. Because I mistook what was going on between the two of you in the parking lot, I asked him if he was responsible for you getting pregnant and he said 'yes.' Why would he say that?"

Cecelia looked confused at first shaking her head in disbelief. She turned towards Bernadette and started pleading with her to believe her, "I have NEVER had sex with Clark. He's been coming to the restaurant for about two years now. If Lisa isn't there or if her section is filled, I try to avoid waiting on him. He's nice but always there with two other guys, and one of them kind of acts a little obnoxious."

Bernadette immediately knew the two Cecelia meant.

"I hadn't really talked to him that much until yesterday.... I don't know why he told you that.... Clay Laurent, not Clark Laurent, is Miki's father."

"Cecelia, how did you meet Clay? How could you get pregnant when none of us even knew you were dating?"

Bernadette was ashamed at the comments she just made. Her relationship with Clark had been just a friendship. When it changed, she never mentioned him to Cecelia or her parents. She fully expected Cecelia to throw back at her, "Like me not knowing about you and Clark dating?" But Cecelia didn't. They were having, for the first time in their lives, a confidential conversation between two sisters. There was full trust between them and a healing was finally taking place. They were forgiving each other for any transgressions from their past and were willing to embrace a new future.

"Remember the program I attended at your alma mater the summer before my junior year?"

"You're talking about the college prep program the university sponsors to introduce high school students to life on a college campus?" Bernadette wanted to add but didn't, "The one you were in when you claimed you were raped in the library?"

"Clay was there that summer too. He was taking some pre-engineering courses. I saw him in the cafeteria, and I fell in love with him right then. I walked over and introduced myself…. I was scared he wouldn't talk to me if he knew I was just in high school so I didn't correct him when he asked what I was majoring in. I let him believe I was taking college classes too. I told him my name was CeeCee, and I used Mom's maiden name."

"Why?" Bernadette was trying to control her anger over Cecelia's deception.

"I thought if he knew my real name he might find out I was just in high school if he was around when the counselors called out the roll to make sure they had everybody."

"But, didn't you have to wear a special camp T-shirt all the time you were on campus to distinguish you as a high school student in the program?"

"I told Clay I was wearing it only because I was a counselor too, and the counselors were allowed to do so since they get a free shirt for being part of the program."

Cecelia hung her head ashamed before continuing.

"I told him we were not allowed to socialize when we were in charge of the kids so I could only meet him at the student center after the program ended."

"I know that campus well. My friend Valerie stayed in the dorm and I spent many nights on campus studying in her room. I also know only the girls' dorm had private rooms. How did you get pregnant?"

Cecelia sighed before explaining. "Clay was not in a dorm. He was staying at a relative's apartment that summer…. The relative was away for the Fourth of July holiday so Clay had access to a car, and we had the apartment all to ourselves. We were over there the entire weekend."

"The weekend we thought the program took the campers to Baton Rouge to visit the Capitol? You lied about that too?"

Bernadette could tell Cecelia was ashamed of her actions….

"The campers did go to Baton Rouge for the weekend. I changed the permission slip after Dad signed it so they wouldn't call the house and ask why I didn't show up. When you dropped me off by the buses, I went around the back of the bus and ran over to the student center…. Clay was waiting for me there."

"Was it Clark's apartment? Was it a condo close to the riverfront?"

"I never met who was living there so I don't know if it was Clark's place. It wasn't by the riverfront. The apartment where Clay stayed was out in New Orleans East."

They both sat on the bed silently. Without knocking, their father suddenly swung the door open and eyed Cecelia. They didn't need to know how much Clay had said to tell he had shared enough of what happened that summer for their father to know Cecelia had played a big part in the events.

Focusing just on Cecelia, he spoke in a harsh voice, "Straighten your clothes. Get in the bathroom and wash your face. Make yourself presentable. That young man is in the den now alone and waiting to talk to you. And this time, baby girl, you're going to listen to what that boy has to say."

Their father's expression was saying it all. They knew that expression well. You better do what he said and you better do it now. Cecelia responded, "Yes, sir," before jumping off the bed and scurrying down the hallway to the bath.

Audra walked in at the moment announcing she had rocked Miki until she calmed down, and the three years old was sleeping. Junior looked at his wife and daughter and stated, "Cecelia's about to have a conversation she should have had almost four years ago. I think we're finally going to clean up this mess."

With that, he turned and walked back to the dining room where he, Uncle Aaron, and Joe began talking about the old times when they were younger. Audra looked at Bernadette and told her she was going to fix them each a plate of dinner.

After her mother left, Bernadette walked to her own room. She sat on the top of the bed with her back leaning against the headboard. Grabbing a pillow and hugging it against her, she thought about everything Cecelia had told her. She now understood every reaction and comment from Clark the night before: why he seemed to wince and groan when she mentioned her Uncle Aaron; why his face was bruised, swollen, and bandaged; and why he seemed so willing to just yield to her questions without bothering to explain. Being Cecelia's sister, it was right for him to assume that Bernadette knew everything about Cecelia and Clay. Bernadette understood now why he didn't challenge anything she said.

Bernadette sat in silence for a while thinking about the months they had been together. Clark was never ambiguous. He said exactly what he meant, and he answered exactly what you asked him. Bernadette had not asked him if he was Miki's father; she had asked him if he was responsible for Cecelia getting pregnant. Now she understood the role he felt he had played. If he knew that Clay had brought Cecelia to his apartment, Clark would feel responsible for whatever had happened there. She had no doubts now that he had found out. She also had no doubts, having been with him for so long, that he would take that responsibility upon his own shoulders.

Chapter Twenty-Seven

Clay entered the condo floating on a cloud. He couldn't wait to tell Clark how well the day had ended. At the end of the day, he and Cecelia had sat with her parents to discuss a wedding date, and they had initially chosen the Fourth of July weekend. With the holiday falling on a Friday that year, the three day weekend would afford out of town family members more time for travel and Clay would be off from work as well. He could catch a flight and arrive in time for the rehearsal Thursday night as long as the priest did not insist the meeting start before 7:00 pm.

Literally running down the hallway, Clay stopped short at the top of the stairs. Clark was neither in bed nor resting in the armchair. He went down the stair and entered his home office on the left. An ominous feeling came over Clay. He retreated slowly down the hallway and climbed the stairs to the upper wing. Arriving at the top, the French doors were open and a breeze was blowing in from the river.

Walking through the French doors, Clay shivered at the dampness in the air. He spotted Clark leaning against the corner column, his right thigh propped on the railing. Being six floors up, it was unnerving to see him sitting that way. He was not wearing a shirt and seemed oblivious to the weather conditions. His left hand was holding a drink against his midriff, and his right hand was holding a cigarette. Clark's friend Willy had started him smoking when they were in college. Between the nicotine in the cigarettes and the caffeine in coffee, they hoped to get enough increased energy and alertness to stay up all night studying for tough tests and exams. The day he graduated from college, Clark had stopped cold turkey and, to Clay's knowledge, hadn't picked up a cigarette since. He was trying to recapture or connect to something from his college days.

Clay grew more upset to see him smoking and drinking. With his current physical condition, Clark would not have driven just to make a cigarette run but an entire carton was on the table on the lanai. "Adrian," Clay thought and wished there was a law against accommodating detrimental requests for tips.

Clay walked up to him, but Clark kept his gaze on the river and didn't acknowledge him.

Stepping closer, Clay questioned, "How are you feeling?"

At first Clay thought Clark didn't hear him because he took two more puffs before responding. His gaze didn't shift as he spoke.

"Glenn called this afternoon…. His father passed." Clark took one more puff before adding, "He's shipping the body back to the states. The services should be Friday."

Clay closed his eyes and took a deep breath. When he opened them again, Clark's position had not changed. He was still silently puffing the cigarette. Not knowing how to reach out to him, Clay turned and retired to the guest room. As he walked down the stairway, he thought about everything that had happened over only two days. "How ironic Clark lost the woman he loved the same weekend Clay found his. Now this…. How much more can he bear?" Clay wondered.

Clay had called the airline and changed his flight from Sunday to that Monday which was Memorial Day. When he woke that morning, his immediate thought was of Clark. He walked down the hallway, and once again, he was not in his bedroom. The scent of bacon frying wafted to his nostrils, and Clay knew he was in the kitchen. When he got to the top of the stairs, Clark was flipping over hash browns.

"Good morning," he called turning to see Clay behind him, "Thought I'd give you one decent home cooked meal before you left."

"Anything I can do?"

"Yes, sit down and eat," Clark responded as he served up the plates and walked over to the dinette.

"So, how did it go yesterday?"

"Clark, she had the baby! It's a little girl, and she is the sweetest little kid I've ever seen!"

Clark started laughing, "I think I'm hearing a little parental pride."

"When I first got there, I had a discussion with her father arbitrated, believe it or not, by Uncle Aaron with Joe butting in now and then. It wasn't as bad as I thought. Maybe I felt that way because, once I saw Miki, I would have walked over hot coals."

"Miki? Is that her name? I like that."

"It turns out that's just her nickname. Her given name is Michelle."

"Michelle Laurent. Has a nice ring...."

"Well, it's not Laurent right now. It's Michelle Julien."

"She didn't put your name on the birth certificate? Your child is carrying her maiden name?"

"No, she didn't!"

"So, you're going to have to adopt your own child?"

Clark's expression indicated woe to the woman who denied his paternity. Trying to ease the tension he knew was building and wanting him to accept his future wife, Clay relayed what he thought was positive about the visit. "After I explained I wanted to marry her but couldn't find her, her father seemed to be on my side. He let us sit in the den and talk, just the two of us. CeeCee listened to me this time. When I explained everything the way I wanted to that day, I felt good she still loved me. Then we sat with her parents and started making plans. Joe and Uncle Aaron left then. Her sister Bernadette brought the baby in when she woke up from her nap. I got to play with her and, Clark, by the time I left, she said, 'Bye, Daddy.' Man, I started crying."

Clark gave Clay a soft punch to his shoulder.

"Hey, I forgot. " Clay pulled out his wallet. "I have a picture of her from her birthday party. She made three last month."

"So this is my little cousin," Clark smiled.

"Okay if I tell her to call you Uncle Clark? It always felt more like we were brothers than cousins."

"I'd like that," Clark answered as he handed the picture back to Clay.

"Clark, is it okay if I crash at your place every weekend, and would you mind if she slept over? I'd really like to get to know my daughter. One of the things we talked about is me getting to visit until we're married. Cecelia is okay with me picking her up on a Friday night and keeping her for the weekend as long as I have her home Sunday morning in time to go to mass with the family."

"I already have your code in the system. I'll just change the file to remove the expiration date and make it permanent. The place is at your disposal."

"Thanks, Clark."

"What time do we need to leave for the airport?"

"Hey, you need to rest. I'll just take a cab."

"No way…. I picked you up, and I'm bringing you back. I'm feeling a lot better today."

"So, what are your plans for the week?"

"Tomorrow Glenn will be arriving with Angelique and his mother so he's coming over to hang out a bit."

"Gwen is not traveling with him?"

"I found out when we talked that they're in the process of a divorce so I doubt I'll see her on Friday."

"What about custody? Isn't that one of the reasons Glenn stayed with Gwendolyn?"

"Turns out he'll be getting full custody. When nothing the doctors here is the states were doing for his father seemed to help, Glenn wanted him to try an experimental cancer treatment the Europeans had developed. Gwen put her foot down. She told Glenn, 'If you bring that smell of death into my house, I'm filing for a divorce.' He reminded her it was his house too and he held his ground this time. When they met with the lawyers, she told him for the right price, he could have Angelique. He told me it hurt his heart to hear a mother speak that way about her child. He knew for certain the only reason she became pregnant was to have a hold on him and his money. After that, he didn't say another word to her. He let the lawyers do all of the negotiations."

"So, how much assets will he have to liquidate to settle with her?"

"None," Clark smiled before continuing, "Gwen didn't care about anything but spending. Glenn told me she never looked over their income tax statements but just signed her name. As long as he kept meeting her demands, she didn't want to be bothered with their financials. When I saw how things were between them that time I was in Houston, I hinted he needed to start filtering money to his Mom so his parents would be taken care of if something happened to him. He took that advice and had a significant sum he had invested in his mother's name. When the lawyers settled on the price for Gwen to walk away and his lawyer assured him it was the best settlement he would be able to get, he said he pulled out the checkbook for his mother's account, wrote out a check for the settlement, and handed it directly to her. He told me seeing her face when he handed over that check was the happiest day of his marriage since Angelique was born. It's ironic that the happiest day would be when it ended."

"Gwen must not have suspected he had other funds he could access and she couldn't touch?"

"She didn't, and the papers were all signed before he played his hand so there was nothing she could do about it. The lawyers told him there was nothing she could have done anyway since it was legally Glenn's mother's account. He hasn't heard from or seen her since. Since his parents were living with them, his mother was there to help with Angelique so all was well.... I felt a little better to hear his parents were still in Europe so he could spend those last days with his father."

"Are you sure you don't need me to stay?"

"I'm fine. I have some other business to handle tomorrow. I finally read the care instructions from the ER so I'll go Wednesday and get these stitches removed and on Thursday I'll be at the lawyers with Glenn. He wants me to have power of attorney over some things back here at home for him and his mother. It may make settling things here in New Orleans easier until he's able to return permanently to the states. His mother is going to live with him and help him raise his daughter. I should be back at work next Monday."

"Clark, if you need me for anything, just call. I'll be on the first flight I can get!"

"Well, if we don't hurry and get you to the airport, that won't be necessary. You can't come back unless you leave."

The two cousins laughed as they rose from the table. After piling the dishes into the sink, they headed for the airport.

When Clay flew in the next weekend to visit with Miki and walked out to where Clark usually met him at the Louis Armstrong International Airport in New Orleans, Clark pitched him a set of car keys.

"I don't think CeeCee's parents will like the idea of you picking up their granddaughter in a Corvette, and based on what you told me, CeeCee needs a new car anyway, especially if she ever makes that drive between Dallas and New Orleans."

Clay pressed the unlock button on the key and the lights of a dark blue Subaru Impreza parked at the curb blinked.

"A wedding gift from me," Clark responded to the glare Clay gave him.

"So, that's the other business Clark had to handle on Tuesday," Clay surmised. He started to argue with his cousin the gift was too extravagant, but he knew it was an argument he would lose. In lieu, he swung his arms around Clark and hugged him gently whispering, "Thank you, cousin."

Chapter Twenty-Eight

Clark had called Robert at home late Sunday afternoon and requested the entire week of the Memorial Day holiday off from work. They were closed Monday anyway for the holiday so it would be only four days officially. Robert hesitated responding because the request surprised him. Clark rarely took vacation. He took a day here or there usually because of a family event, but he couldn't recall Clark ever being away from work for an entire week at a time. Thinking of the years he had been working at the firm, Robert estimated he had used a maximum of fifteen percent of what he was entitled to in any given year. When Robert didn't respond immediately, Clark mentioned the funeral. Robert had met Glenn on several occasions and knew they were as close as brothers. He understood well Clark needing those days. But when Clark returned the following Monday, he wasn't focused.

Robert would pass by Clark's office and see him just staring at Bernadette's picture and twirling a pen in his hand. Robert decided he would give Clark one more week. As tight a ship as Clark ran, two weeks off would not hurt anything. By Friday afternoon Clark still seemed distracted, and Robert could tell his executive administrative assistant, Myra, was also becoming concerned. Robert determined he needed to arrive at the office early on Monday to meet with Clark before the day got hectic.

As the clock on the wall in Clark's office chimed noting the 5:00 p.m. hour, Myra stepped in with her purse slung on her shoulder, "Clark, do you need anything before I leave for the weekend?"

"No, Myra, I'm fine."

"You should call it a night too." She looked at him concerned as he didn't look up but remained focus on Bernadette's picture. He finally turned and faced her.

"I will soon, and Myra, thanks to you and Tyrone…."

"No problem, Clark. With all you've done for me and your generosity to Lisa, loyalty is the least we owe you," she winked at him knowing exactly what he meant. Clark knew Tyrone would have told his wife how Clark got the stitches on his face and he was grateful she hadn't shared the story with Robert. Things had turned out fine and neither he nor Clay had anything on record; but once a story like that got out at the office, there would always be doubts about him. He would have had to keep his guard up.

As Myra cut off the lights in her office, he turned and stared at Bernadette's picture again. He recalled the story he shared with Clay, but he hadn't shared in entirety all that had happened when his father had administered the brutal punishment when he was fourteen.

Despite the harsh punishment he had received, Clark was still determined not to give up his independence. He knew his father was going to start recording the odometer readings as well as watching the trip meter.   When he arrived at school on Monday, he had approached his friend Victor whose father was a mechanic. Victor was confident he could find out for Clark how to roll the odometer back. All Clark had to do was provide him the year, make, and model of the car. Once Victor thought he had figured out how to do it, he'd have Clark bring the car over so the two of them could test the process.

On Monday night, Clark had snuck into his father's office and set the intercom so he would be able to eavesdrop into his early Tuesday scheduling meeting. By then his Dad was traveling a lot acting as a mentor to new Afro-Americans opening their own agency. He'd fly out, meet with them and confirm everything was set up properly, and work with them until he was comfortable they were starting off on the right foot. He also did follow-up visits to ensure everything was operating to their corporate standards. But if the person was really sharp, he wouldn't stay as long. Clark needed to not just know he would be out of town but also the probability of the trip getting cut short and getting surprised by his father arriving home early.

He had removed his pajamas but hadn't started dressing for school yet because he was taking notes at the intercom. The conference call was finally ending so he had placed the notepad on his bed and had turned to pull his uniform out the closet. Still nude, he jumped and turned his head to see who had opened the door to his room.

"Clark, I'm sorry for walking in on you without knocking. I was afraid you had overslept, son. It's almost time to leave for school."

His mother didn't comment on them but had stared at the bruises on his buttocks and thighs.

As Clark dressed, he heard the door to his father's office open and slam shut. He went back over to the intercom and listened to his mother speaking with controlled anger in her voice and emphatically.

"You best mute that speakerphone." She paused for a second, and when the line went dead, he heard her continue, "Calvin, discipline is one thing but, if you EVER hit him so hard that you bruise our son again, that will be the LAST day of our marriage. I WILL file for a divorce and I WILL win this house, both cars, the savings and checking accounts, alimony, child support, and full custody of him! You wanted a son, and it took us six tries to get him. I swear you'll lose him! Is my message clear?"

He didn't hear his father respond but he must have given some indication that he understood a line had been drawn in the sand. He heard his mother's shoes on the hardwood floor. After the door of the study slammed again, his father's office went silent.

When Clark came down to breakfast, he couldn't tell anything had happened between his parents. Everyone was sitting around the dining room table laughing and talking as usual. When he finished drinking his coffee, his father rose, walked over to his mother, and gave her the usual kiss. She was wonderfully receptive and even smiled at him as he turned to leave for work.

Observing the exchange between them knowing what had just transpired, he thought, "That's the kind of marriage I want, one with complete honesty. Say what you have to say and then just let it go. Don't be mad for days and not speaking to each other. Don't hold grudges. Set the ground rules and move on. If something was not negotiable, say how you felt so your partner knew where the line was drawn in the sand." Also in that moment, he knew he would never touch that Lexus again, not after hearing what his mother had said. If he ever wrecked that car, he better die in the accident…. If he didn't then, his father was going to kill him anyway once he got home. He couldn't bear the thought of being the cause of his parents divorcing.

Fridays had become a standing dinner date with Bernadette. Clark continued staring at her picture as he thought about everything he recalled. Had he finally got his wish? Was this the type of relationship he and Bernadette had developed? It's definitely how things had started out as he remembered the first time they had met at Joe's place and her cocky response when he asked her out. *"That sounds like the bet has something to do with you taking me out because I'm FAT? Am I right?"*

A slight smile crossed his face. You couldn't be more open and honest than that. Their entire relationship had begun and been built on that premise. His face turned grim as he remembered the last words she had spoken to him, "I don't EVER want to see YOU again!"

That definitely didn't sound like she was ever going to let the past go. What was unfair is that he had already crossed the line in the sand before he knew it was drawn. One sentence and the woman he had been waiting for had stepped out his life and moved on. After Clay and CeeCee had reconciled, he had hoped Bernadette would call. He could also understand if she didn't after everything she and her family had gone through both financially and emotionally.

Clark sighed, reached across his desk, and picked up the picture of Bernadette. As he stared into her eyes, he began thinking of the years he had sacrificed to get where he was. He had often heard that success was when preparation met opportunity. He thought about the books on leadership he had read, the weekend degree program he had completed to earn his masters, the online courses he continues to take, the seventy hour weeks he had worked. Then he thought about how quickly it all could have been taken from him.

He spoke to the picture in his hands, "Would you have been worth it, Bernadette? Would you have been worth me losing everything I've struggled and sacrificed for?"

He was a man paid to make decisions and, at that moment, he made a final one. Then he rose and cut off the lights in his office as well.

Robert arrived at the office at 7:30 Monday morning. He greeted Myra and was walking past her desk to Clark's office.

'Excuse me, sir. He's in a meeting."

Robert looked at Myra confused, "At 7:30?"

"I know it's early, sir, but he's been sending E-mails to me and his direct reports all weekend. He called each of them last night and said he was having a strategy meeting this morning. Then he called me, gave me a count, and told me have strong coffee and pastries available no later than 6:15. They have been in session since 6:30."

"6:30?" Robert gave her a concerned look before asking, "Has anyone quit yet?"

Myra started laughing before replying, "No, sir. Not to my knowledge."

"Then things must be going well. Myra, I'm not going to disturb them but I would like to peek in for a second using the service area."

"Yes, sir."

"Don't get up. I know the way."

Robert walked out the office and went a short distance down the hall to a small entrance door. Beyond was a kitchen area common to both his office and Clark's. Within this space, Myra and Robert's executive secretary could brew coffee, warm pastries, and serve light lunches. The area was adequately equipped to provide basic amenities if Robert or Clark was meeting with important clients. On either side, the walls could open displaying a counter for serving buffet style. The counter adjoining Clark's office was set with food items known for energizing, and no decaf coffee had been brewed.

Clark was the only one not sitting. Robert observed one person trying not to yawn. Another kept blinking their eyes. Poster boards were hung completely around the office. Clark had an array of colored markers in his left hand. He was walking around the room throwing out ideas, calling on a particular team member for their feedback, and using the different colors to record the facts they needed to capture. The man was energized. Ideas were flowing out of his mouth faster than a secretary could have documented in short hand.

Myra stepped in to brew a fresh pot of coffee.

Robert whispered to her, "It seems our kingpin is back, and he's in rare form."

Myra looked at Clark before smiling at Robert and nodding as she whispered back, "Yes, sir."

Before turning to leave, Robert noticed the space on Clark's desk where Bernadette's portrait stood was empty. He glanced one more time at Clark guessing it wasn't just the death of Glenn's father that had triggered the temporary lapse. Robert had wondered about the wound by his cheekbone. Seeing Bernadette's picture gone, he now assumed they had a terrible argument, and the scar was the result of her striking him with an object. He wondered what Clark possibly could have done to get her that angry. He hadn't pictured her to be the type that would get physical, but one never knew…. After meeting Bernadette at Clark's for dinner, both he and Angela had left hoping a permanent relationship was forming. He'd have to break the bad news to Angela.

Chapter Twenty-Nine

Bernadette, her mother, and Cecelia were having a grand time shopping for items needed for the upcoming wedding. It seems the preparations were bringing them all closer together. Bernadette had never felt such a strong bond, and she knew a new chapter in their relationships was forming. Though her father had provided a set budget for the event, Clay had told Cecelia he would supplement the budget to ensure she got everything done her way. He had given Cecelia a credit card, and based on the number of times she had pulled it out that day, one thing he didn't need was to also provide instructions on how to use it, especially if Cecelia saw something for Miki. Cecelia would turn to her mother and Bernadette and state that the outfit was just so cute that Clay would want her to have it. Cecelia had bought Miki more outfits in one day than the child normally got in a year. The three of them were holding so many bags, Bernadette bumped into a lady as they exited the bridal store.

"Excuse me, please," she muttered before turning to see Angela.

"Bernadette?"

"Angela?"

Bernadette had not seen the wife of Clark's boss since the dinner party when she and Clark had prepared the meal together.

"It's been months. We haven't got together since before Christmas. I enjoyed that night so much. We really need to get together again."

"Maybe for lunch," Bernadette offered trying to guide the conversation away from anything that could involve Clark.

"That would be great. Just us girls...." Angela took the bait touching Bernadette's arm lightly indicating it would be their little secret.

"Did you try any of the recipes I gave you?"

"Yes I did and each came out perfect. Your directions were so clear and the food was so great, I told Robert you really need to consider writing a cookbook. I really feel you'd have a winner."

"I never thought about that. Our recipes have just been handed down, sometimes on pieces of scrap paper. It would be a better way to preserve what has been passed down through the generations. Even if I never get published, I should at least put them on something more permanent. Thank you, Angela. That's a great idea and who knows where it may lead."

Angela smiled and touched Bernadette's arm again. She crinkled her face a little before inquiring, "So, how's Clark?"

Angela's face showed she knew that was a sore subject with Bernadette, but Bernadette remained cordial. Bernadette decided to sidestep the question and not answer it directly.

"Angela, believe it or not, my sister is engaged and about to marry Clark's cousin. That's why we were carrying so many packages. The wedding is the Fourth of July weekend so we're so busy, there just aren't enough hours in the day for us to get together like we use to."

"Maybe it's just the wedding preparations then?" Angela surmised with a questioning look on her face.

When Angela saw Bernadette was confused, she continued.

"Robert told me last night he is a little concerned about Clark so isn't it funny I would LITERALLY run into to you today."

Bernadette knew Angela was trying to downplay the comment, and Bernadette obviously showed enough genuine concern by the comment that Angela felt free to elaborate.

"It's not that he's not performing, my dear. Trust me. Clark's performance has never been an issue but it seems he's been pushing himself even harder. Robert feels too hard. He is also pushing his staff hard, too. He seems to be less patient with them. Not that his feedback isn't on target and appropriate, but it's just different than the way he approached things in the past. He's grown less tolerant. Robert was just wondering if things were going along alright in his personal life. I'll let him know about the wedding. That's probably it...."

"Since Memorial weekend, we have all been a little stressed preparing for a wedding in just about five weeks."

"Bernadette, I believe that is when Robert said he noticed the change in Clark. Last week, Robert had given Clark a special assignment. He thought it would take him at least three weeks to complete it but Clark turned it in last Friday afternoon. Robert commented the report Clark gave him was fit for publication. With the quality and accuracy of what Robert saw, he felt Clark must have been working day and night."

"Clark has so much respect for Robert, I'm sure he just didn't want to disappoint him."

"That's a good point, Bernadette. I'll mention it to Robert."

"Angela, my mother and sister are waiting. I really need to go."

"I'm sorry, dear. I didn't mean to just go on that way. You run along, and we'll get together for lunch soon."

Bernadette stepped away quickly wondering how she would be able to avoid conversations surrounding Clark if Angela called and wanted to set a date. Angela's words reminded her of what Valerie had said the weekend before she and Clark broke up, *"That man's body is just like that can of shaken soda. Girlfriend, after five weeks, he is ready to explode.... His nerves must be shot!"*

Bernadette felt guilty but wasn't sure why. After all, Angela said his performance was exemplary. She just hoped Clark wasn't pushing himself too hard because of what had happened between them.

Bernadette found her mother and Cecelia in the food court. As soon as she dropped the packages she had been carrying on a vacant chair, she noticed a hand waving at her. Recognizing the hostess from Chef Blaine's, she excused herself one more time and walked over to greet her. As she was walking towards the table, she saw Chef Blaine come up, sit down, and hand the hostess a double scoop ice cream cone.

"The lady from the restaurant is walking over. I can't wait to see her ring again."

"What?" Chef Blaine looked up and saw Bernadette approaching.

"Don't mention the ring. The guy told me on the way home they broke up."

"They wouldn't have if she had seen that ring first."

Chef Blaine nudged his daughter as Bernadette got within earshot. He stood, greeted Bernadette, asked if he had ever mentioned the hostess, Megan, was his daughter and offered to buy Bernadette ice cream. She explained she wasn't alone but shopping with her mother and sister for her sister's wedding. Megan glanced at her father who kicked her under the table indicating to be quiet.

"When's the date?" Chef Blaine inquired.

"July 5th? The Saturday of the holiday weekend."

Chef Blaine looked thoughtful for a minute than inquired, "Where are you holding the reception?"

Bernadette sighed and Chef Blaine could tell the thought of the reception was overwhelming. "At our church's parish hall so we get to do all the decorating, cooking, serving, and cleaning up." Bernadette paused and added ironically, "I just can't wait."

Chef Blaine whispered something to Megan and her face lit up. Turning back to Bernadette, he questioned, "Bought the food yet?"

"No, we plan to start buying everything next week."

"How many guests do you think you'll have?"

"A little over two hundred probably, definitely not more than three hundred...."

"Out of town folks or from here?"

Bernadette thought for a moment before replying, "Probably all but about fifty will be from the Gentilly and New Orleans East area."

"Before you buy the food, how would you like to bring your parents and sister to Sunday dinner on me?"

Bernadette looked confused. Chef Blaine started to say, "I told your boyfriend..." but caught his words in time.

"Look... The weekend after the Fourth, I'm opening a new restaurant with my niece. We couldn't do it for the holiday weekend because I'm too busy with tourists in town and I want to be there opening weekend. If you let my niece cater the reception for you that night, it would be a great time for her to test everything out – the kitchen operation, her bartenders, and the wait staff. Then she'd have almost another week to see what changes she may need to make before she opens her doors. We could be doing each other a favor. All your family would have to do is hire a D.J. and get the wedding cake. Everything at the place is new: furniture, tablecloths, china, and glasses. I mean everything! We haven't had all the furniture delivered yet and we can delay the next delivery until after the wedding so you have a dance floor. "

Bernadette sighed, "Chef Blaine, that does sound like a great idea, but to be blunt, my parents can't afford anything that upscale."

"Have you sent the invitations yet?"

"Because we had so little time, we've called everyone so they know about the wedding and the date. We won't do the final proof until Monday. The printer will have the envelopes preaddressed and stamped so, once we approve, the formal invitations will mail out pretty quickly."

"But you can still change things Monday, right?"

"Yes...."

"Look," Chef Blaine pulled out his card and the business card for the new restaurant and handed them to Bernadette. "Call me tonight at my place. All I need is for you to confirm how many guests you think will be there. What time do you go to Church tomorrow?"

"Well, we usually eat about 10:00, and then we go to the 11:30 mass."

"Don't let them eat anything. Let them come hungry. I'll see you at 1:00 at the new place. I'll plan a menu for the reception, and they can taste a sample of everything we'll be serving. You just call me tonight with the count so I can have a price worked up when they get there. Tomorrow is my treat. I insist!"

Bernadette didn't know how to refuse politely so she agreed. Maybe they could afford it if she used all of her savings as well. Based on Cher's wedding, it would be the caliber of reception the Laurents were accustomed to instead of a home spun country version.

Pulling into the parking lot of Chez Jolie, Bernadette was impressed. She remembered an old grocery store chain having this entire block, but it was demolished after Hurricane Katrina. Chef Blaine and his niece had purchased the property and built the restaurant new. There was plenty of parking, and the front of the restaurant was very inviting with carved mahogany doors and gaslight lamps flickering on each side. As they entered, they all were in awe. The place was decorated like a palace.

As Chef Blaine mentioned, the area immediately inside the entrance door had no tables and chairs awaiting the next furniture delivery. It was more than adequate to set up a table for the wedding cake and to allow dancing. The door outside stated the capacity of the restaurant was four hundred and they were expecting only two hundred guests. Bernadette regretted they had come knowing, for certain, they would never be able to afford the place now that she had seen it.

As soon as she stepped inside, Bernadette knew exactly what the chef had planned to do with this facility when she spotted the unopened boxes of computers, cables, and software programs she saw stacked along the front wall. His place uptown was too small to accommodate private business meetings. At the hostess stand was a large fish bowl where patrons could drop in a business card in hopes of winning a free luncheon for two. Chef Blaine had used those cards to study the clientele that frequented his uptown establishment and recognized an untapped market.

The new restaurant had been set up like the ballrooms in upscale hotels. Dividers were hidden behind curtains along the walls that would be used to separate the facility into various sized meeting rooms. Paintings had been hung on the walls disguising what Bernadette knew to be various presentation boards and mediums. He never intended for the normal operation to serve the maximum occupancy but was positioned to accommodate private business meetings for lunch or dinner. The clientele only needed to bring their presentation on a thumb drive or E-mail it to them.

"Hey! How ya doing?" Bernadette heard Chef Blaine's voice behind her.

She turned and greeted the chef and introduced her parents, sister, and Miki.

Chef Blaine took over from there.

"Glad you all could make it. Come right over. We have a table set up for you here and everything is ready to serve. I printed up a menu for you to review to see if it's to your satisfaction. The day of the wedding, we'll have wait staff everywhere. You don't have to worry about people coming in late. We'll be running everything just like a restaurant. They'll still get the full meal whenever they arrive. I'll let you all look that over and get the first course out to you."

"Oh, Junior. Isn't everything lovely?" Bernadette's mother picked up one of the pieces of china and admired the pattern.

Chef Blaine had a waitress and a busboy helping out that day. They were first served two soups. Guests at the wedding would have the option of picking a large bowl of one, or they could opt for a cup of each. So they could taste both, the waitress brought them the cups. The Chef had sent an okra gumbo with shrimp, chicken, sausage, and ham that had simmered in a crab and beef stock. The other soup was a corn and crab bisque.

"Audra, I hate to say it, but this gumbo is better than your mother's, and I thought she made the best gumbo in the world."

Hearing her father's comment and realizing how old her maternal grandmother was, Bernadette was sickened by the thought of a seventy five years old lady trying to prepare gumbo for 200 guests.

Salad selections would be a Caesar, spinach garnished with fried oysters, or fruity coleslaw. Family sized bowls of each were delivered so the Juliens could self-serve. The entrée selections were a grilled rib eye steak with caramelized onions, a rotisserie rosemary herbed chicken, or blackened trout with a seafood sauce. Three orders of each entrée came out with huge bowls of the selections of sides served family style. Since a wedding cake would be served, a dessert wasn't listed on the menu but the chef had prepared a bread pudding for the family.

When the Juliens had eaten to the point they all wanted to take naps, Chef Blaine reappeared. He walked to Bernadette's parents with the estimate in hand.

"How did you like the food? Was it enough?"

Bernadette's father spoke first, "I've never had a meal this fine. I'm a big eater, and even I can't fit in another bite."

Her mother spoke next, "Chef Blaine, everything was excellent. That steak wasn't all bloody like some restaurants serve them and still melted in my mouth. I've never tasted a chicken breast so moist and tender and flavorful and that trout and seafood sauce…. When the waitress left and I thought nobody was looking, I took my finger and licked the plate."

Chef Blaine laughed and placed the estimate on the table between her parents.

"Well, if you like how the place looks and the menu is to your satisfaction, we'd love to have you that day. We also have a system the photographer can lock into if he wants that will show the pictures he's taking on the monitors. I think all of them use digital cameras now. There is no charge for the facility or to clean it up, and the price includes an open bar."

Bernadette gasped. Chef Blaine looked at her and chuckled before continuing.

"The bar won't be for people to line up. The waitresses and waiters will take orders and bring the drinks to the guests so it won't create a bottleneck. You just need to get a D.J. and the wedding cake. We'll have tables set up for that, and if you tell me your color scheme, we'll get someone to make them look pretty for you. I'll let you look over that price while I pack leftovers. I still had more in the kitchen in case we hadn't brought out enough."

When Chef Blaine walked away, Bernadette's mother spoke first, "Junior, I priced buying all the food at the grocery the other day. I priced turkeys, hams, roasts, and everything else I would need. This price is only $800 more and includes drinks and alcohol." She seemed confused. "Am I reading this right?"

Bernadette's father answered, "That food was excellent. And think, Audra, the family can just come and enjoy themselves without having to cook and do all that work. Wouldn't that be nice? I remember for our wedding my finger was so swollen from helping your father ice drinks that morning, you couldn't get my wedding ring on it…. The Chef looks so happy to have us too."

Bernadette's mother looked around one more time, "And, Junior, the place is all new. It's like those fancy dining rooms I see in magazines. Not a speck of dirt or dust anywhere. And, we'd have real china and crystal glasses instead of paper plates and cups. I hadn't priced that and the plastic ware yet. And, look, Junior, he even has a note down here it includes one champagne toast to the couple for all guests."

Bernadette's father turned to Cecelia. "Baby girl, what do you think? It's your wedding."

Cecelia was about to cry. Being a waitress at Joe's, she could imagine what an upscale place like this would cost. She was thinking too that her parents were looking at the price wrong.

"It's beautiful, Dad," she responded before turning to Bernadette for help.

Bernadette rose and picked up the estimate from her parents. When she saw the costs, she KNEW the price was wrong. The food was at least the caliber Chef Blaine served uptown. For everything the chef described, Clark would have spent close to $200 for the two of them, and the estimate was pricing at slightly over $20 per person. There was no way feasible the price could be correct for the quality and quantity of food the chef had prepared. Bernadette doubted the price even covered the wages for the staff and security guards that would have to be on duty that night.

As soon as the chef appeared, Bernadette walked quickly over and stopped him before he reached the table.

"Chef Blaine, you brought out the wrong estimate."

"No, I didn't," and he started chuckling, the laugh he was becoming famous for at the uptown location.

"This price has to be below your actual costs!" Bernadette was getting exasperated.

"I'll admit…. I'm definitely not making any money on it." He smiled before continuing and winked at Bernadette, "Consider it as a little wedding present from me. I like helping out deserving people, and like I said before, it'll be a dry run. It'll help us get ready for opening day, and if what you told me is correct, I'm paying for at least one hundred fifty walking billboards for less than the public relations firm I was using was going to charge me for an ad campaign." He chuckled again and walked past Bernadette to her parents.

Looking at first one parent and then the other, he addressed Bernadette's father, "There is one catch. It's a favor I need. As your guests are leaving, we'll have a hostess at the front door giving each of them some flyers to share with their friends. The flyers will be advertising the grand opening date and our operating hours. Are you ok with that?"

"No problem at all. A place as nice as this? I know folks will want to know when they can come back and they'll be telling their friends how good the food is."

"So, what do you say, buddy? We have a deal?"

"Yes, sir. For that price, I can't say 'no' to a meal so well prepared and a beautiful place like this. This will be a reception I could only have dreamed about for my baby girl. Do I sign anything?"

Chef Blaine flipped the estimate over and showed Bernard Julien the contract language as well as the line for his signature. As their father was reading the contract, the chef pointed to the blank in the contract and stated, "I know the wedding is that afternoon, but I need to know the exact time to be ready."

The chef walked over to Cecelia and warned, "Don't leave the guy at the altar. I don't want all this food going to waste."

The chef let out his famous chuckle again, patted Miki on the head, picked up the signed contract, and told their parents, "I'll have the first row of tables reserved for you, the guy's parents, and the wedding party so I need to know how many. Now, remember, I can't be here that night. I'll be too busy at my uptown restaurant but my niece is good. Here is her business card. I wouldn't have invested in this place if she wasn't. If anything is not right that night, just ask for her. She'll have people here no later than 5:00 that morning starting the preparations. If a photographer or the D.J. has to set anything up, he'll be able to get in with no problem. Delivering the cake at any time shouldn't be an issue either. Do you have any questions?"

"No, sir," Bernadette's father replied. "I can't thank you enough for treating us so grandly today."

"It's been my pleasure. I hope you have a good time at the reception."

Chef Blaine was an astute businessman. Word of mouth in New Orleans could make or break a restaurant and was more effective than any ad campaign, but this was still a Godsend for her family. As he passed Bernadette, she grabbed his hand and looked into his face expressing her gratitude. "Thank you," was all she was able to say as tears welled in her eyes.

The chef patted her on the shoulder and walked off chuckling.....

Anyone watching Clark at the gym would attest he must be training for a decathlon. The trainer at the gym was getting more concerned every time he worked out. From the rooftop of the condos, he saw him running on the levee in the morning. By the time he was opening the facility at 5:00 am to allow the early morning workout crew in, Clark appeared to already have run more miles than most people do in a week. At night, he was hitting the gym too. He hadn't missed a day in over a month. The trainer had observed his technique, and it was perfect. The amount of weights he was bench pressing was impressive. That wasn't the issue. The guy was losing weight, and he was not a man that needed to. He had been pushing too hard and too fast for too long now. The trainer decided to let things go for one more week, and if he was still pushing that hard, he would insist Clark slow down.

Chapter Thirty

Standing on the steps of St. Martha's church, Bernadette remained outside trying to gain control of her emotions. Having learned from Joe that St. Martha was the patron saint of waiters and waitresses, it seemed fitting that the wedding take place there. Bernadette knew once she walked in, she would probably see Clark so she prayed to St. Martha to help her through the rehearsal. It would be the first time she and Clark saw each other since Memorial weekend. Though the break-up had been all her doing, she didn't know how to go about fixing things between them. She kept hoping Clark would call, and his call would open the door once again. When he hadn't, she had begun feeling it was over between them forever. She could well understand why after the things she had said to him. After the months they had spent together, she knew Clark well. She knew he was not the type of man she had painted him to be. How much it must have hurt him to hear her speak such terrible things. After all he had done to show her his love, her behavior had been unthinkable.

Why hadn't she followed her heart instead of letting jealousy push her beyond the bounds of reason? Cecelia had always been petite, and in Bernadette's eyes, the more attractive of the two of them. Boys had started calling her for dates when she was only thirteen. Bernadette had always been jealous of her sister, and those years of jealousy culminated when she saw Clark and Cecelia together. She had surmised that, once again, the model look had won. Bernadette's own low self-esteem had caused her to lose the man she loved. She knew now that her imagination had taken flight. She chided herself for still being that self-conscious about her weight after Clark had done everything he could to ensure her she was beautiful, and he loved her just the way she was. How had she repaid him? At the first test of her love for him and trust in him, she had failed.

Bernadette took several deep breaths trying to calm her nerves. Then she remembered that was a technique she had been taught by Clark and that thought upset her more. Was there anything in her life that would not remind her of him? When Cecelia came out looking for her, she didn't have a choice but to go into the church although her nerves were still frayed. "Just don't look into his eyes," Bernadette thought. "If you don't lock eyes, you can get through this."

The rehearsal was going smoothly until the priest started discussing with Cecelia how the groomsmen would escort the bridesmaids down the aisle. With Bernadette as the maid of honor and Clark serving as Clay's best man, the two would typically be paired as a couple for the wedding. Cecelia stopped the priest and told him Bernadette had recommended a non-traditional approach. As Cecelia explained, it became clear that Bernadette would never have to take Clark's arm.

Bernadette felt Clark's eyes on her as soon as the priests agreed to the alternate procession pattern. She couldn't help but look up and lock eyes with him. As soon as she did, she regretted it. His eyes said, "Is the thought of me only touching your arm that unbearable, Bernadette? Do you hate me that much still?" Seeing the hurt and pain in his eyes was too much. She averted her eyes quickly knowing her recommendation was the same as pouring salt into an open wound. How would she ever get him back now that she had made it clear she could not tolerate the thought of the slightest contact with him?

Bernadette's eyes filled with tears. How could Clark ever forgive her when she could never forgive herself for the way she had treated him? She should have thought about that before she made the suggestion to Cecelia. Now she had just sealed her own fate. She knew without any doubt it was over between them forever. They were too many scars, especially the one on his face. Even if they tried, those memories would always haunt them. It was nice while it lasted, but it was over now. Taking a deep breath and exhaling slowly, she accepted the fact. Putting their relationship behind her was the right thing to do for everyone involved. The tension she was feeling was now gone. She was back to just being Bernadette: the round chimney, the pink elephant, the fat cow. She smiled thinking of those past images of herself but somehow finally being at peace with them in her mind.

Clark saw the smile cross Bernadette's lips. "She's gloating," he thought, "She purposely recommended the change in the procession to make it clear to him she meant the last words she spoke to him. She hadn't forgiven him and wanted him to know she never would."

Clay's parents were adamant they wanted to cater the rehearsal dinner. Arguing Clay was their only child so this was their sole chance to be part of a wedding event, Bernadette's parents had finally yielded. What was going to be a simple meal turned into an elaborate, elegant event with waiters and waitresses everywhere ensuring the buffet line remained full and dirty china was picked up promptly. A photographer was snapping candid shots of all present.

When Bernadette entered the parish hall for the rehearsal dinner, she tried hard to avoid any further contact with Clark. She had now accepted their relationship was over but seeing him in the church at first had been unbearable because it brought back memories of their love making. She had not only missed his company but the pleasures he would give her. She felt so guilty having those thoughts in church and she couldn't seem to stop thinking about what she had experienced in his arms. Even when the priest was giving them instructions, she would have to ask for things to be repeated because her mind had wandered off. When she and her sister went to the hairdresser that morning, the women in the salon were discussing relationships. One of the elderly technicians made the comment, "Once a woman has sex, her body craves it." "Boy, can I attest to that," thought Bernadette. There were nights she couldn't get to sleep, and she woke the next morning tired and irritable. Some nights she dreamt of her and Clark together, and those times made her wake even more frustrated. Though she was succeeding in avoiding physical contact with him, her eyes were looking his way every chance she could.

Bernadette did notice when Clark approached her father. She was too far away to hear anything, but it appeared Clark asked her father if he could have a word with him. Her father rose and followed Clark to the far end of the hall where the two of them were well isolated from the festivities. When Clark first started talking, her father appeared to grow angry. He crossed his arms and stared unblinking at Clark. Soon his face softened, and the two started a dialogue. It wasn't long before they shook hands. Bernadette thought their conversation was over, but Clark raised his right hand with his index finger extended as if he was making one more point. When he finished, the hand changed to an open palm as if waiting for feedback. The expression on Bernadette's father's face and the manner in which he responded indicated he was not in agreement with Clark. He started to walk away, but Clark appealed again stopping him for a moment. There was one time Clark was taking the back of his right hand and slapping it into the palm of his left at intervals indicating he was emphasizing the arguments he was making.

When Uncle Aaron saw the gesture Clark was making to Junior, he walked over and joined them. As soon as Uncle Aaron got there, Junior filled him in, and the conversation became heated. Uncle Aaron started moving towards Clark and began poking his finger into Clark's chest as he spoke. He stopped so close to him that Bernadette felt their faces were touching. Clark didn't budge making it clear to Uncle Aaron he had no intentions of backing down.

Joe was sitting at the same table as Bernadette. He had observed the interaction as well. Throwing his napkin on the table, Joe rose advising Bernadette, "Peaches, if ya' uncle doesn't quit acting like a damn fool, he ain't getting any more free meals off of me. That man has no respect for any opinion but his own. Trying to get him to change is like trying to teach an elephant to fly with a pair of sparrow's wings."

When Joe reached the trio, he put his right hand on Clark's chest and tried to walk him to the left away from Junior and Aaron coaxing Clark to separate. Bernadette knew Joe felt trying to get her uncle to move would be a waste of time. When Joe and Clark had moved a distance from the other two men, Clark started explaining something to Joe, and Bernadette could tell Clark was becoming highly agitated. Still, he looked right into Joe's eyes and listened calmly to everything Joe told him next. When Joe finished talking, Clark put his head down and started rubbing his forehead. After a short period, he looked at Joe and started speaking to him again. Bernadette could tell Clark was trying to convince Joe of some point. When Joe responded to whatever Clark said, Clark linked his fingers and placed them on the crown of his head. He must have pondered what Joe said because he suddenly put his hands down, shook his head indicating a negative reply. Clark walked over to a column in the back of the hall and leaned against it for a while. Joe didn't move from where he and Clark had been standing. It was obvious he knew Clark would be back.

Bernadette saw her father and uncle had been steadily arguing the entire time as well. Suddenly, Clark turned from where he was standing by the column and walked past Joe towards where her uncle and father stood. Uncle Aaron stepped forward a few feet in front of her father with his arms folded in a clear gesture of command. Clark was staring him in the face as he walked towards him. When he got right in front of her uncle, he did a quick sidestep, dodged around him, and walked straight up to Bernadette's father. Bernadette's father smirked when he saw Clark's maneuver. The young man had just scored another point with him by outfoxing his obnoxious brother-in-law.

Uncle Aaron and Joe followed Clark over. The two of them were speaking nonstop but Clark kept his eyes focused only on the face of Bernadette's father. It was as if Clark saw and heard only what her father was saying and was only responding to her father. When Clark answered any questions, he was speaking very slowly and calmly. His gestures were more pleading. At one point, Uncle Aaron put his hand on Clark's upper arm and shoved him back. Clark ignored the egging and walked back up to Bernadette's father as if it didn't happen and again focused only on Mr. Bernard Julien, Jr. Finally, Bernadette's father raised his hand, and the two of them shook on it indicating they had reached an agreement. Bernadette saw her father use his other hand to pat Clark on the shoulder while they were shaking hands. Though she couldn't hear the words being said, she could tell by the movement of his head and mouth that Clark was thanking her father.

Afterwards, Clark turned to Uncle Aaron and Joe and an agitated discussion continued. Bernadette's father had always thought his brother-in-law was the most unreasonable man on earth so he just started laughing and walked away from the trio to return to the festivities. It seems Clark just stood there letting Uncle Aaron blow off steam and didn't respond to his words or the times he shoved Clark's shoulder. Joe was the one that finally pulled him away from Clark and got him to rejoin the guests.

When they walked away, Clark put his head back and did the neck rolls he had taught Bernadette to release stress. He didn't return to the main area where the guests were but went to the end of the bar where he could sit alone. Bernadette saw the bartender walk over and listen to instructions from Clark. He went back to the set-up station and returned placing a bourbon neat in front of him. Clark downed the drink in one gulp, and the bartender quickly returned with another. He sipped that one before he signaled the bartender for a third. Bernadette got concerned. Clark never had more than two drinks when he had to drive. It was a rule he made, and one he never broke. When he signaled for a fourth hit, she started to get up and go over to him, but Clay had been watching his cousin as well. When she saw Clay rise, she sat back down.

Clay walked over and signaled to the bartender not to fill the order. Then he leaned against the bar on Clark's left side placing his right hand on his shoulder. They spoke silently for a few minutes before Clay signaled Cecelia to join them. When Cecelia got by the bar, Clay put his arm around her waist and hugged her while Clark filled her in. Suddenly, Cecelia put her arms around Clark's neck and kissed him on the cheek. Then she moved back to Clay putting her arm around his waist and turning her face up so they could kiss. Clay shook Clark's hand, and he and Cecelia started to walk away until he saw Clark signal the bartender again.

Clay put his hand up with his palm facing the bartender signaling him to stop. He whispered something to Cecelia, and she left his side to rejoin the guests. Walking back to Clark, Clay made a few comments. Clark held up his index finger. Clay held up his index finger and put in right in front of Clark's face. Then Clay turned to the bartender and made the same gesture but with a punching motion. The bartender brought Clark a fourth bourbon. He downed that one with one gulp, pulled out his wallet, and placed some bills in the tip cup. Then Clark turned, and without looking back, walked out the exit door at the back of the bar.

After he left, Bernadette started feeling depressed. Bernadette was also feeling slightly jealous seeing Cecelia first kissing Clark's cheek and then walking away so happily with her future husband at her side. Had Clark championed once again for something Cecelia wanted? It appeared that way by her reaction to whatever he had won debating with her father. Had everyone forgotten that Cecelia had lied and that was why she got pregnant in the first place? She had lied to the university, had lied to Clay, had lied to their parents, and had lied to Bernadette. Everything Cecelia had done in the past seems to have been forgiven. Clark had even made sure she would be driving a new car. Here, Bernadette had tried to always do the right thing, and nothing seemed to ever go her way. Her bratty, spoiled younger sister always seemed to get everything she wanted. Now Cecelia even had Clark acting as a champion for her! Bernadette couldn't wait for everything to end tomorrow though she knew that wouldn't be the last time she would see him. She was certain they would meet at events for Miki, and she was sure they both would smile and be cordial for Miki's sake. The thought of the pretense they would put on for the rest of their lives frustrated her. This time, it was Bernadette who wanted more and wished things could have ended differently.

Chapter Thirty-One

During the wedding ceremony, Bernadette purposely kept her eyes averted. If she saw the pain in Clark's face again, she would burst into tears and ruin the day for Cecelia and Clay. Keeping focused on Miki walking down the aisle painstakingly dropping just the right number of rose petals on the white cloth for her mother helped lighten Bernadette's heart. She was so happy for her niece. As their father escorted Cecelia down the aisle, Bernadette prayed one day it would be her turn, and Clark would be the one waiting for her at the altar. "Could a day like this ever come for her?" she wondered.

When the limousines pulled to the front of Chez Jolie, Chef Blaine had outdone himself. White flowers and lace adorned the entrance way and the computer driven neon sign flashed, "Congratulations to the newlyweds Cecelia and Clay." The waitresses present began acting as hostesses, quickly seating the wedding party and guests. Somehow, Bernadette was able to not lock eyes with Clark until he gave the toast for his cousin Clay. Sharing some of the adventures the duo had experienced growing up kept the family and guests in stitches, except for Clark's and Clay's parents whose faces turned somber as they finally understood some previously unexplainable incidents. Finally, Clark delivered a more serious toast to the couple wishing them a life of happiness together. Bernadette thought the toast was over; but after the guests had donned their champagne, Clark continued, to her surprise, and that of the family as well. At least it was a surprise to all but a few family members.

"This is CeeCee and Clay's day, but I'm asking CeeCee's family, my family, our friends and guests to please indulge me. With CeeCee and Clay's permission, I need to... I need to make one more speech today."

Clark stopped talking, swallowed hard, and had to take a deep breath before continuing. Camille, Connie, and Bernadette were the only three present that immediately sensed something was amiss. The three could tell he was struggling to get the words out. Always at the top of his game, they became totally focused on Clark before anyone else had a clue that something different was happening.

"This is about to become either the happiest day or the most embarrassing moment of my life."

A smile broke out on his face at the thought, and the guests started laughing with him. That seemed to put him more at ease and gave him the strength he needed to continue.

"Those close to my family know that Clay was an only child, and I was the only boy of seven. Though we grew up in different cities, we spent almost every summer together and were more like brothers. Since I was older, like most little brothers, Clay looked up to me as a role model. "

Clark hesitated before continuing. Now all eyes in the reception room were watching, and the room was completely silent.

"He not only looked up to me, but he often came to me for advice and guidance. "

Emphasizing the next sentence, he continued, "He believed I would never lead him along the wrong path…. He believed I always had his best interest at heart…. The summer he graduated from high school, he wanted to begin earning his college credits so he spent that time with me here in New Orleans, and we grew even closer. CeeCee was also attending a summer program at the same institution. That's where they met and fell in love…. That was the first time I failed him."

Clark's voice cracked on the last sentence. He was looking down now obviously struggling to continue. Connie stood up. Camille grabbed her daughter's arm, "Connie, sit down." She spoke the command gently but firmly. "He's always going to be your baby brother, but stop looking at him that way. He's a grown man now. There are some things he has to do on his own and wants to do on his own. I don't know where this is going but I sense he'll be fine. Don't you dare interfere!"

"But he's hurting, Mom. I can tell."

"I know...." Camille was in tears. "But it's a hurt neither of us can protect him from.... I feel it in my heart.... We can't interfere in his life. Not this time. Whatever he's doing, he NEEDS to do this alone."

Reluctantly, Connie sat down fighting back her tears as well. Clark's voice was choppy and filled with emotion. Bernadette also wanted to go to him. It was breaking her heart to watch him. She couldn't bear to see the pain in his face.

"When CeeCee told Clay she was pregnant, Clay came to me NOT for advice, but to TELL me he was dropping out of school and getting a job so they could get married. I pulled out statistics. I showed him a comparison between the hourly minimum wage he would be earning having only a high school diploma versus the starting salary he would make the first week out of college as a graduate in petroleum engineering. I was the one that emphasized to him that he was doing the wrong thing for not only himself but also for CeeCee and their child if he gave up his scholarship and dropped out of school. I was the one that said, 'I've been there, and I know how demanding the curriculum can be. I know you can't succeed in an engineering program unless you spend every minute of every day studying. With a wife, a child, and trying to work, that was a formula for failure, not success.' I was the one that finally convinced him the best thing to do was to wait until he completed his college education, landed a career opportunity instead of a job, and could provide for his wife and child the way they deserved.... And he believed me because he trusted me."

Clark lowered his eyes and gathered his thoughts before continuing. When he looked up, he was staring at Miki.

"So I was the one that caused him, and I, to miss out on the first three years in the life of that precious little child who served as the flower girl for her parents' wedding today...."

Clark paused again before continuing.

"The main way I failed Clay was not giving him the advice he truly needed the most, how to sit down and discuss the issue with CeeCee.

When he came home that night and I asked him how it went, he said he barely spoke one sentence, and CeeCee ran off crying.... I was thoroughly confused. With everything we covered, I felt he had a logical presentation. I couldn't imagine what words he could have spoken to cause that reaction, so I asked him. When Clay said he told her, 'I'm not going to marry you,' my first thought was, 'That would do it.'"

Everyone burst into laughter which helped Clark's nervousness settle, and his voice was stronger as he continued. He rubbed his forehead lightly before continuing.

"Definitely not the way that conversation should have started.... Early June, Clay had to decide whether or not he would accept a job offer with an oil company in Dallas. Since, by that time, they were planning to marry, this was not a decision he could make on his own or could make lightly. Taking CeeCee and Miki away from a loving family was going to be a hardship on her, and he knew that. Clay let her read the contract and agree to it before he signed it. When she saw his starting salary, they ARE moving to Dallas, and SHE forgave me."

The guests burst into laughter again.

"I even got my first hug from my cousin-in-law.... I'm thankful that they met again. I'm thankful for the strong family values Mr. and Mrs. Julien instilled in CeeCee. They had the courage, in these modern times, to raise a daughter who didn't pick the easy way out but chose life and decided to give birth to Clay's baby.... Today, I'm asking them to forgive us for any pain and embarrassment these Laurent guys may have caused you in the past, and I'm grateful for everyone present today joining us as we celebrate Clay, CeeCee, and Miki becoming a family."

Bernadette's father raised his champagne glass to Clark symbolic that all was forgiven. Seeing that gesture, Bernadette was saddened. Was she the only one that hadn't forgiven him? Their relationship was ruined forever because of the hateful words she had spoken. She admired Clark more than ever hearing his speech tonight. She thought about the lingerie she and Valerie had bought for her Memorial Day weekend that was still hidden in the trunk of Bernadette's car. If only things could have ended differently for them, tonight may have been the time for one to come out of hiding.

"If everyone would please indulge me a little longer...." Clark's voice cracked so badly this time, Bernadette knew he wouldn't be able to continue. After looking into Bernadette's eyes, he seemed to find renewed courage. "There's one last thing I need to do before turning control of this reception back to the D.J.."

As a waiter came up to him, Clark accepted and raised a champagne glass to Bernadette's parents as he said, "With Mr. and Mrs. Julien's permission...."

Bernadette's father responded to Clark by raising his own glass and nodding affirmatively.

"What is he doing now?" Bernadette thought.

Clark searched the guests until he found him. Clark took a deep breath and exhaled slowly before continuing.

"With Uncle Aaron's permission...."

Uncle Aaron stood up, took a boxer's stance, and shadow-boxed a one-two punch. Then he laughed, sat down, and raised his glass to Clark. Clark forced a smile and shook his head a couple of times.

Always protective of her younger brother, Connie nudged her mother's arm and said angrily, "I wonder what that was about."

Camille responded, "I don't know.... Private joke among the Juliens, I guess...." But Camille wondered if the gesture had anything to do with the scar her son now had on his left cheekbone and that thought was not sitting well with her at all. It had healed and started to fade, but that scar was permanent. To say that Camille was not happy when she saw it was an extremely mild description of her reaction.

Clark scanned the guests again until he found a third person.

"With Joe's permission...."

Joe stood raising his glass to Clark, but he also made a slight bow towards him as a sign of respect.

"Who's Joe?" Connie asked her mother.

Camille answered her with a slight agitation in her voice this time, "I don't know, Connie." With all unfolding before her eyes, she made up her mind that, from now on, she was going to keep closer tabs on her son. Too much had been going on she didn't know about. He had made excuses why he couldn't be there for the Father's Day celebration she had planned for Calvin. She knew why when she walked into the church and saw him. He was waiting for that scar to fade out more and praying she wouldn't notice. "Yes," Camille thought, "We need to talk and see each other more often." She checked out Uncle Aaron again.

Camille's concern was misplaced. If anything, her apprehension should have been for Uncle Aaron. Beside her, her husband's posture was rigid. His arms were folded across his chest, and his former military training had him on high alert. His face resembled that of a general making a last minute assessment before ordering his troops into combat. Had she looked at him, she would have seen that Calvin knew exactly what Uncle Aaron's gesture meant and the role Joe was now playing in their son's life.

After visiting with the Juliens on Father's Day, Clay had stopped by Clark's family home with CeeCee and Miki and introduced them to his relatives. As soon as he did, Camille had swept the little girl into her arms and his daughters had surrounded Cecelia bombarding her with questions about the upcoming wedding. Calvin had tilted his head at Clay indicating that Clay needed to follow him to his study. Clay nervously took a seat in the chair Calvin designated as Calvin circled behind his desk taking the command position. He could tell Clark had sworn Clay to secrecy by the nervous way Clay's eyes kept darting and the way he licked his lips. If Clark had taken such an oath, Calvin knew he would never be able to break his son no matter what he did or threatened to do to him. With Clay, Calvin only had to lean over the desk with a serious expression and to ask in his angriest tone, "WHERE'S MY SON?" Clay had started singing like a canary.

Calvin was proud of the way Clark had conducted himself. He and Clark had been sparring since Clark was six. He had taught him well, and as soon as he had seen the overweight, middle-aged man, Calvin knew Clark could have easily got the upper hand in any altercation and been the victor. He was proud of him for having handled the situation as he did. Against an 'on duty' police officer, Clark had done the best anyone could have under the circumstances. But Aaron wasn't in uniform today…. Anticipating what Clark was about to do, Calvin was cautiously watching the scene unfold.

Clark signaled a waiter who came over, and he placed his now empty glass on the tray.

"There's one more person whose life was affected by the events of four years ago, a person who had to put her hopes and dreams on hold to help support her sister and help raise her niece."

"Oh, my God," Bernadette thought and started squirming in her chair. "There was no need for Clark to apologize to her, too, especially in public like this." Then she remembered the hateful words she had spoken to him, "I don't ever want to see you again." Realizing she had placed him in that position, she placed her hand on the stem of her champagne glass preparing to follow her father, her Uncle Aaron, and Joe's example. She would gladly raise her glass in a toast to Clark if that meant their relationship could end amicably, and for Miki's sake, there wouldn't be tension between them when they were forced to be in each other's company.

Turning to look at Bernadette, he walked towards her as he struggled to pull something from his coat pocket.

"I've been having this since the Friday before Memorial Day. Plans changed quickly that weekend, and I didn't have the opportunity to do what I intended then…. I KNOW this is the LAST opportunity I'm going to get so I thank you all, once again, for indulging me. "

Clark bent down on one knee in front of Bernadette, presented a ring case to her, and flicked it open with his thumb.

By now the photographer had locked into the restaurant's video system and arranged for the camera to focus in on Clark, and everything he did was showing on four mega screens. The camera zoomed in on the ring.

Connie turned to Camille and slapped her on the upper arm, "F---! Mom, just that center stone must be two carats! I know Clark was doing well, but my baby brother is doing better than I thought to afford that!" Waiting to see her mother's reaction, out of the corner of her eye, she saw her father's stern stare instead. Realizing the word she had spoken, she cowered like a three years old before she whispered, "I'm sorry, Daddy…" She shifted quickly in her seat to watch her baby brother and Bernadette but kept an eye on her father as well remembering past threats she had heard during her teen years, "You're never too old, young lady."

Clark locked eyes with Bernadette before continuing, "Miss Bernadette Julien, I LOVE YOU! I can't imagine my life without you…. Can you ever find it in your heart to forgive me? If you can't but would still agree to become my wife, I PROMISE I will spend every day of the rest of our lives trying to make it up to you…. Bernadette Julien, will you marry me?"

Clark lowered the microphone and spoke softly so that only Bernadette could hear him, "These past few weeks have been hell for me…. I can't make it another day without you, baby." He finally broke down and couldn't speak another word. He closed his eyes for a moment then looked at her waiting for her response.

It was taking time for Bernadette's mind to filter through what Clark had just done and said. She couldn't believe that with her father, Uncle Aaron's, and even Joe' s blessing that he was on his knee in front of a crowd of over two hundred people begging her, overweight Bernadette shaped like a round chimney, the pink elephant, the fat cow to marry him.... Was she dreaming? After the hateful words she had spoken to him and the ordeal he had gone through with her uncle, Clark was the one apologizing to her and begging her forgiveness? The heated exchange at the rehearsal had nothing to do with Cecelia? It was all about Clark debating the three most influential men in her family and in her life for her hand in marriage? It was all about her? The fat girl had won? The fat girl could marry the most handsome, kind, gentle, considerate, intelligent, successful man any woman could imagine.

The words Cecelia had said suddenly came to her, *"He's really a nice guy."* The words she had spoken to Valerie echoed in her mind, *"…he's never said a single derogatory comment about by body or my weight. Instead, he looks at me as if I'm a goddess. He touches me and holds me like I'm a treasured piece of fine porcelain... He makes me feel love.... Clark makes me feel beautiful. He makes me feel good about me and that's something I haven't felt in a long time."*

This had become the moment of truth for Bernadette. He was a nice guy, and he deserved someone who truly loved him. He was the first real relationship she ever had. She had grown up in an overprotected environment. Was what she felt for him just normal for an inexperienced girl who had never known the secret to what could exist between a man and a woman? Was what she felt just the passion he was able to ignite in her? She looked around at the restaurant setting and thought of the fancy places he had taken her, his car, his condo, the lifestyle the Laurents had and the ring! What had that cost him? So, that's why battered and bruised he was sitting at Blaine's that night.... The night she told him she never wanted to see him again was the night he had wanted to propose. Her stomach sank. She had bought lingerie, and he had bought a ring. She closed her eyes tightly and exhaled sharply.

Looking into Clark's face again, she had to decide – did she truly love him? Or, had she fallen in love with the way he made her feel? She could not accept his proposal unless she knew, without any doubt, that she loved the man himself.

She looked at the scar on his left cheek. Every time he looked in the mirror, it would be a reminder of all that had gone wrong between them. What about him? Had he really forgiven her and her family, or was his mind clouded by the way Valerie had described him? *"That man's body is just like that can of shaken soda. ...he is ready to explode. ... He can't keep it bottled up much longer."* Clark could easily get another woman to replace her so, for him, was it just the sexual conquest? She thought about the first time they met and the bet to get her to go out with him. For him, was it just his corporate competitive nature that he had to win the game? What about years after? Would their love last once the game was over and he'd won?

They had talked about everything together.... What about now? Could they still be that way? Should she share her fears? The moment was surreal....

Chapter Thirty-Two

Connie turned towards her mother with tears welling in her eyes, "If she turns him down, I'm going to kick her ass."

Her father's voice admonished, "Connie." In shock, she looked at him not out of fear for the scolding she deserved but because she had never heard him speak so softly or with so much emotion in his voice. As their eyes locked, she knew he was seeing Clark the same way she did at the moment. Both turned to wait for Bernadette's response as they watched a three years old little boy once again with his heart on his sleeve and holding his bubble gum ring in the palm of his hand.

Calvin knew his son well and knew the only answer he would accept at this point was "Yes." Clark had done everything he could to set things right: publicly apologized to the Julien family, accepted complete responsibility for what had happened, and committed to doing whatever Bernadette wanted from him to make amends. After all of that, if the girl gave him some non-committed response like, "I need some time to think about it," it was over between them. Clark would walk away, and she'd never get him back. This was an all or nothing turning point in their relationship, and Calvin could tell by his set jawline that Clark was also demanding an answer now.

Calvin knew his daughter well and that the guy she married was clueless when it came to a woman's emotional needs. If Bernadette turned Clark down, Connie would not be kicking her ass literally but only mentally. He'd be the one that would have to escort Connie outside, hold her tightly in his arms, speak soothing words to her, and let her cry her eyes out on his shoulder until she was calm, and they could return to the reception and behave civilly again for Clay's sake.

Knowing all ties between his son and the Juliens would then be severed, he also knew himself well. He would wait until the reception was over and the majority of the guests had gone. Then he would ask Aaron to have a word with him outside. After punching Aaron's lights out and before he blacked out, he would state, "That's for my son!" If a patrol car came by their house later that night to arrest him, he'd gladly sit in a jail cell.

The room was almost in dead silence with everyone focused on Bernadette awaiting her answer. Even the wait staff had stopped collecting dishes and glasses and just stood at attention. The silence was suddenly broken by a loud, crass voice from the back of the restaurant. Bernadette and Clark both turned towards it immediately recognizing Valerie. Valerie was screaming at the top of her lungs. She had stood, her arms were waving up and down, and she was stomping one foot.

"Bernadette, don't be a fool, girl! A man like that comes along once in a lifetime…. Don't be stupid, Bernadette. Girl, GRAB the DAMN RING! If you don't, that man is going to have women in this restaurant lining up to take your place. He AIN'T getting out here tonight unattached. I guarantee that! And I don't mean just single women either…. They have some MARRIED hussies looking his way!"

Valerie scanned the crowd with her hands on her hips and made pointed looks at a couple of the women seated close to her before continuing with, "You all know who you are!" Her attention then switched back to Bernadette, "And, I don't care if I have to fight my way to get there. My ass is going to be the first one in that line! Bernadette, we've been friends for years but I promise you, girlfriend. If you don't want that man, I'm going to be leading that line! Don't be stupid, Bernadette. Tell the man 'yes' and TAKE THE DAMN RING!"

Valerie looked frustrated before plopping down into her seat exhausted and praying her friend wouldn't turn Clark down.

Bernadette leaned towards Clark and began whispering into his ear. His face was serious at first, and the position of his head didn't move as he listened. Then a smile slowly appeared.

Clark stood turning toward Valerie. He put the microphone to his mouth and softly spoke. "Valerie, my lady said 'yes'!"

Dropping the microphone onto the table, he pulled Bernadette into his arms and kissed her with a passion that had built since Memorial weekend. Some of the guests stood and started applauding. Clark then reached down, took the ring from the case, slid it onto Bernadette's finger, and kissed the back of her hand as if to seal their new commitment to each other.

Cher was making her way to the D.J. He listened carefully as she gave instructions. He quickly dug through several towers of discs before pulling a CD, checking the title, and plugging it into the player before going to his microphone to announce, "And now, the newly engaged couple will lead us in the next dance."

Clark glanced towards the mock stage and saw Cher smiling at them. Turning to Bernadette, he whispered, "Cher is the culprit this time." He added, "And I don't mind at all."

Camille turned to Connie smiling though she kept a watch on Uncle Aaron out the corner of her eye as she said, "I told you he'd do fine."

Audra was wiping tears still as she spoke to Bernadette's father, "Junior, this is too much. Both of our girls meeting such fine young man and being so happy on the same day. This is just too much!"

"I told Bernadette she didn't have to worry about losing weight. She's perfect just the way she is. You know Audra, if anything happens between them and Bernadette comes over to the house complaining about Clark, don't you patronize her. Don't DARE do that! If anything goes wrong in that marriage, it will be Bernadette's fault. I know that. The way that boy approached me the other night, I'm 100% in that boy's corner. I had no idea who he was…. He came up to me and whispered, 'Sir, may I please have a moment of your time?' He asked me so politely, I couldn't refuse him. We walked over to a corner, and he said, 'Sir, I need to apologize to you. I have six sisters and my father would not have tolerated the rude behavior I have demonstrated towards you. Just because Bernadette is almost thirty years old was no excuse for me not to come to you and assume I did not have to ask your permission to see your daughter.' The way that boy was talking, I couldn't do anything but just listen to what he had to say. Then that crazy brother of yours came over and started acting like a fool as always. It seems he kept saying things to try to excite the boy. I felt like Aaron was trying to get Clark to hit him. It got to a point I wanted to punch him myself. Nobody invited him over, and he walked over and forced his way into our conversation and wouldn't shut up."

"Oh, Junior! You punched Aaron?"

"No, I didn't, but he sure would have deserved it. That boy kept his cool through all that badgering, so I know he's level headed. But, out of everything he said and did, what sold me the most and has me 100% in that boy's corner was when he told me that he and Bernadette have sat for hours just discussing the bible and their Catholic faith. He was so sincere when he said how much those conversations had meant to him and had helped their relationship to grow. I knew he wasn't lying because I never met a man that demonstrated more passion about religion. I could see it in his eyes, and his voice got deeper as he assured me their relationship would not have reached the point it had without those discussions."

"Oh, Junior. Isn't that just beautiful? Bernadette got her a boy that's religious too. Most boys that age don't even go to church, and here they are making time to discuss their faith.... That's so nice."

"When I mentioned Bernadette was always stopping by Valerie's and I was concerned over that gal's influence on her, he told me, 'Mr. Julien, I promise you, sir, that once we're married, Bernadette will NOT be stopping by Valerie's nearly as often.' That was music to my ears. Yes, Audra, I couldn't have picked a finer man for our daughter."

Bernard Julien, Jr. was still not happy he had agreed to another request Clark had made of him at the rehearsal dinner. But he had given him his approval, and he would stick to his word. He not only granted Clark's request to marry his daughter but also for them to elope and plan the formal blessing of their vows in the church later. It gave Bernard Julien heartburn, but the guy was convincing. It still bothered him though, and he wondered if it was the right thing to do.

As Clark was guiding Bernadette to the dance floor, the look on her father's face quickly suppressed the joy and happiness he just experienced. Clark felt himself literally growing ill. His heart was pounding, his breath became labored, his head was getting cloudy and perspiration was forming on his forehead. He tugged the tie at his neck, and his only thought became, "He's changed his mind. God help me if he's changed his mind."

Scenes from their past began spinning through his head. When he woke startled from the dream and realized how much he loved Bernadette, he was determined then to make her his wife. When he knew she was still a virgin, he swore that two things would happen. First, he would not make the same mistake he had made with Helena. He wouldn't take that risk again so he was determined to not make her a woman, his woman, until she was his wife. Second, he could not bear the thought of her writhing beneath him that first time. He loved her too much. Though he knew the experience would not be totally pain free, he vowed to begin slowly preparing her both emotionally and physically for that first sexual encounter to make it as easy as possible for her. If everything had gone as planned that Saturday night when he was to propose, he was going to ask Bernadette if she was willing to elope. They could have caught a plane to Las Vegas Sunday when he dropped Clay back at the airport, got married, spent the night, and returned on Monday. The only positive that came out of his dreams crashing on Memorial weekend was that he had been home to receive Glenn's call. Had he been in Vegas, his cell would have been turned off because Clark would definitely not have wanted to be disturbed on his wedding night.

When Clay filled him in on his first encounter with the Julien's, Clark thought about his own family and knew one factor to a successful marriage was having the support of the extended family. The Juliens sounded more old-fashioned than his own clan. To start the marriage on the right foot, he would have to first speak to Bernadette's father personally. When Clay advised the wedding date, Clark felt confident he could make it just five weeks if he didn't see or speak with Bernadette at all. After over a month of preparing her for their wedding night, Clark was on the edge. He couldn't keep holding her without breaking the vow he had made to himself. It was a struggle not to pick up the phone and beg her to come back to him, but he had succeeded knowing a far better goal was within sight.

To try to keep thoughts of her at bay, he had thrown himself into a rigorous exercise plan and set demanding short term goals for himself at work. But those sources were drying up. Robert had called him in that week and warned him he would reorganize and reduce his responsibilities if Clark didn't stop pushing so hard. The trainer at the gym had threatened to deactivate his membership if he didn't slow down on his regimen. He knew they were right. He doubt he had got more than two hours sleep a night the past two weeks, but it was the only way he could keep his mind off of Bernadette. He only slept when he passed out from exhaustion. Many mornings when his alarm went off, his head was on the side of his keyboard instead of on a pillow in his bed. His bed! When was the last time he slept in it? He had started crashing on the upstairs couch. The bed held too many memories of his last moments with Bernadette. Trying to lay there without her had been too torturous.

And now, right when they were about to cross the goal line, Clark saw it being pulled away. If they didn't elope that night, how long would he have to wait? The priest that married Clay and Cecelia had known the Julien family for years, and after talking with Clay's parish priest in Ville Platte, he agreed to make exceptions for Clay and Cecelia because of the baby and the pending move to Dallas.

There were no circumstances that would cut down the marriage preparation time for Clark and Bernadette. They'd have to meet with the priest and complete the premarital inventory. If they were lucky, they'd get the short format and could attend the Day for the Engaged instead of the extended Engaged Encounter sessions. Then they'd still have to meet with a deacon and discuss what they had learned and experienced during the marriage preparation sessions. Worst case, it would be six months. He couldn't go that long without thinking about her, without seeing her, without holding her, without making her his own. And he couldn't live with himself if he broke his vow. His breathing became labored, and Bernadette was beginning to eye him with concern. He again tugged the tie at his neck loosening it slightly.

He had planned everything so carefully. Ever since he was three, he had learned how to manipulate circumstances to go his way but not this time when it mattered most. Before he had approached Bernadette's father, he had developed a template based on Clay's feedback from that initial meeting and based on the composition books his sisters had written. Clark's goal, when he arrived at the rehearsal, was not to see Bernadette but to monitor her father. He watched everything Bernard Julien, Jr. did from the time Clay pointed him out at the rehearsal in the church until the party after was winding down. Clark watched the way he interacted with his daughters, his wife, the priest, his family, and his friends. Clark tweaked the template based on his observations; and knowing it was the best he could come up with having never had a real discussion with the man himself, Clark had moved in and requested a word with the gentleman at the point it became clear the man was bored to tears by the chatter of the women around him. Bernadette's father had been happy to get away from the table.

Clark knew going into the conversation he had a difficult task. Getting to know the family through Clay as they prepared for the wedding, he had succeeded in getting her father's permission to marry Bernadette fairly easily. Trying to get her father to bless their elopement was the hardest challenge Clark had ever faced, especially once her Uncle Aaron butted in. Though her father finally conceded, Clark knew he didn't feel good about the decision.

Think, Clark, think. After speaking with him Thursday night, one thing Clark was sure of was that Bernard Julien, Jr. was a man of his word so he wouldn't go back on an agreement. If Bernadette knew her father preferred her to take the traditional route and have a marriage ceremony in the church, Clark was certain Bernadette would not disappoint him. All her father needed was something to make him feel good about the decision. Clark's mind began rewinding and fast forwarding remembering all of his sister's compositions he had read and everything Clay had shared. He was running out of time, and his eyes went to the clock on the far wall as he watched the hands ticking away.

He thought about the time he was fourteen; and as he turned away from the clock, he locked eyes with his Dad. His father nodded towards him and Clark could read the message as if he was sitting in the home study with his Dad coaching him, "Don't lose your cool, son – FOCUS. I know you used to sneak in the office and steal your sisters' files, but you were learning too from their experiences. You're searching the wrong files, Clark. This isn't that complicated. The answer you're seeking is not in your sisters' past, it's in Bernadette's. Open her file. The contract is already written and signed. You just need the hand shake."

As the music began, Cher had requested the same song they danced to at her wedding but this version was recorded by another of Clark's favorite local artist, Louis Armstrong. It was a duet Louis Armstrong had made with the musical legend Ella Fitzgerald. How appropriate since both Clark and Bernadette were now in tune with the lyrics.

The music helped him remember as he opened the one file that was the most important of all, Bernadette's. His eyes shifted to the left and downward. He started biting the left side of his lower lip as he recalled the first time Bernadette gave him insight to her father. The words she spoke to Clark on their first date after the shock of watching themselves in Cher's wedding video came back clearly.

"We've been friends a long time now, and I don't want to do anything to destroy that relationship. I'm sorry I left without speaking Friday night but seeing the way I was dancing was too embarrassing. My father calls that the 'old belly rubbing' dancing. "

It's worth a shot, Clark thought, and he had to try it because it was the only shot he had.

When they got to the middle of the dance floor, Clark kept Bernadette at arms' length. Then he dropped his hand from hers. He whispered to her so no one else could hear.

"Bernadette, the first time we danced, you were forced into it. The last time we spoke, you said you didn't ever want to see me again. I need to know you're doing this because you really want to. I need to know you didn't just say 'yes' because there's a couple hundred people around us and you didn't want to ruin the day for Cecelia. Bernadette, instead of me feeling I'm forcing you into something you don't want again, can you come to me this time, sweetheart? Can you COME to me and SHOW me you REALLY want this? That you really and truly want me to hold you?"

Using the same words he had spoken to her at Cher's wedding, Clark prompted Bernadette, "Can you, tonight, right now, just throw your arms around my neck and follow my lead?"

Smiling back, Bernadette accommodated him willingly this time. She stepped towards him using the waitress' smile Joe had showed her. She placed her arms around his neck and pushed her body close to his.

Clark turned his head when she reached up to kiss him. He pulled her arms from around his neck and pushed her back to arms' length and asked, "Are you sure, Bernadette? Are you sure? I need to know you're not just doing this for Cecelia and Clay."

Bernadette searched his eyes and responded, "Yes, Clark. I'm sure…. I'm doing this because I love you. I missed you so much but just didn't know how to go about taking back the hateful words I had spoken to you at Blaine's." She pushed Clark's arms aside and walked back up to him, pressing her body against his, and placing her arms around his neck again. She reached up to kiss him.

Again, Clark pushed her back once more holding her at arm's length, and he spoke more seriously this time.

"Bernadette, now that I have met Miki, I have grown to love that little girl as much as you do.... I fell in love with her the first time I saw her and I would do anything for that child.... I need to know you're not doing this just for Miki."

"NO, Clark. Even though I'd do anything for Miki, this is not just to make the family whole. It's because I do love you, and I want to be your wife. I've missed you so much.... I WANT to be with you again."

When Bernadette pushed Clark's arms aside once again so she could walk up to him and press her body against his more urgently this time, he placed his arms on hers for a few seconds but didn't pull her arms down. When Bernadette reached up and starting kissing him, he moved his hands to the small of her back, held her close to him, and started silently praying.

Bernadette's father stood offering his hand to Bernadette's mother, "Let's join them on the dance floor."

As Bernard and Audra began dancing, her father asked, "Audra, did you see the shameful way Bernadette kept throwing herself at that boy? Did you see the way she kept pushing her body up close to him?" He shook his head before continuing, "I wonder when Bernadette learned that 'old belly rubbing' dancing. It must be from that crazy college friend... that gal Valerie, the one embarrassing our family having her as a guest screaming out those obscene words like that. Bernadette hadn't talked about her in years and then remember that night she didn't come home until it was almost time for us to leave for mass? Said she'd stopped at that girl's place.... Sinful, just sinful.... Almost making Bernadette miss Sunday church with her family, and I know she's been filling her head with foolishness.... At least twice a week when she's leaving for work, she's telling us don't worry about her or wait up for her because she might stop by Valerie's. She's been staying nights over there too often.

Good thing she got busy with this wedding and stopped…. That boy has pushed her away at least two times trying to dance respectfully, and she finally forced him into not fighting her off and making a fool out of herself in front of all these people….. The way Bernadette keeps forcing her way on that man is shameful…. If I hadn't agreed to them running off to Las Vegas tonight, I'd probably have another grandchild born out of wedlock. It wouldn't be his fault either. If Bernadette got pregnant, the fault would be all hers. A man can only resist so much temptation before he gives in. The boy asked me respectfully if they could elope and get married because he's trying to start the marriage on the right foot. I admired that but a man can only hold out so long, Audra…. A man can only hold out so long. I feel for that poor boy."

Audra responded, "That's true, Junior. I think Bernadette just doesn't know how she's affecting the boy being so inexperienced in these things. I don't think she means to make things hard for him, she just doesn't know better."

"The boy was begging me because he's trying to do the right thing by her, and she's making it harder and harder for him. You know, Audra…. Though it is not the way I want our daughter to get married, I know now that I have made the right decision. I hope the boy doesn't back out being so religious…. He may feel he needs to try to wait for a Catholic wedding, but the rules are too strict now. If he doesn't get on that plane tonight, he'll regret it. I'll tell him he'll regret it. Bernadette is going to go with him if I have to drag her to that airport myself! The last thing I want is another grandchild conceived out of wedlock. That po' boy can't hold out to all Bernadette's shameful belly rubbing."

Audra smiled and hugged her husband closer.

Bernadette and Clark were in their own world. When the lyrics by Louis Armstrong first started, they had eyes only for each other. During the musical interlude, Bernadette had laid her head on Clark's shoulder and couldn't take her eyes off the engagement ring. So content in his arms, her only thought was that she would be so happy letting him lead her not only for this dance, but through her life as Mrs. Clark Laurent.

Clark had watched Bernard and Audra Julien step out onto the dance floor. He saw the tirade of words that followed between them before he finally put his arms around Bernadette and started spinning her to the music. "PLEASE," thought Clark, "Give me a sign."

As Bernard and Audra danced closer to Clark and Bernadette, Bernard's eyes locked with Clark's. Moving his right hand slightly away from his wife's side, Bernadette's father signaled Clark a thumbs-up sign. Clark respectfully nodded to Mr. Julien.

As the interlude was coming to an end, Bernadette looked up at Clark and said, "I can't wait until our wedding day, and I'm officially Mrs. Clark Laurent."

Hearing those words, Clark thought about the other surprise he had for Bernadette, the one he was holding close to his heart, literally, waiting for the reception to end before he showed her. He didn't want to take any more attention from Cecelia and Clay. He shifted slightly so he could feel the bulky envelope still in place in the inside pocket of his tuxedo. Smiling, he thought about the two first class airline tickets to Las Vegas in his pocket. When he had shared the news and asked her help at the rehearsal dinner, Cecelia had gladly agreed to get him the documents he needed for Bernadette. He had Myra do the research, verify the requirements he had checked on a website, and summarize the notes for him that detailed the hours and location of the Las Vegas Marriage Bureau, the cellular phone number for the driver of the limousine she had ordered, and the confirmation number for the bridal suite she had booked on his behalf and pre-paid. One thing he didn't plan for was luggage. The hotel had all the amenities they would need, and he didn't anticipate much in the line of clothing was required for this trip but Cecelia had secretly packed a bag for Bernadette. By the time they arrived in Vegas on the red eye flight from New Orleans, it would be well after midnight so they'd have to wait until the bureau opened to get the license. Seeing the thumbs-up from her father, he thought, "And, now, the airstrip is finally clear for take-off."

Clark's eyes shifted to the left and downward. He began biting the left side of his lower lip and he whispered, "I SWEAR…. You won't have to wait much longer, sweetheart." Then he thought, "And, THANK GOD, neither will I."

Bernadette laid her head on his shoulder again. Smiling with more confidence now on the outcome of the weekend, Clark laid his cheek on top of hers as they swayed in unison to Ella's voice now crooning the lyrics to what had become their song….

Epilogue

After unlocking the door of their Las Vegas hotel suite, Clark placed the do not disturb sign on the door. Turning to Bernadette, he lifted her into his arms and carried her across the threshold. He smiled remembering this was the second time he had performed that act. The first was the evening she drank too much at a play and spent the night at his apartment. It was the incident that ended up jump starting their relationship. He kissed her softly on the lips before kicking the door shut and carrying her to the bedroom. Laying her gently on the mattress, Clark kissed her more passionately before pulling away. He took the documents they had brought and their marriage license out his jacket pocket and tossed them onto the nightstand before he began removing his sport coat and tie. Bernadette stated she wanted to change first. She got off the bed, pulled a package from her suitcase, and entered the bathroom.

While waiting, Clark undressed completely and slipped into a silk pajama bottom. He got into the bed with the covers drawn up to his waist awaiting his bride. He picked up the marriage license and eyed their signatures. "At last," he thought. A memory from his childhood suddenly came back to him. He wondered why he hadn't recalled the incident until now. He was three years old and had told his sisters, "I'm going to get me a wife so I can kiss her on the lips." He almost laughed aloud as he pondered the innocence of childhood now aware of the other privileges that came with marriage. When he heard the bathroom door open, Clark placed the license back on the nightstand and turned to face Bernadette.

"Damn!"

Bernadette knew she had donned the right gown. It wasn't just the word Clark wasn't able to contain but his overall reaction. His eyes darkened with passion. He licked his lips and swallowed hard as he eyed Bernadette from head to toe.

Having been raised in a house with seven females, Clark knew not to describe the gown as beige or light brown. It was ecru and so close to Bernadette's natural skin tone that she appeared almost nude yet still teasing him of what was to come. The lace on the low cut bodice was accented with gold embroidery and followed the curve of Bernadette's breasts before narrowing along a panel that dipped downward. Held together by only three buttons, Clark's eyes caught the patches of skin exposed down to her navel. Drifting to the slit along her left side that started at the waist, the gown accented the curve of her hips and showed enough of her thighs and legs that he wanted to rip it off her. Clark knew immediately that Valerie had helped with the selection. It was too enticing. "Thank you, Valerie," he thought before pulling the coverlet back indicating to Bernadette she should join him in the bed.

During the lecture his father had given him when he was three, his father had become frustrated when he couldn't get Clark to understand why he shouldn't kiss the girls at school. He finally blurted out, "Son, there are times when some things are just best done in private." His father always did try to give him good advice. Knowing this was one of those times, Clark switched off the lights before pulling Bernadette into his arms....

The End!

www.ingramcontent.com/pod-product-compliance
Lightning Source LLC
Chambersburg PA
CBHW061558170626
46811CB00001B/240